MARRYING MATTHEW

It took all her energy to stand there, holding his baby and keeping the wild collection of emotions from dancing across her face. "You want to marry me?"

"*Jah.*"

"I—I—" She didn't know what to say. *Jah*, she wanted to marry him. Sort of. She wanted a family and he seemed to be the means to get one.

She looked back to her cousins. They stood huddled together, arms around each other and identical grins on their faces. She needed them to direct her, nod or something. Let her know that she was doing the right thing. But they just stood there watching and waiting. She was on her own.

Gracie turned back to Matthew. "*Jah.* Okay."

"Can I ask what you're getting out of this?"

"A family." Her answer was simple. She wanted a family and had for a long time. Once she married Matthew she would have his children to care for and maybe soon a baby of her own . . .

Books by Amy Lillard

Published by Kensington Publishing Corporation

A Family For Gracie

Amy Lillard

ZEBRA BOOKS
KENSINGTON PUBLISHING CORP.
www.kensingtonbooks.com

ZEBRA BOOKS are published by

Kensington Publishing Corp.
119 West 40th Street
New York, NY 10018

All Kensington titles, imprints, and distributed lines are available at special quantity discounts for bulk purchases for sales promotion, premiums, fund-raising, educational, or institutional use.

Special book excerpts or customized printings can also be created to fit specific needs. For details, write or phone the office of the Kensington Sales Manager: Attn.: Sales Department. Kensington Publishing Corp., 119 West 40th Street, New York, NY 10018. Phone: 1-800-221-2647.

Zebra and the Z logo Reg. U.S. Pat. & TM Off.
BOUQUET Reg. U.S. Pat. & TM Off.

First Printing: August 2019
ISBN-13: 978-1-4201-4570-0
ISBN-10: 1-4201-4570-3

ISBN-13: 978-1-4201-4571-7 (eBook)
ISBN-10: 1-4201-4571-1 (eBook)

10 9 8 7 6 5 4 3 2 1

Printed in the United States of America

Chapter One

She could do this. Gracie Glick pulled her buggy to a stop at the end of the red dirt road that led straight to Matthew Byler's house. All she had to do was take the casserole to the front door and wait for him to answer. Easy.

Gracie hopped down and retrieved the glass dish from the back of the buggy. She wrapped a towel around it, but not because it was too warm to handle. Her hands were sweaty. She didn't want to drop it before she even got to the porch.

She sucked in a deep breath to ease the thud of her heart. Her stomach was in knots. Maybe this wasn't such a good idea.

Yet this was the only plan she had.

She wished she had a free hand to smooth over her prayer covering or even to press the tiny wrinkles marring the skirt of her dress. Maybe she should wait until she looked more presentable. Maybe then he wouldn't refuse to answer the door.

Like that was going to happen. He knew she was coming. Well, he knew someone was coming. And that they would have supper.

It wasn't like she could return to the house with the food

she was sent here to give him. She climbed the few steps that led to the big porch with the even larger door.

No. It was a regular-sized door and a large but still average porch. She had to get a handle on herself or she would never make it through this.

Gracie drew in another breath, but it did nothing to ease her nervousness. The best thing to do was simply get it over with. Knock on the door and wait for him to answer. She looked down at the thick glass dish she held with both hands. Knocking might be a little difficult.

But she had come here with a purpose and she was going to see it through.

She looked around. There was a wooden bench similar to the ones they used for church, sitting to the right of the front door. She could set the pan there and knock. It was a good plan.

A plan. Exactly what she needed.

She placed the pan on the bench, then rapped on the wood and waited. Nothing. She knocked once more, then twice. Louder this time. Still nothing. She knocked again, her newfound confidence waning once more. What if he wasn't home? Or maybe just not hungry? Or plain old didn't want to see her?

Now she was just being ridiculous.

Thankfully, she heard the fluttering of movements behind the door. Someone was home. Perhaps one of the children looking to see who was outside. But if there were children in the front room they were certainly quiet. Maybe they were playing that game like she had in school: quiet mouse. Like children played it willingly. Maybe everyone was in the back of the house.

Then she heard it. The squall of an unhappy baby. Before she had time to think about what that meant, the door was wrenched open and Matthew Byler filled the threshold. In his arms he held a screaming baby.

"I just got her to sleep." He glared at her with hard, blue eyes.

Gracie took a step back. Had he always been that tall? That broad? That angry?

"What do you want?" His voice was chipped ice.

Gracie blinked, then managed to get herself back on track. "I—I brought you supper." She nodded toward the casserole on the nearby bench, though she could barely hear her own words over the baby's cries.

He looked from her to the dish and back again. Then before she could move to pick it up for him, he thrust the baby toward her.

"You woke her up. You get her back to sleep."

She fumbled a bit, then got a firm grip on the crying baby. She really did have a set of lungs, as they say. Her head was thrown back, her face red as a beet.

Gracie cradled the infant close to her, inhaling the sweet scent of baby. There was nothing like it in the world. It was the best smell ever. And Gracie had smelled a lot of babies. How many had she gone to help other people with? So many she had lost track, if she had ever really been keeping count.

"Shhh . . ." Gracie murmured. "You're too little to have such big problems."

Matthew had taken the casserole dish from the bench and started back through the house. At her words, he stopped but didn't turn around. "Are you coming in or are you going to put her to bed on the porch?"

"*Jah*. Of course." This was not going as she had planned it in her head. She would come to the house, offer him the food, and the two of them would sit down and discuss her proposal like rational people. Matthew Byler seemed far from rational. He seemed downright unhappy.

Or maybe it was exhaustion that pulled at the corners of his mouth.

Of course he's unhappy and exhausted. His wife just died three months ago.

"Shut the door," he growled as he continued into the house.

Gracie used one foot to close the door behind her and gently bounced the screaming baby. If this was what Matthew had been dealing with before she arrived, she could see why he was so upset that she woke the baby.

"Shhh . . ."

"You're gonna be in trouble."

She whirled around to find four boys, near stair-steps in age, sitting quietly on the couch. The tallest and probably the oldest swatted the one next to him. "Hush up, Henry."

The Amish might stand against violence, but siblings were siblings.

"I don't have to, Stephen."

"When Grace is asleep you do," Stephen retorted.

One of the smaller boys slid from the couch.

"Thomas, sit down," he continued.

"Grace isn't asleep," Henry said.

"She will be soon," Stephen replied. "Thomas."

The small boy climbed back onto the couch and sat by his brother. They were so close in size that Gracie wondered if they were twins, though they looked nothing alike. She knew from personal experience that didn't mean much. Her own cousins, Hannah and Leah, were twins and they looked as different as can be.

The four seemed to be mirrors of each other. Stephen, the oldest, had dark hair like his father, but green eyes she supposed he inherited from his mother. They seemed larger than normal, magnified by the lenses of his black-framed glasses. Thomas was the same without the eyewear. Henry had blond hair and blue eyes. The eye color had to have come from his father, and if she remembered right, Beth, their mother, had blond hair too. Benjamin was Henry's mirror. But only in looks. He sat as still as a statue, waiting for . . . something, she supposed.

She continued to bounce the baby in a comforting manner, though her screams had quieted to hiccups. Gracie patted the baby on the back, rubbing it in hopes of calming her further.

"Thomas," Stephen chastised. The boy was attempting an escape once again. Stephen grabbed his brother by one suspender and pulled him back into place. Somehow he managed to push his glasses up a little on the bridge of his nose as he did so.

"Hey," Henry protested. He was still sitting between Stephen and Thomas.

"Necessary," Stephen grunted. He seemed to have taken on the role of mother and father in his parents' absence. His mother wasn't coming back. But where was his *dat*?

Thomas finally settled back into place next to Benjamin, who Gracie was sure hadn't moved the entire time she'd been standing there. How unusual for a small child to sit still like that for so long. And she couldn't help but wonder if it was in his nature or something else.

Stephen had started bossing again, telling Henry to be still, quit picking his nails, and to stop blowing spit bubbles. Where was their father?

The baby's hiccups were gone. Gracie looked down at the sweet, sweet face to find that she had finally gone to sleep. She felt warm and solid in Gracie's arms, but she knew she couldn't get too used to the feel. Not until she talked to Matthew.

And if he agreed? She would be able to hold this baby, be a mother to Stephen so he could go back to being a child, and maybe . . . maybe even have a baby of her own.

The mere thought made her sigh.

"You okay, lady?"

She pulled herself out of her thoughts and centered her attention on Henry.

Stephen elbowed him in the ribs. "Don't call her lady."

"Why not?" Henry grumbled, shouldering him back.

"'Cause it's not nice."

"But she is a lady."

"I'm fine," she reassured him, hoping that would stop their arguing.

Once again Thomas slid from the couch. Stephen tried to snag his suspenders, but he slipped away, running to Gracie and throwing his arms around her legs and toppling her a bit. She managed to stay on her feet and not wake the baby.

"You're still here?"

Gracie jumped as Matthew Byler loomed in the doorway leading from the kitchen. The baby woke with a tortured wail, and Thomas moved around to the back and hid his face in her skirt. Was he afraid of his father? Maybe this wasn't such a good idea.

"You told me to get her to sleep."

He looked pointedly at his red-faced daughter. The look in his eyes was confusing. He seemed sad, helpless, and small in that one instant, as if caring for the child was more than he had bargained for, then the look was gone. "She's not asleep."

Gracie shifted the child, holding her against her shoulder. She bounced her and patted the thick diaper on her bottom. "She was," Gracie said, her voice timid and soothing all at the same time.

"What was that?" Matthew asked.

Gracie shook her head. Being rude back would not help her argument. Thank heaven he hadn't been able to hear her over the baby's wails. Or maybe he had and he wanted to see if she had the cheek enough to say it twice.

She looked to the children, then back to Matthew. "Is

there someplace we can talk?" The words turned her mouth to ash. "Alone." This was it. She was going to do it.

He frowned. "*Jah.* I suppose." He turned toward his sons. "You boys stay right there. I'll be back in a few minutes."

"How long?" Henry was already beginning to squirm.

Matthew checked the clock hanging opposite the couch. "I told you already. When the big hand is on the four."

Henry screwed up his face and studied the timepiece for a moment. "Then we can get up?"

"As long as you sit there while I talk to Gracie."

Henry nodded. "Okay."

"That's funny," Stephen said, adjusting his glasses once again.

"What?" Matthew asked. She wished he would hurry. All this chatter was making her even more nervous than she had been when she walked in the door.

"Grace and Gracie." Stephen pointed from her to the baby. The baby's name was Grace? The coincidence was unusual to be sure, but Gracie wasn't sure if it was a good omen or a bad one. At least the baby Grace had stopped crying, though she showed no interest in going back to sleep. Those blue-green eyes that seemed too large for such a tiny face were heavy-lidded, opening slower with each blink, but her chubby fingers were tightly wrapped around one of the strings from Gracie's prayer *kapp*.

"That is funny," Matthew said, but his voice was still dry as dust. Did the man only have one emotion: anger? "Come on." He motioned for Gracie to follow him, then he turned and made his way back into the kitchen.

It was a nice kitchen, she supposed. But it seemed a little small. A large table sat in the middle of the room and swallowed up most of the free space. Or was that Matthew himself?

He pulled out a chair and nodded for her to do the same.

Gracie hooked one foot between the legs of the chair and pulled it out without moving the baby. Honestly, she was afraid to shift her too much, scared that the tot would pull the string and strip her prayer *kapp* from her head. How embarrassing would that be?

She eased into the seat and balanced the baby on her lap, carefully extracting tiny fingers from the string. She offered her own finger as a means of distraction.

The baby Grace didn't seem to mind the switch and clasped adult Gracie's finger in her tiny fist. Now if she could get the child to settle down enough to close her eyes. If she did, Gracie was confident that she would be asleep in minutes if not seconds. Well, if the pounding of Gracie's heart didn't keep the child alert. And her heart was pounding.

It didn't help that Matthew—big, scowling Matthew— frowned at her from the other side of the table. He was waiting for her to start the conversation she had asked him for. No niceties. No offer of coffee or pie. No preliminaries. Just straight to the point. She shouldn't have expected anything else from him.

She pulled in a deep breath, but it didn't help anything. She exhaled and prayed for the best. "I think the two of us should get married."

The words hung in the air between them like a burnt smell lingering in the house.

"What did you say?" It was the softest voice he had used since she had walked in the door.

Dear heaven, he wanted her to say it again? She wasn't sure she could manage it. She rocked the baby and gathered her courage. She had done it once; she could do it again.

"We should get married," she repeated. "You obviously need help with the children—"

"I don't need help with my kids."

"Dat, can we get up now?" Henry peeked around the door frame into the kitchen.

"Sit down, Henry." Matthew's voice was stern but held a tired edge.

"I told you he would say that," Stephen called from the other room.

Henry waited a beat more, opened his mouth as if to protest, but was cut off by his father. "Now."

"Okay." Henry dropped his head and disappeared back into the living room.

Matthew turned his attention to her once more.

She half expected him to say something to her. Point out that maybe she was right. That he could use some help. She didn't want to recount all his shortcomings. He was a man, Amish or not, and he had his pride. He could provide for his children, but he needed help with the day to day. She supposed he could hire someone to come in and keep house for him, but who had that kind of money? Their community was close, but not rich.

And she surely couldn't tell him all the reasons why she wanted to get married to him. Well, not to him, but he was the only choice she had aside from moving to Ethridge and looking for a mate there in the larger settlement. But she loved Pontotoc. She had been there almost as long as she could remember. She didn't want to move, but she did so desperately want a family. Badly enough to propose to a man she barely knew.

It was beyond forward and completely out of character for her. And he just sat there staring at her as she held his sleeping baby in her arms and waited for his answer. Why wasn't he answering?

Because he didn't want to get married. It was too soon after his wife's death. He didn't like her. He didn't want to get married again.

Or maybe it was simply God's will, which felt a little

like running away from the truth. And the truth was that he didn't want to marry her. If he did, he would have said so by now.

Every nerve ending she had hummed with embarrassment. She had to get out of there, save what she could of her self-respect. She wanted to jump to her feet and run as fast as she could back to her buggy. She wanted to go home, where she could lock herself in her room, crawl under the covers, and not come out until time ended or Matthew moved away, whichever came first.

But she still held Baby Grace.

"I—" she started, then shook her head. She rose to her feet, careful not to disturb the child. "I'll just put her down." She nodded toward the baby in her arms, waiting for him to rise and show her the way to the child's room.

But he just stood there. One heartbeat. Two. Three, each one more painful than the last. "Where does she sleep?"

Matthew jerked as if he had been poked in the side. Had he been that deep in thought, trying to come up with a way to turn her down gently, so as to not interfere with his regular delivery of food? Slowly he rose to his feet without meeting her gaze. "In here." He didn't wait for her to follow but headed down the hallway to the right. Down two doors, then he turned.

The room was plain, even by Amish standards. The walls were stark white and held no pictures, or murals; the only indicator that the room was occupied by a growing baby was the small wooden crib pushed against one wall. The curtains on the windows were plain white, thin and gauzy to let in light and the breeze, but still add a little measure of privacy. That was one thing they had learned in their district: Other settlements might find curtains to be vain and prideful, but the privacy they offered was worth a great deal more.

"There." Matthew gestured toward the crib.

The sheets were pale yellow, like dreamy sunshine. Gracie would lay her down, even though she wanted to hold her forever. But after Matthew's reaction to her proposal, she knew that was never going to be.

She eased the baby onto the bed, careful not to disturb her slumber, then brushed the blond curls back from her face. It wasn't like she would do this again, and tears pricked at her eyes.

She blinked them back. She wasn't going to feel sorry for herself. She had tried, but God's will would prevail, and it seemed He wanted her forever single. Well, so be it.

Behind her Matthew cleared his throat. She straightened, then walked toward him, refusing to drop her chin or her gaze. She had tried. She had nothing to be ashamed of. Though she felt a little shamed. She wanted a baby, a family of her own so badly that she could almost taste it. Why was it that God saw fit to hold that dream from her? She would probably never know.

She brushed past Matthew and into the front of the house. The baby's room was way too small for the two of them and the hallway even worse. She only had to keep her chin up for a few more steps, then she would be outside, and she could make her escape.

"Where are you going?" he asked, following behind her.

She didn't turn around, just shot a quick wave to the boys as they called good-byes from the couch. "Home."

"But—"

"Enjoy your meal." She escaped out the front door and rushed down the steps like the devil was on her heels. As quickly as she could, she swung herself up into the buggy and turned the horse around. She looked back. She needn't have bothered. Matthew had not followed after her. Another testament to the fact that they were not meant to be a couple. Or maybe she was not meant to be a wife.

And the sooner she came to terms with that, the better off she would be.

"Da-at," Henry called. "Who was that?" The sheer urgency in his voice told Matthew that this wasn't the first time he had asked.

"Shhh . . . you'll wake the baby," Stephen hushed.

"Can we get up?" Henry asked, his voice lower but still more suited for outside than in.

But at least that question kept Matthew from having to answer the other one. "Is the big hand on the four?"

Henry scrunched up his face. "When I look at it like this it is."

"What about when you look at it normal?" He had long since stopped laughing at all of Henry's antics.

The boy's expression fell. "No."

Of all his children, Henry was the biggest challenge. Even the twins together couldn't hold a candle to Henry's capers. Matthew loved him all the more for his spunk and inventive personality, but there were times . . . And this was one of them.

"Then there's your answer." Matthew tried not to sigh, but he was just so tired.

"I told you." Stephen crossed his arms as if completely satisfied with himself.

"Stephen . . ." Matthew intoned the warning in a low, rumbling voice.

So tired he was beginning to wonder who this time-out punished more, him or the boys.

"Five more minutes," Matthew told them while he wondered how in the world he was going to keep them there for another five. They had already been sitting there that long, and that in itself had been a chore. But he couldn't have them jumping out of the hayloft onto the loaded wagon below. Granted, the wagon was loaded high with hay and the fall was no more than ten feet. That was still a lot of distance for a body to get hurt. He couldn't have that. He didn't think he could handle any broken arms or legs or necks. He simply couldn't take any more.

He had been trying to get the baby to sleep when he heard the commotion. He had gone outside to find them doing their jumps and falls out of the hayloft. He had yelled at them to stop, which made Grace cry . . . again. It seemed that was all she did. Eunice Gingerich had asked him at church if she was colicky, but he didn't know what that meant. He had helped Beth as much as he could with the boys, but they had never had to deal with anything like this. So he asked Eunice what it entailed. That's when he decided: Grace didn't have a stomachache. She just missed her mother.

Me too. Especially in times like this. She had a handle on the boys. And she knew what to correct and what to let go. Matthew felt like he was swimming with weights tied to his feet. As soon as it seemed like he had his head above water, something came along and pulled him under again.

And just when he had the boys seated on the couch with a stern warning not to move an inch and the baby was almost asleep, Gracie Glick came knocking at the door.

Asking him to marry her.

He had never heard of anything so bold in his life. Frankly, he didn't know Gracie had it in her. She seemed timid, almost servant like. He had seen her at church a couple of times and never thought about it much until now. But she was always making things better for other people. If someone needed a fresh drink or a paper towel for a spill, she would provide. She was there when he arrived at the service and there when he left. And she wanted him to marry her.

He shook his head at himself. He wasn't getting married

again. He had things completely under control. He didn't need a woman complicating matters more than need be.

"Da-at."

He turned at Henry's summons.

"The big hand is on the four."

Matthew glanced toward the clock. "So it is." He pinned each boy with a separate, hard stare. "You can get up," he started, then had to hold up a hand to keep them from sliding down and disappearing before he said his piece. "But no more jumping off the hayloft. That is dangerous and one of you could have been hurt very badly." He shuddered at the thought of what could have happened, then said a quick silent prayer of thanks that no one had been injured.

"*Jah*, Dat," Henry muttered.

"I'm sorry," Stephen said, too grown-up for his seven years. He had taken on so much responsibility for his siblings in the last three months.

Thomas and Benjamin slid off the couch together and started toward the door behind Henry and Stephen. He was proud of his boys. They might be a lot to handle, but they were blessings through and through.

"Don't slam the—"

Thwack!

"Sorry, Dat," Henry called as Grace started crying once again.

Chapter Two

Gracie's face flamed all the way back home. Except it wasn't really her home. It belonged to her aunt and uncle. She had moved there when Mammi had settled into the *dawdihaus*. Mammi was Abner's mother and Gracie's grandmother. The poor woman had broken her hip and needed extra care, so she moved in with Eunice and Abner. Gracie had followed to assist as always. Her aunt did most of the chores for Mammi. And Tillie had helped, before she left home, that was. Gracie mostly did the cooking and the cleaning and whatever else was needed for the other mournful souls in the community. She cooked for Aaron Zook for a while, but then her cousin Hannah had come back to the Amish and decided to stay. Hannah and Aaron were to be married in the fall and she did his cooking these days. Gracie was glad for them. Their happy ending had been fifteen years in the making.

Gracie had also cooked for Jamie Stoltzfus when he and his nephew Peter had moved into their small community. Gracie had even courted Jamie for a while.

Well, that wasn't exactly true. They had sort of talked about it, and Gracie had agreed that it would be a good idea. She supposed that deep down she knew it wasn't, but she had put her dreams on hold to help out one family member or another until before she knew it, her *rumspringa* was over and she was the only one in their group not married. It had all happened so fast.

She was told that there was no shame in being "that girl," the one who never got married and moved around from family member to family member, helping out whenever she was needed. There might not be any shame, but it sure felt that way. Now she was facing down her twenty-sixth birthday and she had never even been on a real date. How pathetic was that?

So what had she done? She had completely embarrassed herself by proposing to Matthew Byler.

Thank heavens next Sunday wasn't a church day. She didn't think she could handle seeing him there, both of them knowing what a fool she had made of herself.

She pulled the buggy down the packed-gravel drive, past the little cabin where Jamie and Peter had stayed when they first moved to Pontotoc. Now Leah, Hannah's twin, and Jamie were married, providing a loving and stable home for young Peter. He had been traumatized by the fire that killed his entire family and needed the best care possible and lots of love. And that's just what Jamie and Leah gave him. They had even adopted a dog from the local animal shelter.

The house came into sight and Gracie breathed a sigh of relief. Then she chuckled at herself. What had she expected? That Matthew Byler would follow her home, berating her stupid choices all the way?

His dark, brooding face popped into her thoughts. He might be dark and brooding but she didn't think he was cruel. There was something in the softness of his mouth, or maybe it was the little flashes of compassion she had seen in his eyes as he had watched her holding his baby girl.

Dark and brooding, yes. Even handsome. But cruel, no. Never.

She swung down from the buggy, then unhitched the horse and released her into the pasture. From the paddock gate she could hear the buzz of her uncle Abner's tools as he cut wood and sanded corners and whatever else it was he had to do in order to make the sheds he and his sons sold to Amish and Englisch from all around their Northeast Mississippi area.

Jim and Dave Gingerich both had houses on the same property as their parents, just up from the main house. Dave wasn't married and lived on his own, but Jim had plenty of family. He had a wife named Anna and five children: Libby, Joshua, and the twins Michael and Caleb, along with baby Samuel who wasn't such a baby any more.

Now all Gracie had to do was make it into her room without anyone seeing her. Then she could wallow in the mess she had made of things.

Careful to avoid the squeaky step leading up to the porch, Gracie quietly made her way into the house. She kept the screen door from slamming behind her and tried to walk normally down the hall that led to her room. Just a few more steps and she'd be th—

"Gracie, is that you?" Her aunt's voice drifted down the hallway after her.

She stopped mid-step. "*Jah*, Eunice. It's me." So much for wallowing.

"Good. Good. Leah's on her way out with Peter and Jamie. They'll be here any minute."

She had forgotten. It was their usual Friday night supper. Which was basically a madhouse. Hannah would be here along with Aaron and his three children: Andy, Laura Kate, and Essie. Leah, Jamie, and Peter were on their way. Dave would come down from his house, and Jim and his brood would be right behind them. Gracie couldn't say that it wasn't a fun night, but right now she could use a little peace and quiet. Something she wouldn't be able to get with that many people in the house.

"Can you help me with the table?" Eunice called.

"Of course." Gracie forced false brightness into her tone, then made her way to the dining room. Wallowing would have to wait until later.

"You *what*?" Leah's voice was nearly a screech.

"Shhh . . ." Hannah shushed.

Gracie felt the heat in her cheeks once again. Not quite as bad as it had been this afternoon, but close.

"I asked Matthew Byler to marry me." Wow. She had said it twice and the world hadn't come to a halt. She took a deep breath, thankful to have unburdened herself just a bit.

Dinner had been served, eaten, and everything cleaned up. As she had expected, it was a loud affair, noisy. Maybe even boisterous. But how else could it be with so many people in one place.

Now she, Leah, and Hannah were outside on the porch enjoying the early spring evening. The twins were sitting side by side on the porch swing, so different in so many ways. Leah had dark hair and green eyes, Hannah had chestnut-colored hair and hazel eyes. But their differences didn't stop there. Both Leah and Hannah had left the Amish years ago and finally returned only recently. Leah had turned to the Mennonites during her years away, while Hannah had gone full-blown Englisch. But last year, upon their return, Hannah had asked forgiveness of the church and had taken back up with her roots, while Leah had remained Mennonite. It was strange seeing them sitting there side by side, the way they had done so many times while she was growing up, but now they were changed and she hoped for the better.

It was doubly strange not having Tillie around. Hannah and Leah's younger sister was closer to Gracie's age than her sisters'. But as Hannah and Leah had returned to Pontotoc, Tillie had headed out with her boyfriend, Melvin. He wanted to repair Englisch motors and had dragged Tillie along for the ride. Gracie just hoped that she came to her senses before too much had happened for her to return.

"Tell us everything," Leah said.

"And he said yes, right? I mean, it's you and . . ." Hannah broke off as Gracie shook her head.

"He didn't say yes," Gracie admitted.

"He said no?" Hannah screeched.

"Shhh . . ." This from Leah.

"Not exactly."

Leah clasped Gracie's hand and pulled her so she sat squeezed between them. "Tell us everything."

Gracie shrugged, her shoulders bumping her cousins on both sides. "There's not much to tell. I went over there to talk to him and got up my courage to ask, then withdrew my proposal and hightailed it out of there."

"You withdrew?" Hannah asked. "Why?"

"You didn't see the look on his face." Gracie grimaced. "He was not interested." In fact he looked as if someone had hit him in the stomach, hard. Not that she had actually seen something like that happen. But if she had, she imagined his face would be what the person looked like: pain, betrayal, red-faced from lack of air, completely unable to breathe.

"Well, he's a fool then," Hannah said primly.

"Don't let Mamm hear you say that."

"Why?" Hannah asked.

"She sets great store by Matthew. I think she had a circle letter with his mother a while back." Leah rolled her eyes, Gracie was sure over the thought of a circle letter. "Or maybe it was a dish towel exchange."

Gracie let out a small chuckle.

"Well, a fool move is a fool move, no matter how much you like a person."

But Gracie couldn't say that she knew Matthew Byler at all. He and his family had moved to their community a couple of years back, but neither he nor his wife went to any of their group meetings. They had left their buddy bunches behind in their Ohio home and seemed to keep to themselves.

Come to think of it, Gracie wondered why they even moved to Mississippi; neither one seemed very happy here. Perhaps he would move the remainder of his family back to Ohio. Maybe that was why he had looked at her as if she had lost her mind.

She wished.

"It doesn't matter now," Gracie said.

"Can I ask you a question?" Leah asked.

"Of course." She said the words, though she hardly meant them. She was ready to put all this behind her, to stop talking about it and try to forget that it ever happened.

"Why him?" she asked.

"Le-ah!" Hannah exclaimed.

"You know what I mean."

Gracie wished she didn't.

"Tell me," Hannah coaxed.

"He's . . ." Leah searched her brain for the best word. *Intimidating?* Gracie thought. *Daunting?*

"Frightening," Leah finally said. "That man is scary."

"Le-ah!" Hannah again.

"Tell me it's not true, and I'll take it back."

Hannah opened her mouth to respond, but Leah jumped in first. "And no lying."

Hannah exhaled without a word.

Leah sat back, self-satisfied.

"It's still not a nice thing to say," Hannah admonished.

"But true." Leah grinned. "I mean look at the man." She went on to describe Matthew in great and horrible detail. Maybe it wasn't just Gracie who found him to be a big, hulking mass with a scowling beard and cold eyes.

"When did you become such an expert?" Hannah asked. "You don't even go to church with us. How do you know all this?"

Leah shrugged. "He comes into the shop from time to time."

"Really? And you just now decided to share this information?"

"Why not?"

"He comes into the secondhand store?" When Leah moved back to Pontotoc, she opened a secondhand store on Main Street. She catered to Plain people with housewares and modest clothes. She also carried a line of goat-milk products that the three of them made. They got together every Tuesday to fill special orders and restock the basics. So far it was a lucrative endeavor.

"He came in a couple of months ago with a bunch of dresses and aprons."

"Those must have been his wife's clothes. That was right about the time she died," Gracie murmured.

Leah nodded. "He also took some baby clothes. I tried not to watch him, but it's next to impossible."

Hannah rolled her eyes. "Spoken like a true busybody."

But Gracie knew the truth. It was hard not to watch Matthew. Something about him commanded attention. She wasn't sure if it was his sheer size, that black-as-ink beard, or an energy around him that pulled the attention to him. Whatever it was, Leah was right. And yet you couldn't look too long. He emanated a power that was hard to look at for very long. Gracie preferred to think this was the essence of God coming through him, but she didn't know. Honestly, there wasn't much she knew about the man. His name, his wife's name, the fact that she drowned in a creek near their house when the baby was only a couple of weeks old. And . . . nothing. Oh, and that they had moved down from Ohio. Other than that, he was a complete mystery.

Matthew straightened and looked across the newly turned field. In the next day or so he would be planting. He was ready to get his crops in the ground. This year he was planting half and half, peanuts and soybeans. He preferred to grow peanuts, but the rash of peanut allergies that had risen in the last couple of years had hurt the industry. He couldn't solely rely on peanuts as his only crop. Not that he ever had. He'd moved down to Mississippi not knowing that the industry was hurting, and saw a need for peanuts since hardly anyone was planting them. But when his crop came in, he got so much less than he had imagined. Beth had worried herself nearly sick. That next year he had planted only soybeans, but his heart wasn't in it. He wasn't sure why peanuts held such charm for him. They just did. Since then he had been experimenting with different percentages in order to have a crop that he wanted to grow with a crop that he needed to grow. He wasn't sure fifty-fifty was going to be the answer, but for now it would suffice.

He glanced over to the shade tree at the edge of the field. A pram sat there under the branches, the little hood pulled up to further protect the baby inside. He couldn't hear her crying, which meant she had probably tuckered herself out and drifted off. He didn't know what he was going to do with the child. She seemed to hate him, as if she knew that he had somehow been responsible for her mother's death. That maybe he could have saved her.

And maybe he could have. If he hadn't gone to the feed store that morning. But he had. And she had decided to take the baby for a walk after breakfast. She couldn't have planned on being gone long. She left the kettle on the stove, and the twins and Henry playing with the puppies in the barn. Thank heavens Stephen was at school.

But she had fallen into the cold water, possibly even hit her head on a rock, and drowned, leaving Matthew to take care of their five children. Five children he had no idea how to take care of.

He cocked an ear toward the pram, listening for signs that she was awake and crying once more, but nothing. Thank the Lord above. He had no idea what he was going to do come planting time. He had seen an ad in a magazine at the doctor's office for some contraption the Englisch used to tote their babies around. It was about the craziest thing he had ever seen with straps and buckles and quilted pads to hold the baby in place while the *mamm*—or maybe even the *dat*—went about their day with their hands free to do other work. He had stared at it when he saw it, hardly able to believe his eyes. What would the Englisch think of next? And now he was wondering where he could get such a device. Walmart? Maybe. They seemed to have everything else.

The next question was, would the baby allow him to stuff her into it and cart her around all day while he planted? He configured the image in his head and realized it would never work. How was he supposed to keep the sun off her? He might not know a lot about raising children, but of that much he was certain. No sun on the baby. He came in red from the sun on every exposed inch this time of year. But his skin was tough and old. He couldn't imagine her pale, tender skin in the sun for twelve hours straight.

He supposed he could use the pram again. Though he knew she hated it. Or maybe she just hated everything now that her mother was gone.

And there's nothing you can do to bring her back.

The boys could keep to themselves in the house or play at the edge of the field. But they couldn't be trusted to look after their little sister. It wasn't the best idea, but it was the only one he had at the moment.

Then, just like that, Gracie Glick's face appeared before his eyes.

He blinked it away. It had been three days since her proposal. Three days of him pushing the thought from his mind, only to have it rise again a little while later. Her idea was crazy, completely out of the question. He didn't think he would ever get married again. Marriage was hard. It required two people giving their all to make it work. Well, if a couple wanted a happy marriage. He supposed unhappy marriages were as easy as they were miserable. And he couldn't imagine marrying a woman he didn't even know just to have a babysitter and a cook. The thought itself sounded callous. No matter how badly he needed a babysitter and a cook. If the boys were older, they would be in school and he could take the baby . . . well, around. Surely there were plenty of people who would be willing to take care of a sweet baby for a day. All he would have to do would be to find six or seven of them and he would be set. But the boys weren't older and in school. The baby was miserable, not sweet and happy the way babies should be.

Again he saw Gracie, but this time she was holding his baby, rocking her to sleep in her arms. The baby wasn't crying. She didn't seem unhappy, and Gracie seemed pleased to do it.

Even after you thrust the child toward her and told her to get the baby back to sleep.

Even then.

At least he didn't have to worry about the boys. They had been keeping to themselves during the day, playing and working on their chores, helping him out around the house.

They were young, but they were good kids. He was blessed that way.

He looked back over the field, a sense of satisfaction surging through him. He could do this. Without a wife. He could take care of his farm and his children. God would show him the way. And all was right in the world.

"*Dat! Dat! Dat!*"

Adrenaline surged through him. His stomach sank, his fingers tingled, and his mouth turned to ash. Something was wrong.

He turned to see Thomas running across the field. His hat had long since flown from his head as he galloped along, his bare feet pressing into the newly turned earth.

Matthew started toward him, dropping the hoe there at the far edge of the field. He would get it later. Right now he had other matters to attend. "What happened?"

They met somewhere in the middle of the field. Thomas was out of breath from running, Matthew from worry.

"Dat," Thomas wheezed. "Come now. Henry's hurt."

Matthew tapped his foot instead of prowling around the tiny exam room where he and Henry waited.

"I'm sorry, Dat," Henry said for the umpteenth time. His voice was slightly slurred from the pain medication the doctor had given him when they arrived at the urgent care facility.

"I know," Matthew replied. He couldn't say much else. He couldn't grant Henry forgiveness for actions that weren't entirely his fault.

Jah, he had told them to stop jumping from the hayloft into the wagon below. And naturally he had expected them to obey. But they were only boys. And Matthew hadn't bothered to remove the temptation by moving the wagon. He was going to move it soon anyway, up closer to the road to sell to any passersby. But he hadn't. And now this. Now they waited for the doctor to come in and confirm what they already knew: Henry had broken his arm. The question was in how many places. They were blessed that he hadn't broken his neck as well.

Trying something new and showing out for his brothers, Henry had tried a belly-flop dive off the hayloft floor and onto the wagon filled with hay below. Matthew couldn't fathom why Henry thought this would be more fun than landing on his backside, but this was the story he had managed to get out of Thomas. Henry was crying in pain while Benjamin wailed because his brother was crying. It had been hard to hear over all that noise, but the best he had pieced together between Thomas's own sobs was that Henry had tried his belly flop, bounced off the hard-packed hay, and landed on the ground, his arm bent beneath him and taking the brunt of the fall.

This wouldn't have happened if Beth were still alive.

You don't know that.

He didn't. But it seemed like the only thought his brain could form. If Beth had been there none of this would have happened. He wouldn't have left the boys alone at the house and taken the baby to the fields. Beth would have been there to watch the baby and the boys. Matthew would have been finished with the field in half the time. He lost so many precious minutes stopping so often to check on the baby. She had been fine. It was the boys who needed constant monitoring. And Beth knew things like that. He didn't have a clue. How had he gotten so clueless about his own life?

He shook his head at himself. He'd hitched up his horse, bundled all the kids into the buggy, then carted them over to the Gingeriches'. Eunice must have heard Henry's and the baby's cries, for she met them on the porch. Bless her heart, she hadn't even asked Matthew what had happened, just took the kids and nodded at his promise to be back as soon as possible. Then he raced as quickly as he could, doing his best not to cause Henry any more pain than necessary, to the closest Englisch neighbor's house and begged a ride into town. The neighbor, accustomed to such requests, grabbed his car keys immediately and rushed Henry and him to the medical center.

And now they waited.

Matthew whirled around as a knock sounded on the door only a second before it opened and a petite woman wearing a lab coat came in. She wore her long, dark hair in a braid that swung from side to side as she walked. All that hair reached nearly to her waist. He nodded at her but didn't speak. His throat was too dry. He cleared it to no avail. Why was he so nervous?

"I'm Dr. Gilbert. I'm guessing you're Mr. Byler, and you"—she turned toward the bed—"must be Henry."

"*Jah*," the boy said, his voice clearing a bit at the sight of the woman doctor. Henry was nothing if not a boy, and he didn't want any female to think that he was less than a man.

She smiled. "I've got good news and bad news," she said. "Which would you like to hear first?"

"The good news," Matthew croaked. He needed something positive and fast.

"Okay, then. The good news is you don't have to have surgery to repair the breaks."

"It's broken?" Henry looked at his arm in wonder.

"Yep. Which brings me to the bad news. It's broken in three places." She held up the large X-ray film that Matthew hadn't noticed when she came in. With efficient movements, she slid it under the metal clamp on the wall and turned on a light behind it. Then she took a pen out of her lab coat pocket. "Here. Here. And here." She used one end of the pen to point out the breaks, but to Matthew it all looked the same. He squinted but still couldn't tell any difference.

"They're small breaks," she explained as he leaned closer.

He shook his head, and she turned off the light behind the X-ray.

"I guess that's some good news." She smiled.

"Does that mean there's more bad news?" Henry asked.

She nodded. "Unfortunately, yes."

He waited for her to answer.

"Your cast will have to be from above your elbow to the second joints of your fingers."

Matthew hadn't thought about a cast. For Henry, that would be worse than a time-out. He could only hope that this would teach him the lesson that the time-outs hadn't.

A man in a pair of blue scrubs came by with a wheel-chair and took Henry away to the casting room. Matthew wanted to go with him, but the doctor with her sweet smile told him that it was better for the parents to stay in the room and wait.

He reluctantly nodded and once again started tapping his foot to keep from pacing.

"They tell me that he fell out of the barn loft," the doctor said.

Close enough. Matthew nodded.

The doctor made notes on a clipboard that he hadn't seen either. Henry's chart, he supposed.

"And he was unsupervised at the time?"

"He was supposed to have been watching his brothers."

She made another note. "And how old are they?"

"Three," Matthew choked out. "And a half," he hurriedly added as she started to write once more.

"Why was he left alone to watch two boys just a little younger than he is himself?"

Matthew shifted. He had heard about this from a couple of his friends before he and Beth had married. The Englisch didn't understand the Amish way of life. Some called it a hard life, but it was all he knew. He had been hoeing and planting since he was five years old. He had learned how to handle a team a year or two after that and was working a field all his own by the time he turned Stephen's age. It was just part of their lives.

And yet he had heard of Amish parents accused of child abuse and neglect for allowing their children to be "unsupervised," to use her word, or to work jobs that grown men did as well. A ten-year-old who could drive a front loader. A twelve-year-old with a full team of Belgians. No one said a thing until someone got hurt.

"Their mother died a couple of months ago," he heard himself say. "We're still adjusting."

She smiled in that understanding way she had. "Thank you, Mr. Byler. Henry will be back in shortly. The intern will give you a complete list of care instructions for his cast. He'll need to come back in three weeks so we can check his progress." She started writing again, this time on a small note pad. "This is a prescription for pain medication. It's a low dose, but it still might make him sleepy."

Matthew nodded and accepted the paper from her.

"And one last bit of advice?" she said. "Hire a nanny. Boys like Henry are prone to trouble. I see it all day long. They need someone watching over them. I know that you have work to do, but when you're not around, he needs someone there to keep an eye on him and help him make better decisions."

Chapter Three

"Are those Matthew Byler's twins out playing with Jim and Anna's twins?" Gracie shook her head at her own words. Two sets of twins, one identical and the other not. But that wasn't even the strange thing.

"*Jah*." Eunice nodded but didn't stop stirring whatever was in the large mixing bowl on the counter in front of her.

Gracie allowed her gaze to roam around the kitchen. Dough in the mixing bowl, big pot boiling on the stove, the smell of celery and onion floating in the air. "Chicken and dumplings?" she asked.

"I figure this is about the last week we'll have for them before it gets too hot to eat them."

"I love chicken and dumplings." It was one of her favorites.

"Me too." Eunice grinned. "I think Brandon is coming out to eat. He's supposed to bring his friend." She raised one eyebrow into a skeptical arch.

"Shelly?" Gracie snatched a piece of carrot off the chopping block and munched it as she waited for Eunice to reply.

Brandon was Hannah's son, born after she had moved into the Englisch world but conceived before she had left.

Aaron Zook, Hannah's fiancé, was the boy's father, though he had known nothing about his son until Hannah returned the year before. Now the two were trying to find their footing in a relationship that could suit them both. It was rough going. Gracie could see it on both their faces whenever the two of them were together, but they were trying, and that was a lot.

Brandon had met Shelly at the library in town where they both went to check in with their online schools. Shelly's family wasn't Amish, but they were very conservative. Brandon swore that there was nothing between them, that they were just study partners and met in the library to discuss school issues, but everyone in the Gingerich family suspected that there were more feelings between them than either of them was letting on.

Eunice chuckled. "Of course, Shelly. Who else?"

Gracie pilfered another piece of carrot. "Anyone else coming? There is an awful lot of food scattered around for just the six of us." Four was their standard number. Gracie, David, Abner, and Eunice. Hannah was out at Aaron's house each night and Jim's wife, Anna, cooked for her own family. But this looked to be chicken and dumplings for an army.

"I thought you might run a pot of them out to Matthew Byler's place."

Gracie resisted the urge to immediately shake her head. It had been four days since she had completely embarrassed herself. And if she was lucky she would have five more before she had to see him again at church. "Is that necessary?"

Eunice looked up from rolling out the dumplings, her plump face pink from the heat in the kitchen and her own exertion. "Of course it's necessary," she chided. "What has gotten into you lately?"

Gracie stuffed the rest of the carrot piece into her mouth and used that as a reason not to answer right away.

"That poor man," Eunice continued. "Came by frantic this morning needing me to watch his kids. His boy, I don't remember his name . . . he's the middle one. Anyway, he fell out of the hayloft and broke his arm. Matthew had to rush him to town. He just picked them up a bit ago."

And how petty would it be of her to not take him supper after the surely trying day he'd just had?

"What's up, cuz?" Hannah called from the doorway. It was strange and funny to hear her talk like an Englischer though she was dressed Plain.

"You better not let the bishop hear you say that. He'll think you're not serious about your classes," Eunice said. The bishop had been accepting of Hannah coming back into the fold, but Eunice seemed to over-worry that something was going to go wrong and Hannah would disappear once again.

Hannah made a face.

Eunice was constantly worried that something would happen and Hannah's request to marry Aaron or join the church or both would be denied. Gracie supposed she couldn't really blame Eunice. She had lost two daughters so long ago, only to get them back and lose the third to the Englisch world. It had been a while since Tillie had written to them. Gracie wondered how she was faring in the big bad world. She shook off the thought and turned her attention back to Hannah.

"How are the classes?"

Hannah swiped a piece of carrot and shrugged one shoulder. "You know."

Gracie nodded. She did. The classes were meaningful and boring, necessary and a monotonous recap of everything they already knew, and yet they were exciting, for they signified such great change. She supposed that was the real reason behind them. If a person had been raised Amish, which most of them had, they already knew the information told to them again at class. But the class itself signified that something different was happening, a transition. That made them special.

Since Hannah had left the Amish before joining the church, she must join now in order to marry Aaron. And joining the church meant baptism classes.

"What's for supper?" Hannah asked.

"Chicken and dumplings." Eunice gave her a quick glance, then went back to tearing off strips of dough and tossing them into the boiling chicken stock on the stove. The hotter the water the firmer the dumpling, and Abner Gingerich liked his dumplings firm. "I thought you were going to be at Aaron's tonight."

She shook her head. "He got a driver to take him to Ethridge for a couple of days. The grandparents have been pestering for a visit."

"And you didn't go with him?" Gracie asked.

Hannah made a sweeping gesture from shoulder to thigh. "Apparently not," she said, then beamed a bright smile to take the snark from her words. "I don't like to intrude on their time."

"I'm sure they don't see it that way." Eunice tossed the last of the dough into the boiling pot, then wiped her hands on her apron.

Maybe this meant Gracie wouldn't have to take Matthew the dumplings after all. Because now that Hannah was there that was . . . one more person to feed. Like that was going to make any difference.

"Did you cook enough?" Hannah nodded toward the stove as Eunice turned down the heat and placed a lid over the pot.

"Gracie's taking some over to Matthew Byler's tonight."

"Really?" Hannah lifted one questioning brow and shot

Gracie a sassy look. Gracie knew exactly what her cousin was thinking. But it wasn't possible. She and Matthew were not meant to be. And honestly, looking back on it now, she had known it all along. Known it because she knew next to nothing about him. She couldn't marry someone she barely knew. It was crazy!

"Now that you're here, perhaps you would rather . . ." Gracie shot Hannah a pleading look. "I'm sort of tired."

"I don't know . . ." Hannah mused. "I've had sort of a rough day myself."

Eunice harrumphed. "Goodness, what is wrong with you girls? The poor man needs food for his children."

"Hannah . . ." Gracie pleaded.

Her cousin snatched another piece of carrot and thoughtfully chewed. "I'll go over there," she said for them both to hear. Then she lowered her voice for Gracie's ears only. "But you owe me one."

By the time Matthew got all the children home and Henry into bed to rest, his head was pounding.

Thankfully, Grace stopped crying on the ride home, but her wails of betrayal still echoed in his ears. The twins and Stephen had gone out to the barn to do the small chores before supper.

Now Matthew just had to figure out what was for supper. He was blessed to say that the church ladies had supplied him with food enough that he hadn't had to worry about it, but he knew that time was drawing to an end. He had three weeks, maybe a month, and when summer hit in full swing, everyone would be so busy with their own families that they wouldn't have time to give him a second thought, much less cook him a meal.

There had to be some leftovers. He swallowed a couple of Tylenol and was surveying the contents of their icebox when he heard a familiar buggy outside. Maybe it wasn't really familiar, but he would like to believe that it was. He wanted it to be Gracie.

He took a quick peek out the window. It was definitely the Gingeriches' buggy.

Suddenly he knew. Her proposal was exactly what his family needed. He needed a wife. The children needed a mother. They needed someone. She wasn't hard to look at. In fact, thinking back, she was downright pretty. He knew she could cook, and of course she could clean, and she could calm the baby quicker than anyone else who had tried.

And she was pulling up to his house, bringing him salvation once again. He shook his head at himself. He was being overly dramatic, but it was true. On a small scale. She saved them time and time again with food, comfort, even just a woman's attention.

All he had to do was meet her at the door and tell her thanks for the food and he had given her proposal a great deal of thought. He had decided that it was a fine idea. A good idea? A nice plan? A good plan? The way to go?

It was just getting worse. Maybe he should wing it.

He was standing just at the door when the first knock came. He opened it so suddenly the woman on the other side jumped back. She held a large pot in her hands and toppled a bit from the sudden movement.

He reached out to steady her.

"You scared me." Hannah Gingerich. At least he thought it was Hannah. Not that she looked anything at all like her sister, Leah, he just hadn't had enough dealings with them to remember which name went with which woman.

"I'm sorry," he said. "That was not my intention."

She smiled in forgiveness and held up the pot. "I have chicken and dumplings."

"Yum," he replied.

"Mamm said this is probably the last time for them until it gets too hot to eat them." She nudged past him and into the house. "Is the kitchen to the left?"

He nodded. She was bold, this one. Not at all like Gracie. It was hard to believe they were cousins, or even related at all.

"One of us will pick up the pot tomorrow." She brushed past him again and out onto the porch. "You were expecting Gracie?"

He swallowed hard. How did she know? Was he that easy to read? It wasn't like he and Gracie were a real couple. "I thought perhaps."

Hannah-maybe-Leah smiled a little bigger than before. "I'll see what I can do."

Matthew felt a little like a prisoner in his own home. He couldn't go to the fields. He would have to take all three boys and the baby, and that just didn't seem feasible. He supposed he could run over and see if the Widow Kate could watch them for a while so he could . . .

He could what? Plant his crops? He hadn't planned on doing that until tomorrow. Today he thought he would go see Gracie Glick. Tell her that he liked her plan. See if she was really serious about helping him with his children. Lord knows, he needed it.

He settled on getting the garden plot ready to plant as well. He hated it. Woman's work. He took care of the big fields, not the little patch of dirt that sat directly in front of his house. There was a small strip of grass between the porch and the garden, only about twenty yards wide. But he hated the thought that anyone driving by on the road would see him out working in the family garden. It was embarrassing and maybe even necessary. If Gracie decided that she really didn't want the immediate responsibility of five children, he would be the caretaker of that land as well. At least until Stephen was out of school.

When Stephen's days were free, Matthew knew a little of the pressure would be off him. But he remembered the doctor's gentle chastising. She might not understand the ways of the Amish. Not many did. The fact of the matter was they all lived in an Englisch world. If anyone else got hurt, he was sure authorities would be contacted. How would it look to leave a seven-year-old in charge of three younger brothers and a baby?

Gracie's proposal was the only option he had.

His heart started pounding in his chest as he pulled his buggy into the dirt lane that led to the Gingeriches' houses.

Just after their noon meal of leftover chicken and dumplings, he scrubbed the boys down, gave the screaming baby a quick bath, and dressed everyone in their best non-choring clothes. Henry had hated the idea from the start but was further vexed when his shirtsleeve wouldn't fit over his cast. Matthew hated to do it, but he cut off the sleeve much like the doctors had done yesterday to the shirt Henry had worn into the clinic. If he was in this cast as long as the doctors predicted, there would be plenty of time to have a new good shirt made. And everyday shirts as well.

Then the twins started crying when he refused to cut their sleeves from their shirts like their brother's. The baby was still sniffling, her bottom lip protruding as if the tears could start again any moment.

"Isn't this where Abner's Eunice lives?" Henry asked. He remembered Eunice for all the meals she had sent over. Tasty food will do that to a growing boy. "*Jah*."

"Why are we coming here?" he asked. He had taken the seat next to Matthew in the buggy. It wasn't where Matthew liked him to be. He had learned right after Beth's funeral that it was best to keep the twins separated when they were bored. And riding in the buggy was boring. To them, at least. He didn't care one way or the other. Thomas inevitably aggravated Benjamin enough to start a tussle of some sort, and that was dangerous going down the roads where Englisch cars also traveled.

Today he had placed them in the back, side by side, with threats of more than time-out if they didn't behave on the way to see Gracie. So far, so good, but the day and the driveway were long. The baby's seat had to sit in the back as well. Thankfully she had fallen asleep as soon as he started toward the Gingeriches'. He supposed she was exhausted after her trying morning. He knew he was. Now if she would just stay asleep after the buggy stopped. But that was praying for a miracle. These days he didn't seem to have those sorts of blessings.

They passed a little shack that looked like it had been worked on recently. He wasn't much for district gossip, but he thought Jamie Stoltzfus had stayed there with his nephew Peter before they turned Mennonite. Leaving the Amish church, was something he didn't understand but didn't try. It wasn't his business, after all.

"Are we there?" Thomas asked.

"Do we look like we're there?" he returned.

"*Jah.*" Henry grinned from the passenger's seat. He used his tongue to push on his bottom teeth, which were about to come out. Matthew had offered to tie a string around them, tie the other end to a doorknob and slam the door. It was how his *dat* had helped him when his teeth were loose.

Jah, *and you hated it.*

So he had.

And so he allowed Henry to do things his own way.

Like the bright yellow cast he'd come back with yesterday before he was discharged from the medical clinic. It was actually more than bright, the color of one of those highlighter pens people used to emphasize notes.

The bishop wouldn't say anything. But he knew there would be church members who disapproved. That was simply life in a conservative district.

"Are we there yet?" Thomas asked again once the houses came into view.

Matthew didn't bother to answer. As if he could. His throat grew instantly dry and his heart kicked up another notch. The reins slipped as his hands began to perspire. But as nervous as he was, there was no backing out now. He had been spotted.

Gracie, Hannah, and Leah were all outside, clustered around a wooden table covered with bottles of all shapes, sizes, and colors. The taller ones were clear while the smaller bottles were dark amber-brown and deep blue. Three huge bowls sat in the center of the table and contained some sort of milky-looking liquid. He had no idea what it was, but it didn't matter. That wasn't his purpose here.

Hannah-Leah saw him and nudged Gracie with her elbow. Then the other Hannah-Leah turned around and grinned. The two Gingerich women laughed as if someone had told the funniest joke while Gracie stood stock-still in apparent shock.

"Stop." Gracie swatted at her cousins with the towel she held in her hands. He read her lips more than heard the words over the rattle of his buggy.

She swatted at them again and the sisters straightened up, the extra-wide grins not leaving their faces. It was almost as if they were teasing her about . . . him? But that would mean she had told them about her proposal.

His nervousness went haywire. What did it matter? It was a marriage of convenience. He needed someone to take care of his children and Gracie had graciously offered. See? Her name suited her to a T. It was surely a sign that it was meant to be. If he believed in such things. He wasn't quite sure he did.

"Are we—" Thomas started as Matthew pulled the buggy to a stop.

"*Jah*, Thomas. We're there now. But I need you boys to sit in the buggy with the baby."

Groans went up all around. His twins wanted to go play with the Gingeriches' twins and Henry wanted to show off his new cast, indifferent toward the fact that he had showed everyone the day before.

Matthew shook his head. "We're only going to be here a second."

"Then why did we get all dressed up?" Henry asked.

"And clean?" Thomas added. Benjamin sat quietly beside his brother, softly kicking the back of the front seat. Enough that it made a gentle noise but not enough to aggravate. But that was Benjamin.

"Because," Matthew growled. His children seemed undaunted.

The women waited, their curious gazes steady.

He supposed he looked twelve kinds of a fool sitting there arguing with his children. Beth never argued with them. Why did he have to?

But he never came up with an answer. Just then the baby realized they weren't moving and decided to wake up. And squall like a . . . well, like a baby.

Matthew sighed. Why couldn't today turn out like he had planned? Even just a little bit.

"The baby's crying," Henry said.

"*Danki*, son." Matthew hopped down, nodded the brim of his hat toward the ladies, then went around the back of the buggy to get the baby. Like picking her up was going to help. Still, he wouldn't leave her there, wailing her head off while he talked to Gracie.

He unbuckled her from the carrier seat and she arched

her back as if to keep him from actually picking her up. She hated him. That much he was certain of. It was a fact he hated as much as she despised him. Keeping his grip firm but gentle, he cradled her against his chest, her huge tears wetting his shirt front.

What was it Gracie had said? *You're too little to have such big problems.* If she only knew.

"Da-at!" Henry yelled to be heard over the baby's sobs.

"Stay in the buggy," he said without turning around.

His gaze sought out Gracie and he kept it on her alone. He didn't want to see the other women's goofy grins. He couldn't believe that Gracie had told them her plans to marry him. It was such a personal thing to share.

Never mind that. It doesn't matter.

And it didn't. Not today anyway.

"Can I talk to you for a moment?" He raised his voice to be heard over the baby's continued crying. He bounced her in his arms and patted her bottom the way he had seen Gracie do, but his actions didn't have the same effect on the infant. She was as stubborn as her *mamm*.

"*Jah*, sure." She didn't hesitate. She wiped her hands on the towel she still held and came around the table.

"In private," he clarified, walking closer to his buggy. Like that was better. He stopped halfway between it and the table and turned to face her.

"*Jah*?" she asked. Her voice was soft, and he could barely hear it over the baby's crying. Why did the child cry all the time? It broke his heart. Here was another woman he couldn't make happy. "Here," Gracie offered. "Let me." She held her hands out and he gave the baby over. So close to Gracie, he noticed she smelled nice, like lavender and lemon peels, maybe with a bit of vanilla thrown in as well.

Gracie bounced the child, holding her close and kissing the top of her head. The pair looked so natural, even though Gracie was in everyday clothes and the baby dressed in one of her best. Her dark blue dress was one of the first ones Beth had made for her. One of three. The rest had come from the secondhand shop in town. The one Leah owned.

Matthew watched them, trying to form the words in his mind. The baby's sobs turned to hiccups as Gracie continued to rock her from side to side. The baby was happy once again. Well, maybe not *happy*, but at least she wasn't screaming, and that alone was enough reason to marry Gracie as far as he was concerned. He was having a hard time with the four boys and a baby who cried all day.

"There," he said, gesturing toward Gracie and the baby.

"There what?" Her forehead puckered into a frown.

"That just proves it."

She shook her head and kissed the baby's crown once more. The baby was wearing a prayer *kapp* so her lips landed on the dark gray fabric, but the sentiment was there. "I don't understand."

"That right there proves that your idea is a good one. Maybe we should get married."

The minute the words left his mouth he knew he had said the wrong thing. Her face crumpled a bit, then smoothed out into a too-calm expression. He had hurt her feelings. Something he hadn't meant to do.

Matthew frowned, trying to come up with something to repair the situation, but his mind was a fallow field.

"I mean, you came and asked me and I'm giving you my answer."

That calm expression never wavered.

"Did you see my cast?" Henry grinned from beside him, holding up his arm for Gracie's perusal.

"Oh my," she said, the too-calm expression becoming a smile. "That certainly is yellow."

"I thought I told you to stay in the buggy."

"I wanted the orange, but they were out." Henry chattered as if Matthew hadn't spoken.

To her credit, Gracie didn't blink an eye. "I heard about your big day yesterday."

"Henry," Matthew rumbled in warning.

"I even got a shot."

"Back to the buggy now." His voice dropped into the range of a growl. He did not like being disobeyed, and he didn't like to be interrupted, especially when he was trying to find a wife!

She adjusted the baby and leaned a little closer to Henry. "I think you better get back into the buggy like your father said."

Henry smiled at her and Matthew could see the love blooming in his eyes. "Okay." He turned and started back to the buggy, but turned before climbing in. "Next time I'll show you my loose teeth."

Her mouth twitched, but she held in her laughter. "I'm looking forward to it."

Once Henry was back in place, she turned to Matthew. The smile she had bestowed on his son was gone, only to be replaced by that too-calm look from before.

Matthew sucked in a deep breath. He needed to get this done before he ruined it all. "What I mean to say is, you seem really good with the kids and you're right. I do need help." Yesterday just proved it.

She shook her head. "I withdrew my proposal." She hesitated slightly before saying that last word.

And that left him only one option.

"Gracie Glick, will you be my wife?"

Chapter Four

It took all her energy to stand there, holding his baby and keeping the wild collection of emotions from dancing across her face.

There but for the grace of God I go.

"You want to marry me?" She even managed to keep her voice steady and stronger than the squeak of a mouse.

"*Jah.*" He heaved in a deep breath but continued to scowl at her. Why was he scowling?

"I—I—" She didn't know what to say. *Jah*, she wanted to marry him. Sort of. She wanted a family and he seemed to be the means to get one. If she said yes, her life would change forever. If she said no, she would go on being dependable Gracie Glick, the one you can always count on in a pinch.

She looked back to her cousins. They stood huddled together, arms around each other and identical grins on their faces. She needed them to direct her, nod or something. Let her know that she was doing the right thing. But they just stood there watching and waiting. She was on her own.

Gracie turned back to Matthew. "*Jah.* Okay." Her answer was as odd as his proposal.

He nearly crumpled with apparent relief. "Good. Good." The scowl became a smile, then turned back into a scowl again. "Can I ask what you're getting out of this?"

"A family." Her answer was simple. She wanted a family and had for a long time. Once she married Matthew she would have his children to care for and—she gulped at the prospect—maybe soon a baby of her own.

He nodded in an understanding way, but his scowl remained.

Gracie had no idea what to do next. Should they shake hands? Maybe a kiss on the cheek? How did one seal the promise of marriage? Most likely with a sweet buss on the lips, but that was when two people were in love and couldn't wait to start their lives together. She and Matthew . . . well, that was far from the case.

She looked at him.

He looked back.

Someone had to make a move.

"Da-at," Henry called from the buggy. "Thomas won't stop pinching me."

He turned toward his son, then swung back again.

"You had better go," she said quietly.

He nodded.

"I need to get back to work anyway." She tilted her head toward the table covered with bowls of goat-milk lotion, bottles of essential oils, and empty bottles for once everything was mixed together.

"*Jah.*"

"Uh, here . . ." She moved toward him, holding his baby out for him to take. It was a warm day, but she instantly felt cold where the baby had been against her. She took one last breath of baby-scented air, then handed the child back to her father.

Not even a heartbeat later, the baby Grace began to cry.

"Da-at!" Henry again. "Now he's pinching Benjamin."

Matthew tried to soothe her, but her wails only intensified.

Gracie almost forgot. "When do you want to do this?" she asked loud enough to be heard over the baby, but hopefully not so loud to alert her cousins. "Get married, I mean."

"Da-at!" Henry yelled.

What must have been Benjamin's cries joined those of his sister.

Matthew turned back to her, his face creased with tired lines. "As soon as possible."

Two weeks, they decided in that small window of time between her asking when and Henry calling for his father once again. They would go to the bishop tomorrow and ask for special permission to marry.

Gracie had no doubt that Amos Raber would grant them consent, even out of season. Some things just couldn't wait.

Now all she had to do was break the news to her family.

"Well?" Hannah asked once Gracie had watched Matthew's buggy disappear, taking with it the terrible sounds of children crying. Was that something she was going to get used to? Everyone just seemed so unhappy.

Gracie shrugged away the thought and turned her attention to her cousin. "We're getting married."

Leah raised her hands in the air and whooped. Then the twins did some kind of Englisch dance where they locked arms and skipped in a circle.

"In two weeks," she added.

The celebration instantly stopped.

"Two weeks?" Leah screeched. "That's not enough time."

"Like you have reason to talk," Hannah chided.

"Hey, at least I gave you a month."

"Two weeks," Gracie stated. Two weeks was all she

could afford. Any longer and she might change her mind. Even though she wanted this. She really did.

Hannah and Leah stopped their bickering at the sound of her emphatic tone.

Easygoing Gracie was serious about this one.

"Well," Hannah said. "The house is pretty clean since we just had church."

"It'll need a few touch-ups," Leah added. "It always does."

"And we can get the Widow Kate to help us sew the dresses. She usually needs the money."

Gracie listened as they started making the plans. They would need to decide if someone was standing up with her. Second weddings didn't normally have attendants, but this was her first wedding. She wanted to keep a few of the traditions. But if she had attendants, then who was standing up with Matthew? Then the conversation switched to whether or not Matthew's family would be able to make it down for the service and whether or not he had any brothers to serve as witnesses if Leah and Hannah stood up with Gracie as they had just planned.

"We need pen and paper," Leah squealed.

Actually Gracie needed to lie down. This was all happening so quickly it was making her dizzy.

"Wait till Mamm hears," Hannah added. "She's going to love this."

Gracie wasn't certain if she was being truthful or sarcastic. With Hannah you never knew. She had definitely spent too many years with the Englisch.

"Because Gracie caught the bouquet at your wedding," Hannah was saying. Gracie had missed whatever had led them down this road.

"I'm sorry. I don't remember," Leah said with an apologetic twist of her mouth. "The whole day is mostly a blur."

"Well, you looked beautiful and Gracie caught your bouquet."

"Which is supposed to mean she's the next one to get married."

"And now she is." Hannah all but hopped up and down and clapped her hands. "Too bad she can't carry it at her service. That would be so sweet."

"Maybe we can use it as a centerpiece."

"Or the cake topper," Hannah suggested.

"The cake!" Leah exclaimed. "Who's going to make the cake?"

"Mamm, of course."

"We better go tell her the good news," Leah said.

Neither one seemed to notice her silence. She was fine with whatever plans they wanted to make. The wedding wasn't that important. There had been a time when she had thought so, but now she knew better. It was what happened after the wedding that truly counted, and that part had her a little worried.

"Are you coming, Gracie?" Leah asked.

The twins had somehow gathered up all their lotions and bottles and essential oils and were about to head up the wooden steps that led into the house.

"*Jah*." She stirred herself out of her thoughts and followed behind them.

"Two weeks!" Eunice's screech was almost as loud as Leah's had been.

"I think it's best to ge—have the wedding as soon as possible." She had almost said *get this over with*, but stopped herself just in time. She didn't want Eunice to get the wrong impression.

Her aunt threw her hands into the air, then bustled over

to the sideboard and started looking for a pad and pencil in one of the drawers.

"Leah? Hannah!" she called.

The women came out of the kitchen carrying glasses of milk and slices of banana bread.

"We figured we would need something to help us keep our energy up."

"Good plan." Eunice settled her reading glasses low on the bridge of her nose and started to write. "Dress, cake, attendants, shirts."

"Isn't that Matthew's responsibility?" Leah asked.

"He doesn't have any family here. So I suppose we should help him with that."

Hannah nodded in agreement. "And clothes for the kids."

Eunice jotted that on the growing list. "Tomorrow we should go into town to pick out the colors. They may have to special order."

"Just blue is fine," Gracie said. Stick to the basics and hopefully everything would turn out just fine.

"Gracie, there are a hundred different shades of blue."

"Maybe more," Hannah added. She turned to her sister. "Google it on your smartphone and see."

"I will not." Leah frowned at her. "First of all, the service is bad out here and secondly that's not something truly important."

Hannah sighed. "You're right. Guess I just got overly excited there for a moment."

"Focus," Leah commanded. Gracie had heard her say the same thing to Brandon a hundred times. And she didn't need anything called *google* to help her know that. "You're freaking Gracie out."

"I'm not freaked out." Another phrase she had never heard until the twins came back to Pontotoc. Okay, so she was a little freaked out but not about the things they thought.

She mentally shook herself and tried to center her attention on the matter at hand. She needed the women to help her figure out all the details that came before the wedding. There would be plenty of time in the next two weeks to find out what to expect after the vows were said.

With the four of them working together they hammered out most of the plans. Eunice had said simple was best, and anything that could be delegated to another family member would be to help ease their load. But Eunice promised she would make the cake herself. After all, she made the best cake in three counties.

"You okay?" Eunice asked, peeking out the screen door, then coming out onto the front porch next to where Gracie sat on the big wooden swing. The days were starting to get longer. It was almost eight and the sun had just begun to sink in the west.

"*Jah.* Of course." She pasted on a bright smile and beamed it at her aunt as solid proof.

Eunice stepped a little closer and eased down next to her. "Tell the truth," she said in that easy, urging voice that had done her in many times as a child. How could she even think about telling a lie when she knew that voice was coming?

"It's all just happening really fast." Self-preservation, that's how. She needed to talk to someone about the wedding night, but she wasn't ready. Not just yet. The questions were eating up all her thoughts. She just couldn't bring herself to ask those burning questions.

She had heard talk and whispered speculations. She was almost twenty-six and knew the basics, but she didn't *know*. And the unknown was hard to live with.

"Do you love him?" Eunice asked.

The question took her completely off guard. "Do I love him?" She repeated it more to make sure that's really what her aunt asked than to stall for time. "No," she said truthfully. One lie a night was enough.

"Then why are you marrying him?" Eunice held up one hand to stop a quick reply. "And don't tell me anything about Amish marriage being only about convenience and property."

"I want a family." Surely she could say that without all the wedding-night questions escaping before she was ready.

"You have a family. You have us."

Somehow she knew that Eunice was going to say that. But Gracie had lost the rest of her family. Her mother, father, and two brothers. All in terrible random accidents. Those times when God closed His eyes and tragedy struck. Her brothers had been racing buggies on a moonless night on a back road in nearby Randolph. And her parents had died from carbon monoxide poisoning. Gracie had long since come to terms with the idea that she should have been there too, but it was hard being an orphan, even at almost twenty-six.

"I want . . . my own family."

Eunice nodded. "You should have love too."

It was a beautiful sentiment. But a luxury that she couldn't afford. "With who? There are no eligible bachelors my age in Pontotoc." There were even fewer in Adamsville. Her only hope for finding love would be in the parent community of Ethridge near Nashville, Tennessee. But even then, it was a gamble. They married early in these parts, and most men over twenty-six had already settled down and started their own families.

Eunice opened her mouth to correct her, then shut it. She opened it again and shut it again, then shook her head. "I understand. But is this really what you want?"

"*Jah*." But the word had trouble getting out. Was this what she wanted?

Yes and no. She wanted a family, that much she couldn't deny, but she couldn't say that she wanted it with Matthew Byler. Not that there was anything wrong with him. He was handsome. And sort of grumpy. But he seemed to be a good father. Her mind flashed back to the day she had delivered the casserole. His boys had been sitting on the couch, looking almost afraid of him. And his scowl followed soon after. That day she had been sort of scared of him too.

Then she remembered the way he had cradled his baby close to him.

Then shoved the baby at her.

But he was caring. Wasn't he? Worried that his daughter wasn't getting enough rest.

Or maybe he just wanted her to stop crying.

"Gracie?"

She jerked as Eunice touched her hand.

"You were deep in thought there."

"I'm okay." Was she? Maybe she should ask around, find out a little more about him. But that felt dishonest. Like she wasn't trusting him. Like she wasn't trusting God.

"You can still change your mind," she said gently.

Gracie shook her head. There was one thing she knew for certain about Matthew Byler: He needed help, and she was just the person for the job.

But once she closed the door to her room and turned out the light, the doubts flooded in once more.

There, in the darkness, she lay on her small bed and her thoughts swirled around her like some out-of-control dust storm.

She was doing the right thing.

Wasn't she?

Yes, of course.

She thought so anyway.

So she might not know him that well. How much did a person really know about another? And she had already recounted everything she knew about him. What was the use in starting all over? She didn't know anything new about him.

Maybe that was the key! She should go to his house and spend the day with him. Talking, getting to know each other. They could cook and eat. Maybe sit on the porch and watch the children play under that big shade tree in his backyard. She could help him plant and just . . . talk. And if she didn't like him after all that, she didn't have to marry him.

She breathed a great sigh of relief. A plan. She always did better when she had a plan. And this one was perfect. Except . . .

If she discovered that she didn't like him before they got married and she called off the wedding, that would mean no more family. No more options. She would die a spinster.

Then the question became: What was worse? Marrying a man she might not like, or living the rest of her life without a family of her own?

Being alone. That was the worst. Everything else she could get through. With God's help, she would make it work.

Mind made up, she rolled onto her side and went to sleep.

Gracie pulled to a stop in front of the bishop's house and wished that she had taken Eunice up on her offer to come with her. She hadn't wanted Eunice around, poking holes in her plan and making her second-guess her decision. Like Gracie wasn't doing that enough already.

That was one regret. The other was that Matthew Byler

was already inside. Bending the bishop's ear with . . . with . . . did he know anything about her at all? She stumbled halfway to the porch. What if he decided that he didn't want to marry her because he didn't know anything about her, and how could he let a stranger look after his children? Or maybe he had found out some things about her and didn't like what he heard. She was fairly average, she supposed. Not too loud, not too quiet. She hadn't done anything wild or crazy during her run-around years. Not many did in their community. It simply wasn't allowed. But that was good, right? Sure. Unless he wanted someone who was a lot of fun. Like Leah. A person couldn't have anything but a great time around Leah. Maybe he wanted someone like that to be his partner for life.

She tripped again, then stopped before she fell flat on her face. She had to get control of her emotions before she went inside. The bishop would never agree to a union between the two of them if she was as skittish as a newborn colt.

She drew in a deep breath, held it, and closed her eyes. *Dear Lord, I pray I'm doing the right thing. I mean it looks like the right thing to do. What with me wanting a family and him having one that needs someone to watch over them. That looks like Divine Will. That looks like a plan of Your making. If it is, Lord, please give me a sign. Show me what I'm doing—what we're doing is truly Your Will. Ame—*

"Child, are you going to stand out here all day, or are you coming in to discuss this marriage?"

Gracie didn't even get to finish. She opened her eyes to find Elizabeth Raber standing on the porch, eyeing her with a touch of concern. The bishop's wife had a hand braced on one ample hip and a wooden spoon in the other.

Was this her sign? How was she supposed to know?

"Gracie?" The worry in Elizabeth's voice far outweighed that in her eyes.

"*Jah.*"

Elizabeth shifted her weight and cocked her head toward the other side. "*Jah* you're going to stay out here all day, or *jah* you're coming inside?"

"*Jah.*" Gracie nodded her head this time, as if somehow that made everything clearer. She wanted to say she was coming inside, because that was exactly what she wanted in her heart of hearts. And it was, so why was she hesitating?

Because it was a big step and the bishop's wife coming out onto the porch to see what was taking her so long didn't seem like much of a sign.

"I was just putting on a batch of chocolate chip cookies."

Chocolate chip cookies? Those were her favorite. Well, one of them. And surely that was the sign she had been asking for.

Gracie forced a smile and made her way to the house.

"I'm not going to pretend this is a love match," the bishop started, "so I have to tell you, marriage is forever."

Or "until death do you part." Matthew shifted uncomfortably in his seat. They were all sitting around the dining table, plates of chocolate chip cookies in front of them and fresh cups of coffee to the side. No one was eating save Gracie. He didn't have an appetite for anything sweet right now. It was too much to add to his already churning stomach. He was nervous. And he had been praying that he was doing the right thing.

She, on the other hand, was shoveling in cookies as if they were about to be verboten. He supposed all these changes weren't bothering her at all. She was getting what she said she wanted, a family. And he knew for a fact that she traveled a great deal among family members, helping out where needed. Moving into a strange house was probably nothing for her. And if she went to that many houses, surely five children would be a piece of cake. Or maybe a chocolate chip cookie.

She eased another one onto her plate, then glanced around to see if anyone noticed.

He averted his eyes to keep from embarrassing her. Or maybe she didn't mind at all. Who knew?

He should if he was going to marry her. But their marriage was to help them. No, it wasn't a love match. And some called it a marriage of convenience. But he knew that it was just the way life worked. He'd never thought about marrying again. Not really. His first marriage had been trying enough. But he needed help, and the best way to get that was to marry.

And she was getting her family. *Don't forget about that.* That should make him feel better. And it almost did. But the family they had at the start was all the family he wanted. No more children. It was simply too hard. He had put Beth through all that for the sake of family; he wouldn't do the same to Gracie.

"I understand." Matthew's voice sounded hoarse, so he cleared his throat and nodded.

They waited for Gracie to answer, but she was once again busy sneaking another cookie from the platter.

"Gracie?" the bishop asked.

She stopped, looked up at him guiltily. Then she dragged the cookie onto her plate. "*Jah?*"

Matthew had seen enough. At first he thought she was uncaring and so content with her decision that she was plowing through the cookies like she didn't have a care in the world.

But now he thought better. Her eyes were clear blue, but big and scared like a doe in the woods. She chewed on her bottom lip and shook her head, as if somehow that would replay what she had missed and give her the answer.

He reached across the table and took her hand, which

was slightly calloused, but soft in all the right places. That was just Amish women. They worked hard taking care of the kids and the house. They couldn't be expected to have the skin of a princess.

"The bishop was reminding us that marriage is forever. Are you still agreeable to your decision to marry me?"

She swallowed hard but nodded like she meant it.

"Even though there is no love between us?"

"Eunice always says love will come." Her voice was a little muffled from eating cookies, but it sounded steady and true enough.

Still, a stab of guilt shot through him. He couldn't love her. No matter how sweet her eyes were and how cute she looked sneaking cookies like a toddler. Love didn't solve everything. He had loved Beth. There had been a time when their marriage was strong and healthy. That was when he thought nothing could touch them, nothing could ruin their joy. How wrong could one man be?

Perhaps it was better she learn that lesson from him rather than have to go through it herself with another man. His guilt eased a bit.

"So they say," he murmured.

She looked down at their hands, lying on the vinyl table-cloth. His gaze fell there as well. He was rubbing his thumb across the tender skin between her forefinger and thumb. Back and forth, back and forth. He hadn't even realized he was doing it. They looked back up at the same time, their gazes clashing—hers soft and warm. He could only imagine how horrified his looked.

He jerked his hand away, unwilling to give her false hopes.

Her sweet gaze turned cloudy with confusion, but Elizabeth spoke, and she shifted her attention to the bishop's wife.

"Some marriages are even stronger when love isn't

clouding the way." She looked at each of them in turn. Had she seen his caress?

Heat filled his face. He had been caught like a schoolboy making goo-goo eyes at the teacher. Elizabeth Raber didn't miss a thing.

"If I'm understanding everyone's wishes and reasonings, this union will provide a stable home for five young children, one of which is just an infant. How can I deny such a joining?"

Matthew almost crumpled in relief but managed to keep his spine straight and his gaze steady. He turned to Gracie and smiled. Well, he tried to. It felt a little strange on his lips. Then he realized it had been a long time since he'd smiled at anyone or anything. Not even his children. How had he allowed this to change him so much? He had to fix that. Somehow he would.

Gracie smiled in return, but hers looked as hesitant as his did forced. Maybe it was time to start praying. That might be the only thing that would get them through this.

Chapter Five

Gracie looked around the room and smiled even though she felt guilty. She smiled because they wanted her to and she didn't know who might be looking. Today was sewing day. She and Eunice, along with Hannah, Leah, and a couple of women from the church had gathered to get the dresses and shirts done. Normally she would have bought the material for everything, given the yardage for the shirts to the groom, and sewn the dresses herself. But this wasn't normal. Matthew didn't have anyone to sew for him. The truth was he didn't have anyone to stand up for him either. Dave had agreed, and Jim had looked visibly relieved that the responsibility wouldn't fall on him. One attendant was enough for a hurried wedding. Plus Aaron would be at a horse auction that weekend and Jamie had turned Mennonite. The bishop was being generous, but no one wanted to push him any further than necessary.

And then there was the time crunch. There was too much to do for her to go it alone. So everyone had gathered together and made something of an assembly line to sew dresses and shirts. There were two sewing machines at the house and they were manned by Eunice and a woman named Lavina King. She was a kind woman prone to help others, but Gracie suspected that she had agreed for the main purpose of finding out the latest information on the wedding. The four-one-one, Brandon would have said, though Gracie had no idea what the numbers had to do with gossip.

"You know I haven't done this in sixteen years," Hannah grumbled.

"It's good for you," Eunice said. She didn't even bother to look up from her machine.

"Amish women need to learn how to sew." Leah snickered.

"Oh, just because I didn't darn my own socks while I was 'out of the country,'" Hannah returned.

"Jealous, much?" Leah grinned and kept on sewing.

"Girls," Eunice warned, though everyone knew the two were just playing. Twins were like that, Gracie supposed. But she'd wondered when the remarks would come out, since Hannah was standing up for Gracie. Again, Leah was Mennonite and the bishop was already bending a lot of the rules. If only Tillie were there.

She and Tillie had practically grown up together and were truly like sisters. But now Tillie had left to go to the Englisch world with her boyfriend, Melvin, who wanted to work on engines. Gracie missed her so very much and prayed daily for word from her that she was fine and okay. But so far, only the one letter had come, and then there was the one she left the night she disappeared. At least Hannah and Leah were back.

When they had left to go to the Englisch world, Hannah had turned Englisch, married a wealthy man, and lived a life of luxury that Gracie could hardly imagine. Leah went looking for herself. At least that was what she said. Maybe not word for word, but it confused Gracie a bit. She didn't understand it anyway. How could she be lost inside her own skin? But Leah had gone looking and joined a missionary group who traveled to foreign countries and helped out the poor.

That was something Gracie could understand, missionary trips. She had even been on one. She had gone all the way to the Mississippi Gulf Coast to help after the hurricane, but she had heard of other Amish girls who had gone all the way to Louisiana and Texas. She had thought perhaps one day she might do that herself, but now she wouldn't be able.

But she would have a family, and that was worth any sacrifice she might make.

"Ouch." Leah shook out her hand and then sucked on one finger.

Hannah sniggered, and Leah shot her a look. Gracie sighed. She loved her cousins so much. They were the sisters she never had, even with the gap of years in their relationship. And she was so glad they had come back. Now if they could just get Tillie home . . .

"Hey, are you back there?"

All heads turned as someone called from the front of the house. Anna, Jim's wife.

"In the dining room," Eunice called.

Abner had pushed the table to one side, brought in the sewing machines, and took out all the chairs except the ones they needed. It was a lot for one day's work, but Abner didn't seem to mind. He did what he was asked, then headed to his work barn to make his sheds. Too many women in the house would make any man uncomfortable, but Gracie knew that Abner liked to keep busy and most likely had a side project he wanted to work on as well as a shed for a customer.

Anna and her oldest and only daughter appeared in the doorway. Anna held a plate of sandwiches while seventeen-year-old Libby carried a pitcher of iced lemonade. Baby Samuel clung to Anna's legs, seeming unsure of the visit.

Gracie supposed she shouldn't call him a baby any longer. He'd be three in the fall. He wasn't quite potty trained and usually ran around in an Amish dress, but today he wore pants and a shirt. Gracie supposed Anna had put a diaper on him for the occasion and that was what was making him uncomfortable.

"I thought you might could use this." Anna smiled and carried the plate of sandwiches to the table. She set it down and reached into a bag for a short stack of paper plates and cups. No dishes today.

Libby set the lemonade next to the platter, then moved to stand beside Gracie. She looped her arm through Gracie's and laid her head on her shoulder. Gracie resisted the urge to sigh once more. All this wedding business might not be traditional, but she was having the same doubts and anxieties as any bride. Well, maybe not Hannah. She was ready to marry Aaron in a wedding that was fifteen years in the making. Leah had already married Jamie, so they could legally adopt his orphaned nephew and give him the stable home he needed. Anna and Eunice were too removed from their own weddings to fully understand. That had been so long ago for them. But Libby understood. Gracie wasn't too old to remember what it was like at seventeen, dreaming of marrying a good Amish man who had swept her off her feet during her run-around time. But it just hadn't happened that way.

"Gracie, why don't you get the plates ready," Eunice said.

"*Jah*, of course," she answered, but before she moved away, she clasped Libby's hand and gently squeezed it. Libby squeezed back, gave her a smile, then let her go. At least someone understood.

* * *

"You're what?" Stephen's forehead crinkled into a frown.

"He's getting married." Henry nudged him with his shoulder.

Stephen nudged back.

"Boys." Matthew had gathered his boys in the living room, sat them all down on the couch, and shared his news. Thankfully, Grace had finally cried herself to sleep and was down for a nap. Her misery broke his heart, and he had no idea how to make it better.

"Why?" Stephen asked.

"You're not supposed to ask why," Henry chastised. "You're supposed to ask to who."

"To whom," Matthew automatically corrected. Then he shook his head at himself. When had he turned into Beth? Lord above, he needed to get married if only to save himself from . . . himself.

"To whom?" Stephen asked.

"Gracie Glick. You might remember her from church."

"Is she the one who came over here with chicken and ducklings?" Henry asked. "Those were good." He rubbed his stomach and licked his lips to show how much he enjoyed them.

"No, she's the one who brought the casserole. And it's dumplings, not ducklings."

"Is she the one who made Grace stop crying?" Stephen clarified.

"But she started up again," Henry said.

"She's pretty," Benjamin said. His voice was quiet, timid, and almost a whisper. He was a quiet child by nature, but with three brothers like Stephen, Henry, and Thomas, he seemed to melt into the background. Matthew found himself seeking out the child if only to make certain he was fine. So often he seemed lost in the shuffle.

"Yes," Matthew admitted in a croaky voice. She was

pretty, but he couldn't tell his boys that his marriage wasn't about having a pretty wife. Like they would understand. But Matthew needed to work out this new twist his life had taken. His brother was in Ohio and wasn't sure if he could make it down for the wedding. What he would give to sit face-to-face with Jason and talk through this whole situation until it made sense.

"Why?" Henry asked.

Stephen crossed his arms and looked down his nose at his brother. "I thought you weren't supposed to ask why."

Why? Why was he marrying Gracie Glick? Not for any of the usual reasons—love, or even companionship. He searched his brain for a reason. The only thing that popped into his mind was that verse in Corinthians about staying unmarried and if a man can't control his desires he should remarry. Why was that his first thought? He certainly couldn't tell his boys that was the reason, Biblical or not. One, because it wasn't true and two, he would have so much more to explain than he was ready to talk about with them.

"Is it because she made Grace stop crying?" Henry asked.

"I don't like it when Grace cries." Thomas finally found a spot where he could jump into the whirling conversation.

"Nor do I," Matthew assured him. "But she will help me take care of . . . the baby."

"And she'll cook?" Henry asked. Honestly, every thought the boy had centered around food these days. Beth always said that meant they were going into a growing spurt. He pushed the thoughts of Beth away. He didn't want them. But he was finding it hard to let go. He seemed to think of her more and more these days. Not in a romantic way, but in an everyday way. And once again he wished his brother were there. Not that Matthew could tell Jason the truth about Beth's death.

"She'll cook." Matthew nodded.

"And wash our clothes?" Thomas asked.

"With our help, *jah*."

Thomas made a face. He hated wash day.

"I guess that won't be so bad." Stephen nodded as if to say his word was final. He had become such a stand-in parent during these last couple of months. And he was only seven. With any luck, having Gracie around would allow him to go back to being a little boy. But part of Matthew suspected that losing his mother brought out a personality trait in Stephen that had been there all along.

"I'm glad you're getting married," Benjamin said.

The words melted Matthew's heart. He knew they didn't mean everything they implied, but he was glad to hear them all the same.

"One question," Henry said, holding up his forefinger. "Can she get that recipe for chicken and ducklings?"

Gracie pinched the bridge of her nose and willed the throbbing to go away. Of course it didn't work. But she tried. At least it held back the tears that threatened. She had never realized how much went into a wedding until this week. The house had been a flurry of activity, trying to get it all prepared. Food had to be bought and stored and prepared and whew! It was enough to make her head hurt and spin.

Eunice seemed to be taking it all in stride, but that was Eunice. Not much could ruffle her aunt. Gracie supposed that after having children who left the Amish and came back, one who had just left, and everything else that Eunice had experienced in her life, a quick wedding was a piece of cake.

And speaking of cake . . . She took a deep breath and surveyed the mess that had been Eunice's kitchen. She had

had one simple task: Stay and watch the ingredients until Eunice came back.

They had been just about to start mixing the batter when someone knocked on the door. David. His new sow had gotten out and he needed help bringing her back in. She was currently standing in the middle of the road. Just standing there. Not moving an inch. If she kept this up she was surely to be hit by a car. So far two had gone around her while David had tried to urge her out of the road and back toward her pen, but the stubborn pig wouldn't move. Abner and Jim had gone into town on some errand or another and couldn't help. But since Agnes—the sow—was due to have her first litter of piglets since David had started his side business of raising pigs, he couldn't leave her there or get too rough with her. He needed a softer touch. He needed Eunice.

Plus it didn't hurt that Eunice seemed to be the only one the stubborn pig would listen to. So she had wiped her hands on her apron, told Gracie to keep an eye on everything, and headed out with her second son.

"Girl, what happened in here?"

She whirled around at the sound of the voice. Mammi.

"I—I—" she stuttered but couldn't get the words out. How could she explain that she had been too distracted by preparations for the wedding and had accidentally knocked over the sack of flour? She got the broom to clean it up, then tucked it under her arm and used the little hand broom to sweep everything into the dustpan. She straightened and turned to empty it into the trash, but the full-sized broom was still tucked under one arm. She ended up clearing the table with the handle, tipping over the milk and sending the eggs crashing to the floor. The sugar too, flew out in an arc of sparkling white granules. The sack fell over on one side and emptied its contents onto the floor. She jumped then, reaching for the bag to save what she could.

All she succeeded in doing was tossing the newly swept-up flour into the air. Now she had flour all down her front. And dust. She could see it on her cheeks. It was probably in her hair and on her prayer *kapp*. She also toppled the can of shortening and sent the vanilla flying. It didn't spill since it was in a plastic bottle with the lid on tight. There was something to be thankful for. But when she surveyed the remainder of the mess she found it very hard to find any joy in this situation.

Just the vanilla. And that wasn't enough. Tears rose into her eyes once again. Was this God trying to tell her that she was making a mistake? Or maybe He was testing her, making sure that this was what she truly wanted. Either way, she was worn-out, fragile, and unable to hold it all together. In an instant she crumpled onto the floor in a fine puddle of flour, buried her face in her hands, and sobbed.

"What happened?" She heard Eunice's concerned voice over the sound of her own sobs, but she couldn't pull herself together.

"I'm not sure," Mammi said. "I guess I scared her."

Gracie shook her head but didn't take her hands from her face, didn't stop crying.

She didn't want to see. Not just the mess that she had created, but the looks she was certain were passing between her aunt and her grandmother.

"If you'd come out of your room more," Eunice said. "Or maybe not as quietly."

"I can't help that I'm quiet," Mammi said. "Old bones don't weigh much."

Their voices moved around her, but Gracie didn't take her hands from in front of her face. She didn't want to see. Or be seen. Maybe she would stay like this until after the wedding. At least her crying had subsided from racking sobs to little hiccups.

"We're going to help you up now, child."

She shook her head and reluctantly took her hands from her face. "No. I got it." She couldn't let the two of them pull her from the floor like a rag doll. Mammi was just getting over a broken hip and Eunice was spry, but not nearly as young as she pretended to be.

Gracie waved their hands away and reached for the edge of the table to pull herself up. She stuck her fingers in the sugar and her composure slipped a bit. No. She could do this. She had to keep this together. She couldn't fall apart every time the least little thing happened. She would never make it to the wedding.

But the tears came anyway.

She managed to get to her feet, but her dress was covered, front and back. Since she had crumpled onto the floor she was now soaked with milk, bits of eggshell, globs of raw egg, and a mixture of flour and sugar both wet and dry.

"Nerves, I guess," Mammi said.

"Uhmm-hmmm . . ." Eunice murmured as she dunked one corner of a nearby towel into the bucket of water sitting on the counter. Another plus. Gracie hadn't knocked that down.

Eunice dabbed at her cheeks, made a face, then wet the entire cloth. Gracie supposed she was a bigger mess than she even realized. But Eunice didn't give up. She kept on gently wiping until she was satisfied with the result.

"There," she said. "What's got you in such a tizzy?"

Could she tell her? Gracie didn't know if she could bring up the subject of a wedding night. She had never talked about such matters with anyone but Tillie, and Tillie had known even less than Gracie had at the time.

"I—uh . . ."

"Spit it out, girl," Mammi said.

"I'm worried about the wedding night." Once the words were out she wished she could call them back, for several reasons. One being the sheer embarrassment of asking her aunt and her grandmother about such things. She shook her head. "Never mind. It's dumb. You both probably don't even remember your wedding night."

Oops. Not the right thing to say. Eunice looked like she'd been conked over the head with a frying pan.

"What I mean is"—Gracie tried again—"it's been a long time." Still not good. The stunned look remained on Eunice's face. Gracie couldn't even make herself look at Mammi. Meeting Eunice's gaze was enough. "Uh, things change?" She hadn't meant it to sound like a question.

Mammi cackled and slapped a hand against her thigh. "Well, girl, it may have been a long time, but I'm sure it all works the same."

Eunice pulled herself out of her stupor and smiled. Gracie couldn't tell if it was a genuine smile or one meant to hide her real feelings. "I'm pretty sure it's remained the same since I got married too."

And here was the second reason why she didn't want those words floating around. Now she had to actually *talk* to her aunt and her grandmother about matters that were so very, very private. They might not want to even discuss a few things.

Gracie let out an exaggerated sigh of relief. "Whew. That's good to know."

"So what did you want to know?" Eunice asked. If Gracie was correct, the woman's face was a little pinker than normal, especially considering they hadn't even started baking yet.

"It's okay. Really," she said. "We need to clean up a bit."

That was an understatement. Flour and sugar were still strewn about. Milk was puddled on the floor and egg dripped from the edge of the table.

Eunice frowned. "It is a little messy in here."

Mammi laughed. "I bet that was a sight to see. All that flour going everywhere."

A chuckle escaped Gracie as well. She was entirely too high-strung these days, and the laughter just kept coming. She laughed until tears made tracks through the remaining traces of flour on her face. She laughed until she bent over in the middle, her side aching from the exertion. She laughed until Eunice sent Mammi a concerned look that neither one of them seemed to notice she saw.

She just couldn't stop laughing. Or maybe she knew somehow this was the way out of a tricky position.

"I'll go get my broom," Mammi said, and started for the door to the *dawdihaus*.

Eunice wrapped an arm around Gracie and led her onto the back porch. "Go ahead and take that dress off," Eunice said. "It'll have to be washed for sure."

Gracie, still unable to reply through her giggles, did as she was told.

Eunice handed her a thin cotton robe. "Put this on so you have something to wear back to your room."

Again she complied without a word. She needed to get a handle on herself, but she felt as if she were sliding away down some slippery slope of wedding jitters and doubts.

"Go on to your room. We'll talk about this after supper."

Gracie just nodded, unable to stop the wild chuckles that were quickly turning into tears of sadness once more.

Wedding jitters. She wasn't certain those two words were enough to express the myriad of emotions racing through her, but for now they would have to do.

Thankfully the talk scheduled for after supper never came. Eunice and Mammi allowed Gracie to cry herself out, then sleep it off in a two-and-a-half-hour nap. By the time she woke, Eunice was elbow deep in supper preparations.

"It's Friday." And the Gingeriches' usual family dinner. Gracie wiped her eyes to wake herself up. She only succeeded in discovering just how puffy her eyes were after her meltdown that afternoon. "I'm so sorry."

"Leah and Hannah will be here any minute. They can help." Eunice waved away Gracie's apology and sent her to the water pump to wash her face and press a cold rag to her swollen eyes.

Leah and Hannah were coming. And she knew her cousins would have questions. If Eunice and Mammi didn't tell them about her crying jag this afternoon, then surely they would see it on her face. And not just in pink, puffy eyes. Her cousins were too astute by far and they would see through any hastily pasted-on smile she might conjure between now and then.

She managed to get a little of the redness out of her skin and some of the puffiness, but it wasn't enough. Hannah took one look at her and nudged Leah. Thankfully neither one said anything. All through the meatloaf and mashed potatoes, the green beans, salad, and peanut butter spread. Not even during the pie, though she felt their gazes land on her from time to time. They were biding their time until they could get her alone. After dessert and the table was cleared, after the dishes were washed and put away, the floor swept, and the counters wiped down. After the men had gone outside to have a smoke, then back into the barn for a last minute or two of work before Bible reading and bed. It was the in-between that scared her. The in-between when she would be ambushed. Her cousins would grab her by the elbows and steer her out onto the porch. Then they would push her—albeit, gently—into the swing and plop down, one on either side of her.

"Spill it," Leah said, not giving Hannah time to speak. "We want to know everything."

Chapter Six

Gracie swallowed hard. How could she answer her cousin and still save face? "There's nothing—"

"We don't believe that either," Hannah put in.

She didn't think she could say the words again. Yet these were her cousins, as close to her as sisters, despite the age difference and the time they had spent away.

But they were closer to her age than either Mammi or Eunice. And perhaps they could help her . . .

No. She couldn't say all of that again. She knew the basics, and that should be enough. She was just experiencing wedding jitters, just as Mammi had said.

"I'm just nervous." Perfect. She had managed to dodge Leah and Hannah's caring probing and still tell the truth.

The twins shared a look, one that she had seen them exchange too many times to count. They were trying to decide if she was telling the truth or not. From there they would decide if they would call her on a lie and push further into the truth.

"Nervous?" Hannah finally asked.

"*Jah*." Gracie cleared her throat.

"About what?" This from Leah.

Gracie froze. They believed her, but they wanted to know more. That's just how they were.

She shrugged as if the whole thing was hardly worth mentioning. "You know, like what to expect when I'm married."

Leah and Hannah exchanged another look. Every time they did that, Gracie's heart skipped a beat. It was as if they knew what she was thinking, and they knew that the other knew as well.

Or so she thought. That idea was so twisted in her head she wasn't sure what she meant.

Hannah leaned forward and captured Gracie's gaze. "Are you talking about in the bedroom?" Her voice was quiet and still seemed to echo. The men in the barn probably heard. They were most likely out there laughing at her right now.

"No," she said, shaking her head. Was she shaking it too much? Should she calm it down? "No, no, not at all." Her voice had taken on the tone of the bishop when he started blustering about things. Not his preaching, but little things like hemlines and apron colors. Could the twins hear the difference?

She stopped shaking her head, only then realizing that her words had long since ended. Yet her denial continued and had turned into something akin to the motions of the little dog with the loose head that Sam Yoder had put into the front window of his buggy. Of course the bishop made him take it out the very minute that he saw it, but Gracie had caught a glimpse. The dog was sort of cute. She suspected that she looked a little *ab im kopp*. Off in the head.

"It's just . . ." she started, hoping to recover a little of her dignity. If only her mother were alive. She would have explained everything a bit more. Or not. The Amish weren't known for talking about such private matters. Even among family members. But Leah and Hannah were different. They had both lived Englisch lives. If someone were truly going to talk to her about something so intimate, it would be them. They were the only two people she knew who might be able to prepare her for this . . . event. She should ask. Yet she found herself saying, "What will we talk about?"

Another look passed between the twins.

"The kids, most probably."

"Yes, of course." She hadn't been thinking about the children. She had only been thinking of endless hours— daylight hours—that had to be filled with something. That was almost as scary as the nighttime hours they would spend alone. At least part of that time they would be asleep. As for the other . . . she had changed her mind. She didn't want to know any more than she already did.

"Just be yourself," Leah advised. "Everything else will fall into place."

Just be yourself.

That was a bigger chore than it sounded, considering she felt like a stranger in her own skin.

After Leah had given her the questionable advice, the subject had changed and Tillie was the focus. What she might be doing. If she was happy. When they would hear from her next.

Talking about Tillie gave Gracie a whole new set of emotions to deal with. Growing up, she and Tillie had been close. Gracie had always imagined that Tillie would be a part of her wedding. Now her cousin didn't even know that she was getting married. Gracie more than wondered if she was happy. She wanted to go find her and bring her back before she did irreparable damage to her standing in the community. It was a miracle that the bishop was allowing Hannah to return. If not for Aaron's three little ones and the son that Hannah and Aaron shared, he might not have. Only the good Lord knew for certain.

And Gracie wanted Tillie back. It was as simple as that. She had never really liked Melvin, only did stuff with the two of them out of her love for Tillie. But Melvin was no good. He had a wandering heart, a desire to work on Englisch engines, and a gleam in his eyes that Gracie knew meant he was dreaming of faraway places.

Tillie was more like her. Amish through and through, wanting nothing more from life than a strong house, a stable husband, and a passel of little ones running around. Gracie somehow knew that with Melvin, Tillie would never have that. At least Gracie wouldn't have to worry about that with Matthew. He seemed to be well grounded. Another plus.

She wondered what Tillie would think of Matthew. She would like him, Gracie decided. After she got to know him, of course. Matthew could be a little intimidating at first. Okay, a lot. But Gracie saw through most of it to the hurting man underneath. She was fairly certain Tillie would be able to see that as well.

Or maybe that was just what Gracie wanted to see.

She shook the thought away. And turned to the sound of a buggy rattling down the lane. She couldn't believe this. She and Matthew were going on a date. Well, no one had actually called it that, but it's exactly what it was. They were headed out to Sarah Hostetler's sweet shop. Matthew had suggested they get a special treat for the children for after the wedding. Sort of a wedding surprise. Gracie thought the idea was brilliant and sweet, and she hoped with all her might that Matthew was the one who came up with it. Big, tough, glowering Matthew deciding to get candy for his kids. But she had a feeling that Eunice or Anna fed him the idea. Or maybe Hannah, since she was in a similar situation with becoming a stepmother. That made more sense. And it made Gracie a bit sad. Though she was impressed that he was going through with it.

Gracie could hear the commotion even over the rattle of
the buggy on the packed gravel. It sounded like a very unhappy child. The sound grew louder as the buggy grew
near. It was nearly deafening by the time Matthew pulled
to a stop. He got down from the buggy, barely acknowledg-
ing her with a dip of the brim of his hat. Then he went
around to get the baby. Stephen climbed down from the
front seat to get out of Matthew's way, leaving Henry and
the twins to crawl out of the driver's side.

Henry jumped down without any help. He landed
solidly but managed to graze both knees on the ground.
Thankfully it was only dirt, but she wasn't sure Eunice
would take kindly to all that coming into the house.

"The baby's crying," he said to no one in particular.

"Thank you," Matthew replied, his exasperation apparent. Gracie wasn't sure if it was all directed at his son or
some of it was saved for the fact that once again the baby
Grace was crying. Did she just wail nonstop?

She noticed the twins were struggling and went to help
them. The dark-haired one, she thought his name was Benjamin, looked up at her with such gratitude it made her
heart melt. If only all of them looked at her that way. Or
maybe just Matthew. But she was asking too much too soon
from this impending marriage. Uh, upcoming marriage.
That sounded better.

"I'll just take the baby inside," Matthew hollered over
Baby Grace's cries.

She nodded. What else could she do but stand there and
nod as Matthew carried the screaming baby into the house,
his boys following behind him like a trail of ducklings?

Matthew felt beyond guilty walking out of the house
with the baby still crying. He couldn't make her happy—

so much like her mother—that much was notably apparent. So there was no sense in trying. But when she got like this it seemed no one could help her, and he hated to hand her off. But honestly he could use the break. Did that make him a bad father? He felt it did. And though he might still be angry with Beth, he had gained a better understanding of what she went through every day.

It was pretty obvious that the baby didn't like the carrier, but if he was being honest she still cried when he took her out of it. Only Gracie had been able to quiet the child. Gracie and sometimes Eunice, depending on how wound up the baby was before Eunice got her. Today just might be a disaster.

"Don't worry," Eunice called behind him. "We've got this." The *we* was made up of Eunice and her mother, who was at least ninety. They had said that Hannah had gone for a bit and would be back later, but who knew exactly what that meant. Hopefully she wouldn't be gone long and the three of them would be able to take care of his rowdy brood. Henry alone really needed two people watching him at all times so if one blinked the other would catch it.

"*Danki*," he called over his shoulder, guilt burning a hole in his stomach. It mixed there with the nervousness of a date. Thirty years old and he was going on a date. With a woman he was going to marry in less than a week. Next Thursday, five days away.

He caught Gracie's gaze and made himself not look away. There was something in her eyes that seemed to know him. More than he wanted. It was as if she could see all his secrets. And he had a few. Ones he didn't want to share.

She looks at you with compassion now. How would she look at you if she knew the truth?

He frowned at the thought. In the house behind him the cries abruptly stopped. The lack of sound made him stumble, his ears ringing from the almost quiet that surrounded him. Had they stuffed a rag in her mouth? He couldn't say he blamed them. He loved the baby. He did. He was her father, but it was hard to live with someone who seemed to hate the very ground you walked on.

"Are you ready to go?" His voice sounded rough and stern. Why did he always sound angry?

Gracie took a step back instead of toward the buggy and he had a flash of feeling that she was about to tell him that he could go alone.

Then the creases in her forehead smoothed out and she gave him a tentative smile. "*Jah*," she said. She was really pretty when she smiled. It made him think of blue skies and daisies swaying in the wind.

What? He must be going crazy from listening to the baby cry. Thinking about daisies and the sky.

He shook his head at himself.

"Are you okay?" she asked. There was that compassion again. Where did it all come from? She had more consideration for others than anyone he had ever known. And she was giving. That he knew from talking to some of the members of their church district.

"I'm fine," he growled.

At least this time she didn't shy away from him. It was a start. Maybe he would make it through this dating thing.

Or not, he thought after they had been on the road a while. It had seemed like forever because she was just sitting there beside him on the bench, back straight, eyes forward, chin in the air. She hadn't said a word since she asked him how he was, back at the house. It was as if she had shut down. But why?

Because you're not nice.

He didn't want to be nice. He didn't want to scare her, but he also didn't want her to get any ideas that their marriage could be anything more than it was right then.

But it was tricky. They could be friends, but nothing more. Married, but not *married*. It was complicated.

Still, he wanted her to talk to him from time to time. Like now.

He cleared his throat. She didn't move.

"Nice day," he grunted. Why did he always sound so rumbly? He didn't want to scare the poor girl.

You don't scare your children. At least not unless you mean to.

But that didn't matter. His children and his soon-to-be wife were two entirely different matters.

"*Jah.*" She dipped her chin just a smidge but otherwise didn't move. She didn't turn to look at him, to smile, or any of the things that Beth would have done back before they had gotten married, before they had started their family.

They rode in silence a bit more. What had happened to his ability to hold a conversation with another person? It seemed to have left town. Or maybe he had been talking so much to his children lately that having the attention of a willing adult was more than his stunted brain could deal with. He definitely needed to get out more. Other than his trips to church every other week and his occasional jaunt into town, his associations with adults were nonexistent. Could being alone for three months make such a difference? But it was really more than three months. Beth had been born a quiet person and there at the end . . .

He pulled that thought in. He didn't want to think about Beth today. He had loved her, but as it turned out, love wasn't quite enough. That love was part of the past, and the woman beside him was the future. It was time to stop looking back.

"It's going to get hot soon," he said. He glanced her way. She was still sitting prim and proper, staring straight ahead. One hand was resting in her lap, the other braced on the bench between them to keep from swaying in that direction and accidentally touching him, he was certain.

She waited a beat, then she shifted, turned her entire body toward him. "You don't really want to talk about the weather, do you?"

He stared at her blankly, then shook himself out of his surprised stupor and faced the front. They were driving down back roads made of red dirt and gravel. There were never many cars on these country lanes, but the ones that were usually traveled fast. And one thing he had learned about Mississippi roads: They curved around like nothing he had ever seen. Every quarter mile, sometimes less, there was another bend to go around. And in the early summer months, like now when the kudzu was thick and full, those curves became dangerous, blind corners. He needed to keep his eyes on the road instead of staring gape-mouthed at the woman beside him. Regardless of the surprising things she said.

"Do you?" she asked again. Her tone was nearly a challenge. If he said no, she would be right. He could almost see her nod in self-satisfaction. If he said yes, as a matter of fact he did want to talk about the weather, he suspected that she would call him out.

He cleared his throat. "Not really."

There went that nod he'd been expecting. "People always feel that they should talk about something when they're together. And two people who are just acquaintances will talk about the weather."

He understood her implied message: They weren't just acquaintances. They were about to be married. "What would you like to talk about?"

"Tell me about your children." Mission accomplished, she turned back to the front and relaxed. A little. Sort of. Her back was still ramrod straight and her chin still high in the air.

"Stephen is the oldest." He figured that was the best place to start.

She nodded. "He's very mature for his age," she said.

"*Jah*. Always has been. I think he takes his role as the oldest very seriously. And since Beth passed . . ." He trailed off. He wasn't going to talk about Beth today.

"It's okay," Gracie said. "You don't have to act like she didn't exist. That would be ridiculous."

"It's not that." He wished he had kept his mouth shut. He didn't want to explain, didn't want to tell anyone about his relationship with his wife. Now the woman he was about to marry was going to ask, *Then what is it?* And he wouldn't have the answer. Not one he was willing to share anyway.

"Whenever you're ready," Gracie said.

Once again he was so shocked by her words he turned to stare at her. "When I'm ready for what?"

"To tell me whatever it is you're stewing about over there."

It was on the tip of his tongue to tell her that he wasn't stewing about anything when she continued.

"Or you may not be ready to ever talk about it. And that's okay too."

He had no words, so he simply nodded.

"But I'm here for you," she prattled on. "Whenever you're ready. Just say the word."

He smiled to himself, glad that she had said that last part. Here he was thinking that she was some sort of super wife sent from heaven or God Himself. He wasn't sure what to do with a wife like that. Beth had been a good wife, mostly, but not necessarily a wife he could boss around without question. He pushed the thoughts away. He wasn't thinking about Beth today. But he had been the head of his household and she had been his partner. He was about to think that Gracie would be too agreeable and wouldn't challenge him. She had seemed better than good, saying he could tell her about Beth when he was ready. Not that it was ever going to happen. He had thought her emotions to be detached maybe. Not of this world. But after her little spout off, he knew she was bothered by what secrets he kept, and that reduced her to human. *Jah*, he'd rather be married to one of those instead of an angel sent from above. Even if the marriage wasn't one rooted in love.

So he said the only thing he could. "*Danki.*"

She nodded, then reached out a hand and braced it on the dash as the buggy lurched to one side. "What's happening?"

"I don't know." He tugged the reins to keep Cotton, his horse, from taking off. He was usually even-tempered, a good gelding for the job, but something had spooked him, and bad.

Gracie let out a yelp of what he hoped was surprise and moved both hands to the dash to keep herself steady as the buggy pitched again.

Something was wrong. Very wrong. He stuck his head out the window to get a better look.

"What is it?" Gracie asked as the buggy began to shake. She managed to keep her voice steady, but inside she was quaking worse than the buggy she was in. She had read stories about buggy accidents caused by spooked horses. Her biggest fear was to be pulled unwillingly into traffic. She closed her eyes at the thought, then opened them again as the crazy sway made her sort of queasy.

"I'm not sure." Matthew leaned his head out the window for what seemed like ten minutes but could only have been a couple of seconds, then he ducked back in. "The wheel is coming off."

Panic shot through Gracie. "The wheel is coming off?" It took everything she had not to take the reins from Matthew and pull on them with all her might. Why were they still moving if the wheel was coming off?

"Not the whole wheel," he explained. "Just the metal rim."

That was better, she supposed, but her fingers still tingled with panic. And his horse didn't seem to care about the difference. He was dancing sideways, tossing his head as Matthew struggled to control him.

Then the buggy started to slow. Thank heavens. Finally, after what seemed like forever, Matthew was stopping the buggy. Maybe not as quickly as she wanted him to, but most probably at a safer speed. Then the horse reared his head and started off once again.

Chapter Seven

She had never been as grateful for someone's size as she had in that moment. Not many men could control a horse the way he did. His sheer strength and a calm demeanor saved them from what could have been a very terrible accident.

Once the buggy was actually stopped, Matthew jumped down, throwing the reins to her. "Stay put," he tossed over one shoulder as his feet hit the ground. Gracie wasn't sure she liked being bossed around like that, but she couldn't move just yet anyway. Her body parts seemed to be in all the wrong places. Her heart was in her throat, her stomach somewhere around her ankles, and the remainder of her legs had been replaced with spaghetti noodles.

What could have happened kept circling in her thoughts with various ends, none of which were pleasant and most dealt with death.

Matthew muttered something, and though she couldn't understand the words, his tone was unmistakable. He was angry. Very angry.

She slid from the buggy, somehow managing to make her wobbly legs support her body. This was a lot like the time she and her cousin Abby got into the secret stash of muscadine wine that Abner didn't think anyone knew about. A couple of swigs of that and she felt as unsteady as she did now.

Trailing her fingers along the side of the buggy for better balance, she walked around the back end of it. She didn't want to spook his horse any more than he already was.

Matthew was forcing the rim back on the fiberglass wheel. His face was red with the effort. They couldn't travel without it. He let out a final grunt, then stood back to survey his work. Thankfully, the entire rim hadn't come loose, just one side. Even more thankfully, he had managed to push it all the way back on. Now they could go again. Once the horse calmed down, of course.

Yet Matthew smoothed one hand across the rim, stepped back, and shook his head. He took off his hat and wiped his sleeve against his brow.

"What's the matter?"

"It's not going to stay," he said with a grim slant to his mouth.

"It's not?"

"No. The rivet that was holding it on is missing. Here," he said, pointing toward the little hole where the piece once was. "It's just going to slip off again and I don't think Cotton can handle that."

Cotton could only be the gelding who was still snorting out his displeasure over the whole ordeal.

"What do we do?" She asked the question, but she already knew the answer.

"We walk." He squinted down the road in the direction they had come from, then walked around the back of the buggy to look in the direction they had been going. Gracie mutely followed. "Where are we?"

She could only blink as his words settled around her. "You don't know where we are?" Not to panic. She had lived here since she was a child and she knew these roads like the back of her hand. She looked in both directions. There were no houses in sight. There were a couple of badly dented mailboxes, so there had to be some, but they were so far back from the road that she couldn't see them. The kudzu-covered trees kept them hidden from view.

But her biggest concern? She had no idea where they were either. Her heart jumped back into her throat, but she swallowed it down and did her best to remain calm. "We must have missed a turn somewhere."

"You don't know where we are either."

They had been so engrossed in their conversation, neither one had paid any attention to the signs directing them to Sarah's Sweet Shop.

She sighed. "We just need to walk back in the direction we came and eventually we'll get to someplace we know."

"Good idea."

She grabbed her wallet out of the buggy, thankful that she hadn't brought her big purse. She would hate to lug that thing down the road. Hannah was always teasing her about it. She filled it with everything she needed, then so many times left it at home, opting instead for the convenience of carrying only her wallet.

Matthew unhitched Cotton from the buggy, talking to him in soothing tones. The horse seemed calmer than before, but she could tell that he was still upset. He had some personality, this horse. Now she wished she had her purse. Then she could give him a peppermint candy as a treat.

Without a word, Gracie and Matthew headed back down the road, leading Cotton behind them.

They walked in silence, but her mind wasn't still. It was swirling around, trying to piece together the little parts of this situation that seemed . . . off a bit. Like the fact that they were now in the middle of nowhere, walking away from their broken buggy, when they had started out to get candy.

She had heard about Englisch boys who took girls out on some back road, then feigned car trouble in order to be alone with them and not have to leave, because they were "stranded." She was certain there had to be more to the trick. She didn't know all the particulars, but she had a few ideas.

She wanted to ask Matthew if he had done this on purpose so they would be forced to spend more time together. But why would he do that? She was more than willing to spend time with him. They were getting married! But more than that, once she got past his perpetual scowl, she found she liked spending time with Matthew Byler. And that was good.

But finagling an "accident" could be dangerous, and Matthew didn't seem like a risk taker to her. He looked strong and steady. And if he had wanted to spend more alone time with her, all he had to do was ask Eunice to keep his children longer. Her aunt had taken to Matthew as well. But then, Eunice loved everyone.

Only one way to find out. Gracie should ask him right away if he was playing tricks on her. She opened her mouth, but this came out, "You were telling me about Stephen."

He drew back a bit and looked at her. He seemed surprised. That she had remembered their conversation? Or maybe that she wanted to know more about his children? Maybe he just thought they wouldn't talk about anything. Lord, help her! She couldn't go through a marriage not speaking to her husband.

Matthew turned his attention back to the road ahead and pressed his lips together as if he was thinking. "He's the oldest," he finally said.

"You already told me that. How old is he?"

"Seven going on fifty."

Gracie chuckled. "I saw that the first time I came over." And that was the time she had asked him to marry her and embarrassed herself like she never had before—even that time she fell backward out of the pony cart while Benuel King and his buddies were watching. She had been trying to look interesting, with her chin lifted and her gaze to the side and the reins loose in her hands. She hadn't reacted quick enough when the pony decided to kick it up a bit without any encouragement from her and off the back she went.

"*Jah*," he said, his voice sort of soft as if he were remembering that time with fondness. But that couldn't be right. She had made a fool of herself. And the casserole hadn't been that good. She might not have stayed for supper, but she had made the dish too many times to count. It was filling and warm, but nothing worth getting dreamy-eyed over.

"Has he always been so serious?" she asked, hoping to bring them back to the real conversation.

"*Jah*," he said with a small laugh. "Then there's Henry. He's five."

"Oh, I know Henry. But tell me, whose raising are you paying for?"

"What?" He tilted his head to one side as if trying to decipher her question.

"Eunice always says that when a couple has a child who's something of a handful, the parents are paying for their own raising. So who was the handful? You or Be— their mother?" Why she didn't want to say his late wife's name was beyond her, but she felt that if she said it out loud, somehow Beth would be there. And this conversation was between the two of them, her and Matthew. Strangely enough, she wanted to keep it that way.

"Me," he said with a smile. "I was always getting into

trouble. Well, my older brother Jason was always putting me up to something, and then I would get into trouble."

"You have a brother?" She had never heard anyone talk about his family other than the one that lived in Pontotoc. "Does he live in Ohio?"

"*Jah.*"

"Is it just the two of you?"

"No," he said with a wry grin. "We have six sisters. Three older and three younger."

Gracie laughed. "That's quite a brood."

"So you see why Jason and I had to stick together."

"I suppose," she jokingly replied. "But I really think it's just a ploy to justify the orneriness of boys."

"Whatever." But his grin kept the word from stinging.

"Are any of them coming down for the wedding?" The very thought made her even more nervous, if that was possible.

"Jason was thinking about it, but he's got the farm. He can't get away this time of year." The problems with having a wedding out of season. "The sisters all have little ones. It's too hard to travel with them. For no—" He broke off, but she knew what he was going to say. For no reason. His expression went from thoughtful to sheepish.

"I know what you mean," she said, completely letting him off the hook. He meant it was his second marriage, and they weren't treated as special as first marriages. It was her first marriage, but that didn't affect his family at all. At least that's what she thought he meant and if it wasn't, she didn't want to know the real reason.

"Jason said he might come in the fall, after harvest. What about you? You don't talk about your family."

"I do too. All the time."

"I'm not talking about Eunice. I mean your close family. *Mamm, dat,* siblings."

Her family wasn't something she really wanted to discuss,

but she knew that she would have to share this at some point. "My brothers were racing buggies one night."

Matthew made a sharp noise. She didn't have to say anything else; he understood.

"And my parents both died in their sleep." She hated to bring up the reason why, but she knew he would ask. "Carbon monoxide poisoning."

He shook his head sadly. "That's quite a blow. Both of them at once."

"*Jah.* But then I went to stay with Eunice and Abner. And other family members who needed help. I stayed with my cousin when she had a baby and her mother couldn't come. I stayed with my uncle's family when he fell and broke his leg. So it's been something of an adventure." She didn't tell him a fraction of all the family members who had called for her help. And she had gone.

She had never really thought about it before, but she had gone searching for more family. Everyone thought she was just being kind and helpful, but really she was looking for the one thing she didn't have: family.

"What about the twins?" She had to get them back on the conversation that wasn't about her. She didn't want to think any more about her unwitting quest to find where she belonged.

He smiled. "They are something else. Benjamin is the gentlest and sweetest child a person could ever ask for."

"And Thomas is a bit on the ornery side, like Henry."

"I think they have meetings and training sessions."

Gracie laughed. "Surely not."

"Just wait. You'll see, once you move in."

The air around them suddenly turned thick. She didn't want to think about that, and yet she wanted to plan every detail so she knew what to expect. How was she supposed to balance that?

She had no answer, though she searched for one. She

needed to say something, but any thoughts were lost as something nudged her in the back. She skipped forward, glancing over her shoulder. Nothing.

She shook her head and was thankful that the moment with Matthew had passed, and she must have imagined that nudge.

"Hannah and Leah are twins. Fraternal, like your boys. Then Jim and Anna's twins are so identical I don't think they can even tell each other apart." She jumped again as the same prod came at her back.

"Did you push me?" she asked.

"Why would I push you?"

Good point. She turned back around. "I think the boys are great."

He smiled. "They're good boys, but you can't let them think they have any power in that house. Or you will never get control back from Henry. He's something of a—"

"Leader?" she supplied.

"I was going to say instigator."

Same thing.

Henry Byler, the Amish kid who would take over the world.

"And the baby?"

Again the atmosphere changed. The temperature seemed to drop, the air got thick, and Matthew seemed to almost dull at the question.

"She's not happy with the current situation." He said the words so slowly, each one succinct. It was almost as if he had to spell them out in his head before he could speak them.

"Is she colicky?"

"No, just unhappy."

She missed her mother. Gracie knew that pain. Perhaps she could ease the loss for Baby Grace. She knew exactly how it felt. Maybe kindred spirits would come together.

She liked that idea. She and Baby Grace helping each other get through this life. This wonderful, sometimes-so-hard-she-didn't-think-she-could-go-on life.

"Listen," he started, his voice a little choked, as if he didn't want to say the words gathering in his thoughts.

"What is that?" Terrible of her to interrupt, she knew, but somehow she didn't want to hear what he was about to say.

"What?" he asked. She breathed a small sigh of relief that he had allowed her to change the subject. She had a reprieve.

"Up there. Is it a cat?"

"I don't see anything," he said.

Great. Now it looked as if she were making things up.

"Right there."

"Still don't see it."

"On the side of the road there. That black thing."

He leaned in and squinted, looking hard in the direction where she pointed. "Maybe a sweater."

"It's coming toward us. Sweaters don't walk."

He straightened. "A dog?"

Sure enough, about ten paces later the little black dog came bounding up, pink tongue lolling out one side of his mouth.

"Well, aren't you a cute little thing."

She reached down to pet it and the dog flopped onto one side and rolled over so Gracie could pet her belly. "Sweet dog," she crooned, squatting next to her.

From a distance the animal had looked fuzzy, but up close that frizz became silky. A long-haired, solid black dog that surely belonged to an Englischer. Most of the Amish in these parts kept hunting dogs but not house critters. Everything had a job, including pets.

There was no collar on the pooch and no tag. But Gracie knew that this wasn't the kind of dog that people let roam about. She had to have an owner somewhere, and if they left her out here she would surely get hit by a car.

"Give me your suspenders," she said, standing up and holding out one hand. The dog immediately popped up beside her, short little tail wagging.

"My suspenders? Why?"

"So I can make a leash from them."

"No," he said. "My pants will fall down."

"Not if you hold your pants up."

"I have the horse." As if asserting his position, Cotton snorted and stomped one foot.

The dog danced around his legs and barked at the beast.

To Cotton's credit, he didn't seem to mind. A miracle, she supposed, considering how skittish he was when they first unhitched him to walk for help.

"And you have two hands. Pants in one and reins in the other."

He frowned even more than usual. "No," he said emphatically. "The dog follows or he doesn't come." He started walking again as if to solidify his decision.

"She," Gracie corrected, starting after him.

Matthew kept going but bent at the waist to check the puppy's underbelly. "She," he agreed.

Gracie felt the heat rising into her cheeks and could only hope that her face had turned a pretty shade of pink instead of the fiery red it felt like.

This would be the perfect time to bring up their wedding night. If she was still worried about it. And she wasn't. They should be able to talk about such matters if they needed to. They were about to get married. It was only natural. But she didn't bring it up because she wasn't worried about it. Not at all.

Instead she allowed the conversation to take its natural turn toward the dog now trotting happily alongside them. Gracie was glad the pup followed them. She couldn't convince Matthew to give up his suspenders and she was afraid to leave the little dog behind.

"She belongs to someone," Gracie said for the fifth or sixth time. She had lost count. "She has to." She no sooner finished the words than she felt that familiar nudge behind her. Someone had pushed her again. Not hard enough to make her stumble or fall, but just enough to get her attention. She had thought Matthew was doing it. But with his longer stride he was slightly in front of her and couldn't have pushed her from behind.

She turned around just as Cotton tossed his head, bumping her in the side. She gasped and laughed, rubbing his velvet nose. "You just want attention, *jah*?"

The horse blew out a breath as Gracie turned completely around and walked backward so she could pet the horse.

"Really?" Matthew asked. That ever-present frown marred his forehead and had even fallen to his mouth. "It's going to take us twice as long if you walk backward the entire way."

"Horses need love too." Everything needed love. Even if some weren't destined to get it.

"He likes you, I guess."

Gracie smiled. "I like him too." She gave the horse one last brush of her hand, then turned around. Walking backward was not only slow, it was hard too.

She was no sooner facing front than Cotton nudged her from the back. This time harder than the last.

"Bad horse," she scolded, then tried not to laugh at herself when she realized she sounded like a kindergartner. "I'll give you a peppermint when we get home, but you have to promise to behave until then."

"You're talking to that animal like he can understand every word."

"What if he can? I read about these dolphins one time that could do all sorts of tricks, like jump through hoops and watch themselves on television."

"That's something hard to do?"

"You know what I mean. They can follow the story."

"And where did you read all this?"

She shrugged. He had his secrets and she had hers. "I really do believe that the dog belongs to someone." Nice change of subject.

"Then we stop at the next house and leave her there. Surely she belongs somewhere close."

"Not necessarily," Gracie countered. "Someone could have dumped her." But she didn't think that was the case. The pup was cared for and loved attention. She had somehow gotten lost and needed help finding her way back to her family.

Just like me.

Gracie locked that thought away. She was about to have her family and she would search no more.

"There." Matthew pointed ahead toward a tin-colored mailbox decorated with dents and rust spots. The owner's name wasn't painted on it, just the house number for emergency vehicles.

As silly as it was, the closer they got to the mailbox the sadder Gracie became. The pooch trotted along as if she had been following them her entire life. Head held high, she chased off the random butterfly but otherwise happily stayed right by her side.

What if this wasn't the right house? What if the owner lied and said the dog was his when she really wasn't? What if he was a mean man who would hurt the dog? How could she live with herself then?

Hush up, she told that worrisome little voice in her head. It was always telling her the worst of everything, and somedays it took all she had to control it. She supposed it was from having so much loss in her life, then being shuffled around, wanted only when she was needed. Except Eunice. She had always treated Gracie like one of her own.

"Are you coming?" He had already turned and started

up the small hill that led to the house. The drive was made of light-colored stones, not quite like the ones that made up the road. A strip of grass grew up the middle.

"*Jah*," she said and started after him.

The sound of barking dogs met her ears as she walked behind Matthew and Cotton. Not the best place to be, she decided. Even though back there she didn't have to worry about him nudging her or knocking her down. With each bump being a little harder, it was likely he would push her to the ground. But behind a horse was not where she wanted to spend much time at all. She sped up to swerve around him. She'd take her chances with the nudges.

The pup, thinking it was a game, ran on ahead to greet the canines who lived on the property. The three dogs that came out from under the house didn't seem to know the little black beast. They barked and sniffed at each other, all four of them wagging their tails so hard their rears were swinging back and forth as well.

"Hidey," the man on the porch called. He had stood when he caught sight of them and now patiently waited for them to get close enough to talk.

"Hi," Matthew returned. She could barely hear his voice over the barking.

"Hush up," the man said, clapping his hands at his dogs. They immediately fell silent, even the black dog. But they all continued to wag their tails and visit with each other. Just more quietly now.

"Our buggy broke down about a mile back that direction." Matthew gestured with one arm to show him. "Then we found this guy—er, girl, and thought maybe she belonged to you."

He studied the dog as if he had never seen anything like her in his entire life. "Nope. Not my dog."

His dogs had lost interest in Pepper and had started after Cotton. The horse snorted and stomped his foot, pawing at the ground in warning. The dogs understood and went back to see if Pepper smelled any different than she had a couple of minutes ago.

Pepper. Gracie wasn't sure where the name came from. One minute it was simply there and fit so perfectly, she couldn't stop herself from calling the little dog by that name. *Pepper* was much better than *little black dog.*

"You need some help into town?" the man asked.

"I don't want to put you out," Matthew said.

The man spit off the side of the porch, then grinned, his smile colored yellow from tobacco. "I'm retired," he said. "I ain't got nothing else to do with my day."

"Much obliged." Matthew nodded his thanks.

"Eugene Dover," the man said, holding out a hand to shake.

Matthew shook it as he introduced himself.

Gracie watched their interaction, then plopped down onto the ground so she could easily pet Pepper while she waited for Matthew and Eugene Dover to conduct their business.

"Go ahead and put your horse in the pasture. It'll be there when you come back to get your buggy." He stopped, narrowed his eyes. "You aren't planning on leaving it here for a week or two, are ya?"

Matthew shook his head. "I'll be back for him sometime this afternoon."

"What about your dog?" Eugene asked.

"It's not our dog," he replied.

Eugene jerked a thumb over his shoulder toward her and the little black dog. The pooch was on her back in the grass, squirming from side to side as Gracie rubbed her exposed belly. "You better tell her that."

But Gracie could tell from the look on Matthew's face that he wasn't sure if the man was talking about Gracie or Pepper.

* * *

And that was how Gracie found herself in Eugene Dover's car.

Why did riding in the back seat with Matthew at her side feel more intimate than sitting together in the buggy? Because in the buggy he had driving to worry about. Riding in the car he could give her all his attention. She wasn't sure how she felt about that.

Pepper must have been accustomed to riding in a car. Eugene had placed her in the front seat and rolled the window down just enough for her to stick her head out as they rode along. The sight of it made Gracie want to giggle. She was such a sweet dog; Gracie was going to miss her when her owner was found.

Until then, Gracie had convinced Matthew to care for the dog and she would hand out flyers and post a notice on the bulletin board in Leah's store. It was the only way to keep Pepper safe.

He had argued with her at first, citing that they had too much to do with the wedding preparations, and she admitted that he was right. She was actually going to have Brandon and his not-girlfriend, Shelly, handle making the flyers and posting them. Her cousin's son had been raised Englisch and lived with Leah and her new husband, Jamie. Now they all attended the Mennonite church, which was very progressive and would allow him to take a picture of the pup. Exactly what they needed to find the owner. And the responsibility would lie with them while she took care of wedding things.

Matthew could get Stephen and Henry to care for the little pooch. They took care of the small chores in the barn. What was one more animal in the mix?

Plus, she thought the boys could use a little good turn in their lives. Sure, she was going to be their mother soon, but they weren't sure how to feel about that. As far as they knew, she could be a mean person just as easily as she could be a nice person. And if she was mean that would be a terrible turn of events. Their mother had died, their little sister cried constantly. A sweet puppy who wanted to be loved and play fetch would surely take their minds off any troubles they had, real or imagined.

"Turn left here," Matthew said from beside her. He was so close she could feel the rumble of his voice roll through her. He should have sat in the front so he could see better, but he had climbed into the back, accustomed to always riding behind the driver.

Thankfully it wasn't very long before they found their way back to familiar ground.

"Do you think Abner or one of your cousins will be home?" Matthew asked.

He hadn't said anything to her since they had climbed into the car, and the question caught her off guard. She started a bit, then turned to look at him. He seemed even closer than he had before. She should scoot over, toward the door, but the car was small and there wasn't much room.

"I—uh, probably. One of them is usually there in case a customer comes by." And it was Saturday, a traditional "off" day for Englischers. His shop seemed to always be extra busy on those days.

"Good." Matthew nodded. "They'll be able to help me get a new wheel and get back to my buggy."

"Don't forget your horse," Eugene called from the front seat.

Gracie wasn't sure if he was joking or if he really was worried that Matthew would leave his horse there indefinitely. Maybe someone had taken advantage of him before. But Matthew was a man of his word. She knew it. Instinctively. He was that sort of person. If she could see it, she was certain that Eugene could too. Anybody who came into contact with Matthew could see that about him. Strange how you can just look at a person and know something so core and basic about them.

A little of her nervousness over the wedding disappeared. She was marrying "one of the good ones," Mammi would say. He would provide for his family and care for them until his last breath.

The thought was both comforting and nerve racking. How could she ever be good enough for a man like that?

Matthew and Gracie never made it to the candy store that day. He took her home, tried to give Eugene some money for the ride, but the man absolutely refused.

"Then for stabling my horse," Matthew had said.

The man looked at the money then back to Matthew. Maybe he had him this time. But Eugene shook his head. "You leave that horse longer than today and we'll talk about it. Until then, keep your money. I'm just being neighborly."

Gracie thanked the man again and they watched him drive away. Not every neighbor was so kind to the Amish and their simple ways. For the most part they were, yet Eugene Dover seemed to be a head above them all.

The boys squealed over the dog and begged to keep her. Matthew tried to explain that it was a temporary situation for both them and the pup. As soon as the owner was found, the dog would be gone, but he had a feeling no one was really paying him much mind.

Gracie stayed there with his children while he went with Jim to get a new wheel for his buggy. By the time he got the wheel all changed out, it was nearly dark.

There was the trip to the wagon supply shop, the ride back out to Eugene Dover's house, this time in a buggy so it took twice as long. Then he had to get his horse, give him the peppermint that Gracie had insisted he take for him, walk back out to where he left his crippled buggy, then actually switch out the wheels.

And that's when he realized he never got to ask her again how she knew so much about dolphins.

Chapter Eight

"I have one more thing to talk about today."

Matthew's heart kicked up a notch. He was as nervous as a schoolboy and all because of the blond-haired woman sitting across from him. The bishop's words were not helping.

Actually, Matthew had been nervous all morning. Today was the day. The day the bishop would announce their intent to marry and ask if anyone in the congregation had any objections to the union. No one was going to stand up and say anything, especially not when he arrived with the crying baby who could only be comforted by Gracie's grandmother. Once she had settled down, Mammi Glick handed her off to Gracie, who had been holding her ever since. There hadn't been a peep out of her in three hours. Everyone would want the two of them to marry, if only to keep his baby from screaming her head off.

But still he was nervous. Someone could object. Someone could say no, and then where would he be? This whole marriage plan hadn't been his idea, but it had taken root. He could see all the benefits. He knew what he needed, and he could see the solution. Gracie may have come up with the idea, but it certainly belonged to him now.

"Matthew Byler and Gracie Glick came to me this week and asked if I would grant my permission for them to be married. Now as you may know, Matthew is recently widowed and has young children who need both parents, a mother and a father. Gracie—"

Matthew held his breath. He prayed that the bishop wouldn't embarrass her. Matthew himself still wasn't sure exactly what Gracie was getting out of the marriage. A family, yes. But a wagonload of responsibility and three days' work with two days to do it. She knew that, and she still wanted to marry him. She had met Henry and she still wanted to marry him. He wasn't under the misguided notion that she was somehow secretly in love with him even before Beth died and had been waiting for a chance to make him her own. He wasn't that sort of man. His mother always said he was too gruff. And that was when he was eight! Many more years of disappointments and failures had ingrained that nature into him. Now it was as much a part of him as the fact that his eyes were blue. There was no getting around it. And he knew what people said when they thought he couldn't hear. He didn't try to dissuade them. What did it matter what anyone thought of him?

But now it wouldn't be just him. It would be them, and he didn't want people to look at Gracie with pity in their eyes. Maybe if he knew for certain why she was marrying him, then he would feel better about it. Or maybe that was something he didn't want to know.

"So if no one objects, I will announce that Gracie and Matthew will be married this week in a small ceremony there at the Gingeriches' home. And we welcome this union into our church."

Matthew had never heard the bishop say anything like that before. They welcomed them? Did he expect that they wouldn't? Or maybe it was a blessing since it hadn't been very long since his wife died. But one thing the bishop didn't know: Beth had been gone from him much longer than three months.

They made it. They got through the church request and no one said anything, like they shouldn't get married. Or they were all wrong for each other. Not even a peep about how Matthew had been a widower for barely three months. There was a baby at stake and everyone knew it.

But for a moment there, Gracie had thought Hannah might say something, but then she looked over and gave them a little smile—her and Baby Grace—and Gracie knew they were home free. She also knew that Hannah had her best interests at heart. Maybe seeing her there with the baby made Hannah realize just how much Gracie wanted . . . no, *needed* a family of her own.

"Now what happens?" Henry looked around as if he might be overlooking something. "I thought she was going to come home with us and cook."

Matthew sighed. It had been a long and stressful day. Now he only wanted to get the Sunday chores done, sit down, and prop his feet up. And maybe pray a bit that the baby's good mood continued. So far she hadn't cried any more since they handed her over to Mammi Glick, but Matthew wasn't about to start counting chickens.

"Marriage is about more than someone coming to cook for us," he gently explained.

"Then what's it about?"

This was definitely not a conversation he wanted to have right now. "We'll talk about it when you're older."

"Ah, Dat," Henry grumbled.

"In the meantime, you and your brother can go out and brush down Cotton and make sure he's settled for the evening. Pepper needs water and food." He still couldn't believe he let Gracie talk him into taking care of the dog until her owner was found. They had a wedding to get through. They didn't have time to search down an errant dog owner.

For a moment Matthew thought Henry might protest, but Stephen shook his head and waved him over to the door. They had promised to look after the pup and Stephen was definitely the one to make sure the other boys kept up their end of the bargain.

"I was still hoping she could come cook," Henry fussed as he followed Stephen out.

Whew! That was one tough question Matthew managed to get around. And thank the good Lord for that miracle. But he wasn't sure how much longer he would be able to avoid those topics. How was he supposed to tell his son what marriage was all about when he wasn't sure he even knew himself? And not just the one he was now facing. There had been a time, long ago, when he thought he knew what marriage was about, but he'd been wrong. Since then nothing had taught him any differently. He knew the whole love-and-children speech that everyone recited by heart, but he didn't know what it all meant. And in four short days he was marrying Gracie Glick. Considering the limitations he wanted to put upon their relationship, he might not ever know. Maybe it just wasn't in God's plan for him. Only time would tell.

He heard the rattle of a buggy and got up with a groan to see who was coming down the lane that led to his house. His was the last house on the drive, so when buggies came down this far they were definitely there for him. Cars, on the other hand, were a different story.

A quick peek out the window revealed Aaron Zook, Hannah Gingerich's fiancé. Aaron had been a good friend to him when he first arrived in Pontotoc. He had welcomed him into the community and made him feel at home. As much as he could, anyway. Not long after they moved, Beth had become pregnant with the baby and everything had changed. Still, Matthew considered him a good friend. They both knew what it was like to lose their spouse and the pain it entailed.

Matthew pulled his suspenders back into place, grabbed his hat from the hook by the door, then walked out onto the front porch. "Hey there, Aaron Zook. What brings you out today?"

Aaron jumped down from his buggy, hobbled his horse, then made his way to the porch. "Just thought I would come for a visit," he said casually.

A little too casually. They had just been at church together. If he had wanted to talk, they had had plenty of time after the service. Hours even.

"Come on in," Matthew said, motioning him toward the house. "I would offer you some pie and coffee, but Henry ate the last of the pie this morning before church, and I wouldn't ask anyone to willingly drink coffee that I've brewed."

Aaron laughed good-naturedly and shook Matthew's hand when he got to the top of the stairs. "I didn't expect you to have either."

Unlike Matthew, Aaron had become an accomplished widowed father. He'd had more practice at it than Matthew had, having been widowed for years. But he'd also had more help. Aaron had family all around them in Pontotoc and they, along with kind souls like Eunice Gingerich, helped to keep him going in his time of need. So much so that he had just now decided to marry again. Or maybe it was simply because Aaron was getting a second chance to marry his first love.

"Come on in and sit down." Matthew opened the door

and followed Aaron into the living room. He was proud of the way the room was kept. It was hard not to be. Beth had of course set up the furniture, where the couch would be and which corner the china hutch would go into, but he had kept it neat as a pin. He had the boys pick it up every evening before bed and dust it once a week. That was a Saturday chore, so it was still pretty clean as they walked into the room.

Matthew gestured toward the couch and sat down in the padded rocking chair across from it.

"Where'd the dog come from?" Aaron said, gesturing toward the general vicinity of the yard.

"Gracie." Her name was a sigh on his lips and again he wondered how she had so easily convinced him to keep the dog. "We found her yesterday." Matthew went on to detail how they had come across the pooch and their plans to find the dog's owner. He didn't mention that he felt that person would never be found, and he had just adopted himself a dog.

Aaron shook his head with a chuckle.

"What?" Matthew asked.

"As if you didn't already have enough to do."

"The boys are taking care of her and I think they like having a dog around." Was he defending Gracie? When had his focus shifted? Had Aaron noticed?

He looked up to find his friend watching him with searching eyes. *Jah. Jah*, he had.

"If you didn't come for pie and coffee . . ." Matthew trailed off expressively. Aaron was there for a reason. "And you didn't know about the dog until you got here."

"I wanted to talk to you about your upcoming marriage."

Matthew tried not to stiffen at the words. Aaron was a friend and was only trying to help. But Matthew had had enough of everyone's so-called help. "What about it?"

The words came out softly and a little more forced than he had planned.

Thankfully, Aaron didn't seem to notice. Or maybe he just wasn't deterred. "Are you certain of your decision?"

He tried to relax. Perhaps Aaron would be easier on him than his own brother had been. "Why would I not be?"

Aaron scooched back a little into the sofa cushions and leaned forward to brace his elbows on his knees. "It seems to have come about awful sudden like."

"So did Beth's drowning." That wasn't the truth, but Aaron didn't know all that. No one in Pontotoc, or even his family in Ohio, knew the whole truth behind his wife's death.

"I know. I know." Aaron shook his head sadly. "But you shouldn't rush into anything right now. You're still grieving, and the children—"

"The children need a mother," Matthew said coldly.

To Aaron's credit, he didn't draw back. "They do," he said. "They all do, but they also deserve a family that's a unit. Not two people marrying for questionable reasons." He shook his head. "That didn't come out right," he said. "I want you to be happy more than anything in the world. But I'm afraid that you're about to waste a future chance at happiness by getting married now." He paused to let that sink in.

"You think Gracie is a waste."

"No. But what if one day you meet someone else?"

"You think I should wait?" With all the problems he now faced. Impossible.

"You know what?" Aaron stood. "I think I'd better go while you're still in a forgiving mood. I came here to help and instead I've made a mess of things."

Or maybe his reasons were so unsound that all the words came out wrong. Perhaps that was some sort of sign that what Matthew was doing was the right thing. Aaron almost had him there for a bit, almost had him doubting. Now he wasn't completely, one hundred percent positive that marrying Gracie was the best plan, but he was definitely doubting it less.

Matthew stood as well, and as if on some sort of timer, the baby started crying. He paused, hesitating between going to pick her up or walking Aaron to the door. There was this part of him—this big, big part of him—that wanted to walk with his friend and thank him for his concern, however misplaced. And another part of him that was even bigger that felt riddled with guilt and remorse. How could he leave her in there to cry? Even if he knew that picking her up, shushing her, changing her diaper, getting her a bottle, or tucking her into his chest and nuzzling the top of her fresh-smelling blond curls was not going to stop her cries. If anything she might even cry harder, howl louder, until he placed her back into her crib and she fell asleep once more. This time from sheer exhaustion.

It didn't change matters. It was his job to pick her up, care for her, even love her while she sobbed out her unhappiness.

"Are you going . . ." Aaron asked, nodding a bit down the hallway and the baby's room.

"Of course. Just a minute." Matthew started toward the hall, his steps heavy, tired. How long could a man endure? How long could he outwardly act like what he already knew wasn't the truth? How long could he pretend that his daughter didn't hate him, and he wasn't beginning to resent her back? That it was getting harder and harder to respond to these summonses, knowing that he would be rejected. And how terrible a person was he for even thinking such things?

Matthew still managed to make his feet take him all the

way to the crib. He leaned in and saw that she was crying real tears, like she had suffered the utmost of betrayals. He supposed she had. Her face was bright pink, her cheeks wet as she shook her tiny fists toward heaven and kicked her legs with all her might, as if that alone would somehow right all the wrongs that had been dealt her.

He ran a quick finger down the leg-edge of her diaper to see if she was wet. Thankfully she was dry. Maybe a bottle would ease her cries for a bit. But Mammi Glick told him that she had given the baby a bottle just before she had fallen asleep. That had been less than an hour ago. Surely she wasn't already hungry.

He was beginning to worry that he was so calm when she cried and yet so reluctant to take care of her. Was he losing it?

Making shushing noises that were as dumb as they were ineffectual, Matthew raised the baby from her crib, her legs still kicking as if she were trying to knock herself from his grasp. But that was ridiculous, right?

She was still screaming when he tucked her against his chest and turned around to find Aaron standing in the doorway of the room. He had thought perhaps his friend already left. Yet there he stood.

"She's very unhappy about something." Aaron gave a rueful smile.

"Life," Matthew replied, and brushed past him to take her into the living room. The boys were outside and he would have stayed in her room to help insulate the noise from the rest of the house, but he didn't want to leave Aaron alone in the living room. This could take a while.

Matthew settled down into the padded rocking chair, acutely aware of Aaron's blue-gray eyes on him. He rocked the baby, willing her to stop crying, forgive him, and let them begin again, but her tears continued. He pressed a small pacifier into her mouth, but she shook her head and batted it away. It was going to be one long night. Made even longer by the fact that they had had a few moments of peace where she was concerned, and now those moments were gone.

"Here," Aaron said. He was still there? Why? His friend reached his arms out toward the baby. "Let me."

Matthew tried not to let his relief show as he turned the baby over to Aaron. He shouldn't feel relieved. But he was, and the emotion mixed with his shame and left a bitter taste in his mouth.

As he watched, Aaron performed the Quiet the Baby Dance that parents Englisch and Amish alike had been doing for thousands of years to soothe their babies. He cradled her close, patted her back, gently bounced her in place, and made a collection of noises that were a strange language that adults could speak, but only babies could understand. Within minutes she was quiet, hiccupping a bit and breath still heaving from time to time, but no screaming, no tears, no horrible, undetermined distress.

Matthew wanted to crawl onto the floor and lie there, not moving, and see if God would just take him. He was apparently not fit as a father and only the baby was astute enough to pick up on it. Everyone else could calm her, could make her stop crying, make her happy even. Everyone but him.

Aaron kissed the top of the baby's head, then shot Matthew another rueful smile. "Sometimes—" he started, but Matthew held up one hand to stay his words.

"She hates me. She cries whenever I'm around. She won't let me help her." He heaved in his own shuddering breath, hardly able to believe that he was admitting this to another person. "I have to marry Gracie Glick. If only to retain my sanity."

"Are you saying the baby cries like this all the time?" Aaron's eyes widened.

Matthew nodded miserably. "Constantly."

Aaron pressed his lips together and made a noise of both anger and sympathy. "No wonder you're willing to marry someone so quickly. You've had months of this."

"*Jah*. The women from the church come over and help. That gives me a break, but . . ." He stopped before he could say the rest, that he was so exhausted these days that there were times when he didn't trust himself with her. Stephen was too young to take care of her, so he had taken over most of the care for Henry and the twins. He was too young for such responsibility.

Between her constant crying and having to rely on his eldest to help where he could, it was almost more than Matthew could accept. Then, adding insult to injury, the baby cried every time he cared for her. It was as if she were telling him, *You killed my mother, now go find me a new one.* So that's just what he had done.

"I should be getting home. Where would you like her?" Aaron asked.

"The playpen, I suppose." Matthew bit back a sigh. "I've got to go check on the boys and make sure they have all their chores done for the night."

Aaron placed the baby in the playpen set off in one corner of the room closest to the window, but still in the shade. He adjusted the mobile plaything so she could reach for the objects, then turned back to Matthew. "Why don't you try to relax for a little while and I'll go check on the boys," he offered.

Matthew did his best not to fall completely apart at the offer and settled back in his seat. "*Danki*," he said, his voice just a bit choked. Maybe that was all he needed: a rest. A little break from the tragedy that had become his life.

"I'll come back in if there's something amiss out there," Aaron continued. "Otherwise I'll see you sometime this week."

Matthew nodded, glad he didn't say *at your wedding*. It was looming ever closer, necessary and troublesome all at the same time.

The baby needed someone to take care of her, and aside from allowing her to go to Ohio and live with one of his sisters, where he would most likely never see her again, he opted to marry Gracie Glick. He and the boys could get along fine, he was fairly certain, but the baby was another matter altogether. He didn't want to send the baby away and have the boys remember what a coward he had been. The only other option was to send all the boys, along with the baby, to Nannie's house.

The thought was like a knife through his heart. He couldn't send them to his sister's. He would never be able to handle that, losing Beth and the children in just a matter of months. He might as well have someone shoot him, like you do an old horse when it's gone lame. There's nothing more you can do but put them out of their misery.

Or move back to Ohio.

He pushed the voice aside. It had been whispering to him lately, patiently explaining how he could move back, closer to his family, where he could . . . what? Move back in with his parents and Jason while he waited for someone to die, or for some Englischer to move so he could buy their farm? Land was scarce all over, but Ohio Amish country was so full up of farms it was next to impossible to get one unless someone left it to you or you converted an Englisch farm to an Amish one. That in itself was costly and time consuming, and the very reason he and Beth had moved south.

And then this . . .

But he didn't want to think about any of that right now. He needed this time, thanks to God and Aaron for giving it to him. Time to regroup and set his mind and his heart right. Time to not worry about anything. Time when there was nothing but peace in his world.

Their footsteps across the porch was his first warning.

"I told you, you should always empty the water trough completely before trying to add more," Stephen said in that bossy voice he had adopted recently.

"Only when there's too much dirt in it," Henry protested. "It was practically clear as a window."

"There was dirt in there," Stephen argued.

"You're just wasting water," Henry taunted.

"Am not!" Stephen retorted. "You just don't want to get your cast wet."

"The doctors told me to make sure and keep it dry," Henry shot back.

The boys burst into the house, their argument over chores escalating as they saw him.

They rushed him, the twins following behind, not really in the argument but not wanting to be left out of the fray.

"Dat! Dat!" the boys called.

And the peace so sweet and brief was shattered.

The baby began to cry, the twins joined in with their own versions as Stephen and Henry vied to get their father on their side.

And then this . . .

Chapter Nine

Gracie scooched to one side on the porch swing so Leah could join her. Confident, bright Leah eased down gently, that in itself unusual. Normally she would plop down beside her and use her heels to get the swing started once again. Something was up.

"I guess you were voted to be the one to come out here and talk some sense into me," Gracie said.

Leah grimaced. "We drew straws."

"And you lost."

"Actually, I won."

Gracie turned sharply to stare at her cousin. "You wanted to do this intervention whatsit?"

"I wanted to talk to you and make sure you feel you're making the right decision."

"You know how I feel about marrying Matthew."

Leah nodded. "I know." She started the swing once again, using the heels of her bare feet. "But is that all?"

"What else would there be?"

Her cousin shrugged. "I don't know."

"Come on," Gracie said. "Surely one of y'all has some crazy idea about my motives."

"Hannah said it could be all about the dog, but I pointed out to her that you had only found her yesterday."

Gracie laughed. She couldn't help herself. "You guys are sweet to be worried about me, but I know what I'm doing is right." *Do you?*

"We have to worry about you. We love you."

"And I love you." She laid her head on Leah's shoulder. "I wish Tillie was here for this. She doesn't even know I'm getting married."

Leah heaved a sigh. "I know. We were just starting to connect again."

"Maybe she'll come back," Gracie said, wishing like everything her words would come true.

"She won't. Not without Melvin, and he isn't coming back. Not now."

Melvin's parents had taken it hard that their only son had wanted to join the Englisch world and had packed up everything and moved. Gracie had no idea where the Yoders were living now. This was the only Amish community in Mississippi. They could have gone back to Tennessee, but someone in Pontotoc would have heard. No, Linda and Johnny Yoder had set off to be lost to the community where they had raised four daughters and a son. Now it was as if they had never even been there at all. Their house was now abandoned, but Gracie figured it was only a matter of time before someone took it over. Melvin wasn't coming back because there was nothing for him to come back to.

"She might still change her mind," Gracie said. There was a chance, but it was a slight one. Still, they could hope.

They sat in silence for a moment, listening to the sounds of the night around them. The call of a whippoorwill, the chirp of tree frogs, and the deep croaks of the bullfrogs in the nearby pond. Night bugs sang to one another and a dozen or so lightning bugs tried to stab holes in the black cloak of night.

"He's a good man," Gracie finally said.

"Melvin?"

"Matthew." She paused for a moment. "He seems all burly and tough, but he loves his children and he does the best he can. He's a good father and I know that he was a good provider for his wife. I know it." She thumped her fist to her chest just over where her heart beat. "He'll be a good father to our children as well."

She was thankful for the cover of darkness that hid the pink she knew was seeping into her cheeks. She still wasn't entirely sure that she was prepared for her wedding night, but surely the good Lord would see her through. After all, she wasn't the first bride in history.

"I just want him to make you happy." Leah's words held a fierceness that both pleased and shocked Gracie. She loved her cousins so very much.

"I never thought about it much," Gracie said, "but after Jamie—"

"I'm sorry," Leah murmured.

Leah's husband, Jamie, had started off trying to court Gracie. Until that time she had pushed her dreams of having a family of her own to the back of her mind. There was no sense pining after something she couldn't have.

"Don't be." Gracie patted Leah's hand where it lay on her denim-covered thigh. As a member of the local Mennonite church, Leah didn't wear the traditional Amish dresses, but instead wore long skirts that nearly reached the ground and tops with sleeves that never went up past her elbows. She also wore a prayer covering, though many of the women in her church had foregone that tradition. "Jamie made me realize that I could have the family I have dreamed about my whole life."

Leah tilted her head to one side and was quiet a moment

before she spoke. "I suppose Jamie was about as desperate for a family as you are."

Desperate. It was such a lonely word.

And Jamie was trying to provide a home for his nephew, Peter, who had fallen into his care after the death of Peter's parents and only sibling. Peter didn't speak for months after the tragedy and still suffered from his own injuries caused by the house fire that took their lives. Only after having Leah in their lives had Peter started to speak again. Now he was a chatterbox, full of life and energy. So much that even his pronounced limp couldn't dampen it all.

"We all have things we need," Gracie finally said.

One of her favorite Bible verses came to her. *For He satisfieth the longing soul, and filleth the hungry soul with goodness.*

They all needed, and the Lord provided. In all things.

On Monday, the Widow Kate came over to watch Henry, the twins, and the baby. Yesterday it had become more than apparent to Matthew that he was in dire need of a break. He would have one soon, but not soon enough, he feared.

After Henry and Stephen had clamored in, arguing over who knew the correct way to refill the water trough and the baby had started crying once again, Matthew had lost his temper. He roared at his children, a voice tone way above a mere shout. He sent them all to their rooms, put the baby in hers, and prayed that he made it through this without completely losing his mind. And that's how he felt, like he was losing his mind.

His mind was in a jumble, a tangle of sharp edges and stringy thoughts that slithered away each time he reached for one. He couldn't remember the last decent night's sleep he'd had. That had been before Beth's drowning. He had been the nighttime caretaker, the one who got up for those midnight feedings. The baby hadn't seemed to mind him then, but her mother was still alive, maybe not as attentive as she could have been, but still breathing. At least when Beth was alive there was a chance. It was after she died that the baby had turned on him. He was still the one who cared for her in the middle of the night, but something had changed. She no longer responded to his touch, his soft words, his gentle pats. It was as if she knew that her mother was never coming back, and it was all his fault.

He shook those thoughts away. There were times when he honestly felt as if he was losing his mind and this was among them. He just had to wait, get that one good night's sleep and he would be back on top. It was a struggle to stay there, and eventually the emotions and failures would pull him under again, but he always managed to make his way back to the surface. He just had to be patient and wait. But there was something nagging at him.

Matthew wasn't sure why the thought had occurred to him, but it had. Maybe it was something that Aaron said to him the day before. He didn't know, but the thought was there in the night and had plagued him all through the dark hours. As if he didn't have enough to keep him awake. Now he had this. And he came to talk to the only person he thought might be able to help him. Aaron Zook.

Matthew set the brake, hopped down from the buggy, and hobbled his horse. Aaron Zook's house sat directly across from the schoolyard, and Matthew hoped that Stephen wouldn't see him pull up or drive away. He needed this information, felt as if his life might depend on it.

As suspected, he found Aaron in the corral working with a large black horse whose coat was so shiny it was almost hard to look at. Even though he was wearing his hat, Matthew shielded his eyes from the midmorning sun and made his way over to where Aaron worked.

Matthew knew so very little about horses. Just what a

farmer needed to know to pull a plow or a buggy and help his family get around. But watching Aaron with the beast was like watching water flow from one stream into another, fluid, beautiful, transcendent. And he was unwilling to interrupt. So he simply watched, transformed to another place by the beauty of their movements. He had heard through the rumor mill, also known as the church ladies, that Aaron had always wanted to work with horses, but just in the last year or so was able to make that dream a reality. It was good to know someone's hopes had been realized, their prayers answered.

He stopped at the fence, loath to speak lest he break the spell between man and horse. Besides, he wanted to watch a bit longer, enjoy the poetry that was before him.

But only a few short minutes later, Aaron gave the horse a carrot stick and patted his strong, shiny neck. Then he turned the beast out into the main pasture and walked back to where Matthew watched and waited.

"This is something of a surprise," Aaron said as he came near.

"I didn't want to disturb you," he replied. Maybe he shouldn't have come here.

"You're fine." Aaron took a rag from the back of his pants and wiped his forehead under his hat band and rubbed the sweat between his fingers. The day had turned out quite warm.

"Don't you need to brush him down?"

"It can wait a minute. He likes to roll around in the dirt anyway. If I wait, then I can get some of that out of his coat at the same time." Aaron smiled, then asked, "What brings you out today?"

Matthew hesitated. "I wanted to ask you about something." *Something that's been bothering me for a while now.* But he didn't say that last part.

Aaron patiently waited as Matthew gathered his words.

It wouldn't be this hard talking to Jason about this, but Aaron . . . he was such a pillar in their community. He didn't want the man to look at him differently if he disapproved of his plans. And if he disapproved, would it make any difference in Matthew's decisions? No. So why was he asking?

Because he wanted someone, anyone to say that he was doing the right thing by marrying Gracie. Yesterday Aaron had acted like he understood, but if he knew the rest of the story would he be as accepting?

"Matthew?" Aaron's voice was quiet and questioning.

Matthew shook his head. "You know what? Never mind." He started to turn around and leave, go back home, forget this burning need he had for approval.

"Where are the kids?" Aaron asked, effectively stopping him in his tracks.

Does he think I left them at home alone? Matthew turned to face Aaron once again. "Widow Kate came over to watch them."

"So you hired a babysitter to come talk to me and you're going to leave without even asking me whatever it was you came here to ask?"

When he put it like that . . .

"It's about Gracie . . ." Matthew started.

Aaron nodded politely and once again waited for Matthew to continue.

"I know she wants a family," Matthew said. "She's told me that much. But I don't know what else she's getting from this marriage."

A frown creased his brow as Aaron mulled over what Matthew was saying. "What is it you think she wants?"

He shrugged. "She said a family. I have to believe that's it."

"But you think there's more." It wasn't quite a question.

"Maybe. I don't know."

"'There's something fierce in the heart of a woman.'"

"What's that?"

"Something my father always said. I really didn't understand it until Hannah came back."

"And you think Gracie . . ."

"I think Gracie has been taught her entire life to please those around her, at the expense of whatever it is she herself desires."

Matthew let that wash over him. He could see that in her, that pleasing nature.

They both paused for a moment, letting the sounds of the morning wash over them. From somewhere a truck engine rumbled, but it was too far away for Matthew to care.

"I don't want to have a traditional marriage with Gracie."

Aaron turned swiftly to stare at him. "How's that?"

"You heard me." He couldn't say it again. Nor could he bring himself to explain.

"You said she wants a family," Aaron pointed out.

"She's marrying a family. We will already have children to care for. Five of them. Do we really need more?" So what if the average Amish family had something like ten kids? Five was plenty. Besides, he knew a whole slew of families that only had three or four kids. It was a sign of changing times.

"You said she wants a family," Aaron said again, patiently.

"But she didn't say that she has to have her own children."

"You honestly don't think that's what she meant?"

That's what he wanted to believe. "I don't know," he said, avoiding the real issue. He should have never brought it up. It was too personal an issue to talk about, even with someone he considered to be his best friend.

If he was being truthful, being his best friend wasn't saying much. Matthew hardly had any friends at all in Pontotoc. And even less in Ohio now that he'd left. Still, this wasn't the sort of thing a man talked about with just anybody.

"You have to talk to her," Aaron said. "Before the wedding. You have to let her know that you don't want more children."

"You think so?"

"I know so," Aaron said emphatically. "And as soon as possible."

Chapter Ten

As soon as possible would have been for him to go over there that afternoon, but he managed to find his way home instead. Maybe he had just forgotten. But once he was home, it was awfully hard to leave again. He had been doing that so much these past few days. He just wanted to rest, that was all. Maybe tomorrow.

After all, he had prayed for a miracle and surely that had happened by way of Gracie Glick. Perhaps it was wrong to mess things up when they were just going so well. He wouldn't want to bring them ill fortune by not trusting in God to do what He had promised.

Not that he believed that God would send bad fortune raining down on top of their heads. He wasn't sure God was all that interested in their day-to-day lives. Most people he knew were bored out of their minds. Would God be doubly so? Maybe even triply.

He couldn't say his prayers hadn't been answered. God had sent Gracie Glick to propose to him. How strange was that? Amish women weren't so bold as to just up and ask a man to marry them. Especially not one they barely knew. And yet she had. Was she bold or stupid? Or maybe just fulfilling some divine insight that would pull the two of them together forever. Who was he to stand against God? And if God had indeed sent Gracie to him, then at least some of his prayers had been answered.

Except when he got back to the house, Stephen was home from school and Henry fit to be tied.

"I don't understand why we can't have chicken and ducklings," Henry said for the umpteenth time.

Stephen had heard about the wedding meal from someone, most likely his teacher, Amanda Swartzentruber. She was engaged to be married this fall and like most young girls was wedding happy.

"Dumplings," Matthew corrected, "and it's not part of the wedding meal."

"How come?" Henry demanded.

Matthew shook his head. "It just isn't."

"Why not?" he asked again.

"Because it's not."

"That doesn't make any sense." Henry folded his arms and scowled. Matthew knew that look well. And hated it.

"It doesn't matter if it makes sense or not. That is just the way we do things."

"I don't like it," he said. "Why can't chicken and ducklings be a part of this wedding meal?" The boy was not giving up.

"It's not how we do things." Matthew was beginning to lose his patience. He didn't even correct *ducklings*.

It was true; Henry had been born precocious, always questioning and saying whatever crossed his mind. The teacher was going to have a fun time with him when he started to school in the fall. Especially since it would most likely be her first year teaching.

"Well, I think we should change it. Who do I need to talk to? Amos?"

Matthew nearly choked. "You cannot talk to the bishop about adding chicken and dumplings to the wedding menu."

"Can you do it for me?"

"No."

"What about Gracie? She could do it." He started away
from Matthew as if intent on finding Gracie and convincing her to speak to the bishop about chicken and ducklings.

Matthew caught the back of his suspenders and stopped
his progress. "No one is speaking to the bishop about any
part of the wedding food. Understand?" He hated to be so
stern, but once Henry got something in his head it was near
impossible to get him to think about something else. And
truly, what did the bishop care about what they ate at the
wedding? He wouldn't, but Matthew wanted Gracie to have
as many of the traditions that come with a first wedding as
possible. She was only having one attendant, but some
second marriages had none. Her wedding would last half
the day instead of all day with two meals, two cakes, and
hundreds of guests. Most girls started planning out their
wedding in the second grade. By the time they had joined
the church and actually found the person they were going
to marry, they had gone through countless guest lists, cake
flavors, second meal menus, and dress colors. Gracie only
had those schoolgirl dreams to hold on to and he felt another stab of guilt. Did such things mean something to her
too? Not every girl was like that, but most were. Beth was.
How cheated Gracie had been. Would be. Was it worth it?
He had no idea.

Henry stuck out his lower lip. "*Jah*, Dat." He wasn't
happy but at least Matthew wouldn't have to explain it all
to Amos, why his son was so adamant about having ducklings at the wedding.

For the rest of that day and most of the next morning
Matthew managed to ignore Aaron's warning. Gracie had
said that all she wanted was a family. Why should he read

any more into it than that? He had almost convinced himself that he was doing the right thing by not bringing it up to her when Nancy Byler knocked on his door.

"Hi there, Matthew Byler who is not kin to me." She grinned as she said the words. Then she nudged past him and into the house. She carried a cardboard box full of containers and packages with a bunch of different smells. He supposed that, separately, they probably smelled amazing, but collectively it was a little overwhelming. And nauseating.

"Hi, Nancy." He forced some brightness into his tone. She said that very same thing to him every time they happened to cross paths and had since the first time they met. It was charming and annoying all at the same time. Mostly annoying.

"I brought you some food." She beamed him a big smile, thrust the box into his arms, then waddled her way into the kitchen. They had done this before and he knew now that she expected him to follow.

That was the thing about Nancy Byler No Relation. He had learned early on that she was . . . odd. That was the only nice way he knew how to say it. She had never married and never intended to. She babysat when needed, took care of those around her, and smiled . . . all the time. It was a little unnerving, but Matthew told himself that he should be so happy as to walk around with a perpetual grin. He had just never managed to achieve that level of joy. Now he wasn't sure he would ever be able to.

"I've got you the rest of the peanut butter spread from church in here," Nancy was saying. "You'll have to get some bread though. I didn't have time to bake any. But there is a fresh strawberry-rhubarb pie in there. Well, the rhubarb is fresh from the garden, the strawberries are from Walmart. Mine haven't come in yet. Neither have Strawberry Dan's. Bless it all, if this keeps up he'll have to change his name."

That was highly unlikely, but Matthew understood what she meant. The strawberries hadn't come in yet. Good, fine, moving on . . .

"There should be enough to last you until the wedding—" She kept talking, but Matthew couldn't listen any longer. He was looking at the size of the box and thinking, *By the time we eat all that food, we'll be bringing home my new wife.*

So little food; so many changes.

"*Danki*," he managed. He wanted to say more, but what was there to say? *Thank you* about covered it and yet was nothing at the same time. "You still need that back-porch step replaced?"

She smiled again and waved a hand in the air between them. "*Jah*, but it can wait for another week or two. You'll be pretty busy for the remainder of this one. But I appreciate it, I do."

"I'll be over tomorrow afternoon," he promised.

"No, really, it can wait." For a minute there he thought she actually blushed. Why? He had no idea.

"Tomorrow afternoon," he repeated. His food hadn't waited, and she had taken care of his family for several days. The least he could do was replace a rotten porch step so she didn't fall.

"*Danki*," she said with another one of her bright, slightly vacant smiles, then she bustled out the door.

He watched her go, the wheels in his mind turning with thoughts of food and weddings and all the turmoil that was his life. But his contemplating was short-lived. A few moments later, Henry burst through the door, hollering about something Stephen had done. The dog followed him in, yipping and barking at his heels. Then the baby started to cry.

* * *

Tuesday. He had forgotten that Gracie and her cousins had a "cousins' day" each week to make goat-milk lotion, soaps, and other beauty products that Leah sold in her shop in town.

Matthew had wanted a moment alone with her just to . . . talk about things. He might bring up the fact that he didn't want more children. Or he might not. Mentioning it would mean that he felt it was important, maybe even as important as Aaron seemed to think it was. Matthew had yet to convince himself either way. So he'd had Nancy Byler No Relation come over and sit with Henry, the twins, and the baby while he went over to work on her porch steps. This was just a side trip.

But now, as he pulled his buggy down their lane, he spotted them out front, their worktable set up with all these bottles and bowls. How was he supposed to get her alone for a minute and talk . . . about whatever? He couldn't take long. He still had to get over to Nancy's and fix that porch step.

Or he could turn around and pretend he was never there.

Too late. They spotted him.

All three women waved big and he could see their smiles. He was committed now.

He raised a hand to them and forced a smile.

They watched and waited as he drew closer. He parked his buggy under the big oak tree next to the barn and hopped down.

His legs felt stiff, as if he had been riding for a long time.

"Did you come to sample the lotion?" Leah asked.

Matthew was grateful for her wisecrack. It helped him put things into perspective. He shouldn't be uncomfortable. He was about to marry Gracie in two days. After that, they would all be family.

"Of course," he returned. "Do you have anything in strawberry?" He wasn't sure where the words came from, only grateful that they were there.

The girls laughed, and Leah elbowed Hannah in the ribs. "Strawberry. That's a good idea. Thanks, Matthew."

He nodded his head and turned his attention toward Gracie. "Can I talk to you for a minute?"

She nodded but didn't move out from behind the table where she stood.

Did he need to see her alone? Did it matter? What was he going to ask her? Not about children. No. Not that.

"I just wanted to warn you about something." The words came without any instruction from him. And he was grateful. "Henry has it in his mind that we should serve chicken and dumplings at the wedding. Except he calls it 'chicken and ducklings.' He loved it when Eunice sent some over last week and now he's stuck on them." He was rambling, but he couldn't seem to stop himself.

Once he finished, she just looked at him for a bit as if maybe he was a little off-kilter. "Chicken and ducklings?" she finally asked.

"That is so cute," Hannah said.

"Adorable," Leah agreed.

All three women started laughing.

Now it was Matthew's turn to stare. It was sort of cute, but he was exhausted. He'd had enough of Henry and his brilliant nature. But seeing these women laughing and smiling at his son's antics had him grinning as well.

"What did you tell him?" Gracie asked.

Matthew recounted the story, from his response to Henry's request to his son's threat to talk to the bishop so that chicken and dumplings could be added to the wedding menu.

"Why not?" Gracie asked.

"What?" Matthew felt as if he had missed something kind of important.

"Why not serve chicken and dumplings?"

"Ducklings," Leah corrected.

Hannah laughed.

"Because that's not how we do things?" His response came out more like a question than he had planned.

"So?" Gracie shrugged.

"We already have all the ingredients," Hannah added.

"I say you should." Leah gave a satisfying nod.

"But—" Matthew started to protest, but the girls were already discussing the benefits of having chicken and ducklings versus the traditional chicken and filling.

"*Jah*?" Gracie asked, finally turning to him.

"Are you sure?" he asked. What happened to the bride wanting a traditional wedding? Or maybe that required a traditional bride. One thing he was quickly learning was that Gracie Glick was no traditional bride.

Thursday dawned bright and beautiful. The sun was shining, and it seemed like the perfect day to get married. If there was such a thing. Was there? Maybe Gracie should ask someone. Who would know?

What difference did it make? She was getting married today whether it was the perfect day or not.

She jumped as a knock sounded at the door. "*Jah*?"

The door opened, and Eunice poked her head inside. It was just the thing Gracie needed to see, that smiling face.

"Leah is on her way," Eunice said. "Is there anything you need until then?"

Gracie ran her hands down the front of her dress. It was a beautiful blue, dark, and shot through with black threads that gave it a depth that her everyday clothes didn't have.

She would save this dress, wear it for church and special occasions. It was too special for anything else.

As she looked at herself in the mirror, Eunice let herself into the room and picked up her snow-white apron. White aprons were an indulgence in their community. When a person had to tote water, then heat it with a wood stove just to wash a single load of clothes, white became a time-consuming luxury.

Eunice shook out the apron and helped Gracie wrap it around herself and then tied it in the back. She patted the bow, then clasped Gracie by the shoulders and turned her around.

"If your mother could see you now." Eunice brushed an errant hair back from Gracie's face as they both blinked back tears. This was a happy day. Not a day for tears. She was getting just what she wanted and neither one of them should be crying.

"Stop that," Gracie said, brushing tears off Eunice's cheeks. "I'll just be down the road."

"I'm still going to miss having you around."

"I'll be around," Gracie promised. But would she? She would have a new family to care for, a husband who would need meals and clean clothes, five children to keep in line, and a dog, if they didn't find Pepper's owner soon.

Eunice smiled, then brushed away Gracie's tears as well as her own fresh ones. "Look at us." She laughed, but the sound was a bit choked. "I didn't mean to come in here and make you cry." She sniffed and turned back toward the door. "I'll send Leah in when she gets here."

"*Danki*," Gracie said, watching Eunice walk toward the door, yet unable to call her back. Anything she could say now would bring them both more tears. She wished her mother could be there; she wished Tillie was there; she wished she could somehow get the family she so needed and also remain there with Eunice and Abner. She supposed all brides felt a little like this, torn between two loves, two needs, and two desires.

At the door, Eunice stopped, one hand on the knob. "Tell me one thing," she said, not even turning around to look at Gracie. Maybe that would just make it harder. "Tell me . . . is this really what you want?"

That was the question she had been asking herself, and one she thought she had known the answer to since she was a little girl. And she answered the only way she knew how. "*Jah*," she said. "Of course."

Matthew had to get out of the barn and away from all the well-meaning male guests. "A small wedding" sounded cozy and intimate, special even. But what they were was a pain. Normally he would have been surrounded by his own attendants, as he waited to get the call that it was time for the ceremony. These attendants would have been his closest relatives with maybe a couple of good friends hanging around to wish him well. But at a small wedding, over half of the male guests were milling around next to him out in the barn. They wanted to treat this like a before-church meeting or a boys' night out, laughing and slapping him on the back as if his nerves weren't already shot.

But why would they be? He should be marrying for love. Instead he was marrying for a housekeeper. When he put it like that, it sounded cold, not at all what he wanted from the relationship. He wanted to do things with Gracie, go on trips, picnics, to softball games, and adult singings. He wanted to be a family with her, raising the kids and growing old together. And that's what she had said she wanted as well. A family, togetherness. It suited them both and that was why they were getting married. So why was he feeling so nervous?

The thought of growing old with Gracie Glick at his side

filled him with a sort of unexpected peace. That should have been what made him anxious, not all the chatter around him. But it was the boisterous men who had him looking for a way to escape.

He eased toward the door, laughing and talking, taking a sip of water from time to time. Just a couple more inches and he would be home free. The men around him turned to look at something Abner had in the barn, most likely ornate molding to go in one of the playhouses for Englisch girls that he had been making lately, and Matthew made his escape.

If he remembered right, the girls were supposed to be in the downstairs sewing room. Since this was his second wedding, traditions were broken. There would be no "seating," when the bride picked the couples who were supposed to sit together at their table. There would be no pre-ceremony with everyone filing down the stairs to get into place.

And the sewing room was toward the back, off to the left opposite the kitchen.

He spotted the window and started toward it. Surely by now she was dressed. The ceremony was about to start.

So why are you out here running around instead of in the barn where you are supposed to be?

He had to talk to her once more before the wedding. One last time to make sure this was really what she wanted. Maybe he should tell her about his decision not to have any more children. But there was so much baggage tied to the decision, he didn't have time to explain it all before they would be summoned. And he would need to explain, that was for sure. And yet he didn't feel he was ready for all that would entail. After all, Beth had only been gone three months.

With light knuckles, he rapped on the window. A scream sounded from inside. He'd obviously startled them. Then

someone brushed the shade aside and opened the window.
It was her cousin, Abby. Then Gracie was coming toward
him, a vision in her wedding blue.

"Matthew?" Her brow was furrowed into a concerned
frown. "Is everything okay? The children?"

That was just like her, worried about others before herself, worried about his children.

"They're fine."

Hannah and Leah had taken the boys while the baby had
gone with Mammi Glick. She had taken the girl back into
the *dawdihaus*, telling them to come and get her when the
cake was served. Then she shut the door so neither side
would be disturbed.

Matthew had laughed out loud at that one. Too funny.
Or maybe it was his nerves again. He just couldn't stop
thinking about Gracie and what else she might be getting
from the wedding. Family and . . . But he had never found
the time to ask. Nor had he found the time to tell her about
his adamant desire to not have any more children. People
could go around and say that it was beautiful and natural
and pretend like it was the greatest thing, but he knew. It
was torture for a woman. Torture. And he never wanted
Gracie to go through something like that. She had been
through so much already.

"What's wrong?" Her voice changed, became guarded.

"Nothing." He shook his head and searched for the
words he needed to tell her. "Why are you marrying me?"

She laughed, but the sound was nearer to a choke than
to mirth. "It's a little late to be asking me that, isn't it?" She
glanced behind her as if checking to see where everyone
in the room was. Of course they were right behind her,
listening to every word. News of his question would be the
talk of the reception.

Gracie shooed them all away and leaned out the window.
"I told you what I wanted."

"And what about more children?" he asked. It really wasn't the time, but he couldn't go through with this without knowing for certain.

She blushed a pretty pink and fanned herself a bit. To her defense it was beginning to get hot out and he could feel himself beginning to sweat through his shirt. Thankfully the dark color would mask that. Or so he had been told.

"I'm happy with what the Lord gives me. He already has a plan. He already knows."

Matthew nodded. Spoken like a true Amish woman, ready to accept God's will. He couldn't say it was the easiest thing to do in all cases, but they had been raised to say the words until it was so. But he found them bitter and offensive.

"Gracie, come on," someone called from across the room.

"I need to go." She bit her lip, her nervousness rising back to the surface.

"Just one more thing," he asked. "How do you know so much about dolphins?"

Chapter Eleven

The wedding went off without a hitch. Well, without any major hitches. Both Henry and Thomas had a hard time sitting still during the preaching, and Hannah had to take them outside. Stephen and Benjamin had complained early on that their shirts were itchy, and they spent most of the service rubbing their necks where the fabric touched. Baby Grace was the only Byler child in attendance who behaved, but that was only because she was asleep. Mammi was good with babies; so many years of practice would do that. Matthew seemed to believe that the baby had something against him, but Gracie knew the truth. He was just worried, and that emotion was carrying over to the baby every time he held her. Once Matthew's concerns had been addressed, then she would go back to being the loving child that he claimed she was before Beth died.

They ate and played a couple of silly wedding games, then it was time to load up and head home. Jim and David had already taken all of Gracie's things to Matthew's house. Now she had the rest of the afternoon to get settled in before supper and bedtime.

The thought made her warm all over again. She never did find out the proper way to act on her wedding night.

She supposed now she would just have to play it as it came. But it was the deliberateness of getting all the children into Matthew's buggy, sitting in the front beside him, Baby Grace in a seat on her lap. Her friends and family all watching as they waved and drove away. All those people knew what tonight would bring. Or they were speculating. It made her feel . . . strange. Exposed somehow, that her night was known to all while she had no idea what would be going on behind their closed doors.

Maybe she was just nervous. After all it was only natural. And then there was Matthew coming to her right before the ceremony, asking her about having other children. He had looked so relieved when she told him that she would take whatever the good Lord gave them. She supposed Matthew wanted a score of children. Most Amish men did. The more children the more hands to get the work done. But she couldn't hope for too much. She meant what she said. She would happily take whatever the Lord saw fit to bless them with, be it two or ten. Though ten was highly unlikely at her age. And she said a small prayer of thanks that she and her husband had agreed on such a delicate matter.

On a bus ride to the Gulf coast to help the hurricane victims. That's how she knew so much about dolphins. The girl who sat next to her had been watching a movie on her phone—a feat Matthew hadn't even known was possible—and Gracie found it so interesting that she couldn't help but watch it over her shoulder.

He should have known it was something like that. Of course Gracie was going to help others. That's just the way she was. And of course she found this movie to be particularly interesting since it dealt with animals and humans helping dolphins all around the world.

The thought made his heart warm once again. She was

a good girl, his Gracie, and he was blessed that the Lord had brought them together. So what if theirs wasn't a "normal" meeting. If nothing else, he could say their courtship was interesting.

"What are you smiling about?" she asked as they traveled toward his home, the home they would now share.

"Nothing." He shook his head.

"Are we there yet?" Henry asked.

"Does it look like we are?" Stephen retorted.

"Boys." Matthew gave a stern warning in the one word.

"My shirt is itchy," Thomas complained.

"I have to pee," Benjamin said. "Bad."

"Benjamin Byler, we do not talk like that in front of the womenfolk. If you must announce that condition, please say I need to use the outhouse."

"But I only need to pee in there," Benjamin protested.

"Benjamin," Matthew said. He wished he could see his son's face. Maybe he would install a couple of those fancy dash mirrors so he could see what was going on in the back without having to turn away from the road.

"Get it right." Henry nudged him in the ribs.

"Ouch. I need to use the outhouse. Real bad now."

Matthew dropped his head, then promptly settled his gaze back on the road. Now was not the time for forgetting to pay attention. "You're just going to have to wait until we get home," he said to Benjamin. To Gracie he said, "I'm sorry about that."

But he could see that she was doing her best not to laugh.

"It's okay. Boys will be boys and all."

"Yes, and there's a lot of boy going on at my house." He paused. "Our house."

She smiled, and he realized that it was the first time she had smiled just for him all day. At the wedding she had a smile for everyone, but this one was his first. "Our house," she repeated. "I like the sound of that."

And strangely enough, he did too.

Getting home was a frenzy of activity. She supposed she would get used to it. Matthew seemed to take it all in stride, so she had to believe that every homecoming was about the same. All the boys had to be unloaded, which resulted in someone pushing someone else, mostly Henry pushing Stephen and then one twin pushing another, with equal pushing time for each boy. Benjamin had come out of his shell for her, if he'd ever really had one. He had seemed so quiet the first time she met him, but now he was somewhere between Stephen and Henry. He was a little bossy and preferred his way above all else.

"It's your turn to go check the messages," Henry was saying as they climbed down. It might be her wedding day, but it was still a Thursday and life kept going. Chores had to be done, children fed, and they still had a dog owner to find.

"Whose turn is it really, Thomas?"

"Mine and Stephen's," he admitted.

Stephen kicked at a clot of dirt with the toe of one shoe. Every day they had to go to the phone shanty to check the messages and see if anyone had called about their signs.

They had put signs up from their house clear over to the other side of Eugene Dover's house. So far no one had said they were missing a dog, but it was still early yet. But the boys loved the little pooch, that much was obvious. And no one wanted to be the one who got the message that she belonged to someone else.

"You boys get on in the house and take off those Sunday clothes," Matthew said. The boys grumbled a little but did as he said, running as fast as they could to the front door.

"And hang up those shirts in your closets. You can wear them to church again on Sunday."

"Ah, Dat," went up from all four of them, along with protests that the material was scratchy and uncomfortable.

"I guess I'll go get Baby Grace settled in."

He nodded but didn't tell her there was something else that she needed to be doing. So she picked up the carrier and headed inside, even as she was so very aware of her husband walking behind her.

The house was much as it had been the day she was here a week and a half ago. Clean, with just a little clutter around, the kind that comes from living in a space. There was a stack of mail on the table, a pair of muck boots by the door. Judging by their size, they belonged to Matthew. The quilt that had been thrown over the back of the sofa was pulled down, as if someone had slept there the night before and not returned it to its normal resting place.

She unbuckled Baby Grace, who kicked her legs with glee at being released from her confinement. She gurgled and cooed, and Gracie wanted to bury her nose in that soft-scented neck and inhale that sweet baby scent.

She could hardly believe it. She was here. Married. With a ready-made family of four rowdy boys and the sweetest baby girl any *mamm* could ask for. Truly God had blessed her.

And her husband . . . well, she might not know everything to expect, but he was a good man, a fine provider and a loving father. Surely everything else would fall into place.

With a contented sigh, she snuggled Baby Grace to her chest and started toward her bedroom. "Let's go check your diaper, *jah*?"

She said the words, then walked from the room, so very aware of Matthew's gaze on her. Was he feeling the same weirdness that she was?

They liked each other. That was to say, she didn't think

ill of him, but they hadn't had much time to learn anything about the other before they got married. Of course it was going to be a little awkward for a while. But with time everything would smooth itself out.

She opened the door to the nursery but stopped in her tracks. "What's this?" she asked, gesturing toward the space.

Matthew came up behind her. He scratched the back of his neck and dropped his gaze. "This is your room."

"My room?"

This had once been Baby Grace's room. With nothing more than a crib and a rocking chair in one corner. Now there was a small chest of drawers and a twin bed added to the mix.

"My room?" She couldn't help but repeat herself.

He nodded but still didn't look her in the eye. "I thought you might want to be close to the baby."

Her room. Close to the baby.

Close to the baby was right. There was hardly any space to walk. Just enough to come in and turn around. But it was clean, and the furniture seemed sturdy enough. She had stayed in worse. Still, this put quite a crimp in her life plan.

"I—" She had been about to say *I thought we would share a room like a normal married couple.* The house wasn't that big, and his room was just down the hall. She would be able to hear the baby if she started to cry at night. But the words got lodged in her throat. That was okay because Matthew interrupted.

"Our marriage is . . . unconventional and I thought you would be more comfortable here. We can change things around if you want. Paint, or buy new sheets." He said the last as if just then realizing that the furniture would be impossible to move. There simply wasn't enough space for rearranging.

"No," Gracie said quietly. "This is fine." She couldn't hide her disappointment. But surely her life wouldn't revolve around separate beds. There would have to come a time . . . and she should be grateful for this grace period to get to know him better before jumping into an even more intimate relationship with him.

Or maybe he just wanted to sleep alone but would visit her from time to time. She had heard of such arrangements. Sometimes when a husband snored and kept the wife awake or stole all the covers. No one had come right out and said that, but women talked. She had overheard many a conversation about marriage. Yet none of it told her how to deal with this situation.

She would just have to wait and see how everything went. Give it a try and trust God.

"Right," she said with a quick smile. It would all turn out. It always did. The Lord had gotten her this far. There was no turning back now.

She could feel his gaze upon her as she crossed the room and let down the side of the crib. There was no room for a changing table, nor had there been one in there before he had her things moved in. It was a luxury anyway and there were plenty of surfaces that could be used to change diapers without taking up precious space.

He watched her as she changed Baby Grace's diaper. She knew he was watching and she decided to pretend he wasn't. Or maybe that it didn't bother her that he was. At any rate, once she finished her task, she turned, and he was gone. Thank heavens. He was beginning to make her nervous, like she was not capable of a simple wet-diaper change and would mess it all up or drop the baby on the floor. When neither happened, he moved on, most probably going out to check the boys and the chores they were to complete.

Gracie cuddled Baby Grace against her chest and gave her room—their room—a hard once-over. Nothing was lacking. Bed, mirror, chest of drawers, crib, chair, nightstand, lamp—though *nightstand* was a kind word for the tiny square shelf barely big enough to hold the lamp. Nothing was lacking but nothing was striking either.

She felt a little like that girl in the Englisch fairy tale she had read once when she was younger. She had sneaked the book into the far corner of the library and devoured it right there on the carpet. Something about the cover drew her in. Wasn't that the way with books? But she had known from the start that her parents wouldn't approve. But she had to read it.

Now she had something in common with Cinderella. There were no evil stepsisters or stepmothers in her life, but she was sort of tucked away to be forgotten until she was needed. She wasn't positive, but she was pretty certain that was not how a healthy Amish marriage should be, even one that was for the sake of children. And she was also certain that day one of the marriage was not the right time to bring it all up.

"One day," she murmured into Baby Grace's hair. "One day soon."

She couldn't ever remember feeling so out of place and awkward in a space that was supposed to be her home. After she had changed Baby Grace's diaper she had dug around in drawers and found one of those newfangled baby carriers that was something akin to a bedsheet with a jumbo safety pin to hold everything in place. She read the instructions and figured out how to work the contraption and only after four tries.

Baby Grace seemed to like her new vantage point and it freed up Gracie's hands for other chores. She was fairly certain that most brides didn't come home and immediately start sweeping and reorganizing cabinets. But she needed to get a feel for what was in the house so she would know what they would need when she went to the store.

But that could wait for later when the baby went down for a nap. Now it was time for a walk around the property, a look at the garden, and a check in at the little shop up near the road.

The garden plot was pretty standard. Big enough for a young family of six, but now they were seven and growing. She would most likely need to double the size by next year. This year, however, a couple more rows should suffice. And she needed to get started on planting as soon as possible. Tomorrow would be great, but Monday at the latest.

The little red shop was built out of one of the simple sheds that Abner Gingerich made. It was a staple for his business. People could do almost anything with one of his sheds since it was basically a box with a floor, a door, and a roof. Something told her this one hadn't been used in a long time. She hadn't noticed or heard anyone say that Beth Byler wasn't opening her shop this year, but now that she was gone, it was sort of a moot point.

A rusty-looking padlock held the door closed and kept out visitors, but if Gracie knew anything at all . . .

Careful not to bang the baby's head against one of the two small windows the shop had, Gracie lifted onto her tiptoes and ran her fingers along the edge of the window trim. *Jah.* There it was. The key. Well, a key, she just assumed it was the key she needed. Why would it not be?

The door creaked when she opened it, further testament that the little shop had been closed for a while and certainly longer than the three months since Beth passed. But that didn't mean a whole lot, since Beth had been pregnant and taking care of four rowdy boys. Still, these shops they sported in front of their property were the way most made ends meet.

A cloud of dust poofed from over the door as she stepped inside. She waved it away from her nose and the baby's and tried not to sneeze. How long had the place sat unused? Longer than she had first imagined.

She took a minute, blinking to allow her eyes to adjust to the dim light inside the shed. The two small windows were opposite each other; their placement would add both light and a breeze as the summer heated up. But mostly a breeze.

Gracie left the door open and eased into the shop. There was a faint smell inside like rotting plants and melted candle wax. A strange combination for sure. But once her eyes had adjusted she could see the cause. The vegetable bins had been cleaned out, but judging by the stains in the wood, not before the produce turned. Each bin was carefully labeled: cucumbers, tomatoes, squash, okra, potatoes, green beans. Not a great offering but enough to bring in a little extra. On the far wall, the bins had been replaced by a flat table with packages of . . . she moved closer to inspect them. The cellophane baggies were tied with tiny pieces of raffia, but inside the contents were nothing more than misshapen blobs—blue, green, purple. Once upon a time they had most likely been hand-dipped candles. Some of the transparent lumps might have been glycerin soap. But the Southern heat had taken its toll and reduced the product to nothing more than a glob of wax in a bag. But Gracie knew one thing: Whoever made them had taken care to make them attractive. Each one had a handwritten tag with the scent clearly labeled and a tiny image drawn to illustrate. A strawberry for the strawberry scent, a pine cone for the pine scent, and on down the line.

"What are you doing?"

Gracie screamed and whirled around, one hand bracing

the baby's head instinctively. The other she pressed to her pounding heart. "Matthew!" she gasped. "You scared me."

"Obviously."

Not *I'm sorry, forgive me*, or *I didn't mean to*. He had been the epitome of a gentleman all morning long, but now he seemed . . . angry.

He raised a brow as if waiting for something. *Oh, for me to answer him.*

"I, uh, I just came out to see what I would need to do to get the shop running this season." She looked around her at all the ruined candles and soaps and the many shelves coated in a thick layer of dust. "It's going to be some work, but I think we can handle it." She patted the baby's bottom and smiled.

Matthew didn't smile in return. He just stood there, staring, looking as if he wanted to say something but was trying to find the right words. The words to express his anger? Or perhaps to keep from sounding so angry. She had no idea, but for a brief moment she wondered if he had that disease she had heard about where people had wide mood swings and could be happy one minute and then incredibly sad the next. Except Matthew only ever looked moderately happy, if at all.

"You're going to spoil her," he said with a terse nod toward Baby Grace.

Gracie ran a loving hand around the curve that was the baby's back and bottom, so snug in the carrier. "I just want her to get used to me."

"She looks okay to me."

And then it occurred to her. He was jealous because the baby was always crying around him. She had to say, if he went around with the same sourpuss attitude all the time, no wonder the baby sobbed when he came near.

"We're bonding." She held her ground. She wasn't going

to apologize for taking care of his daughter. Wasn't that one of the main reasons why they got married in the first place? The marriage wasn't even twelve hours old and he was already regretting it?

Matthew shook his head as if he wasn't sure what to make of it all. "You don't have to open the shop this year." His voice was gruff, gritty like sandpaper.

"I don't mind. It'll give the kids something to do this summer."

"You don't have to," he said again.

But she was already on a roll. "I figure we can keep the vegetables here, but over here I'll put some of our lotions and soaps. Not many, since I don't want to damage sales fro—"

"I don't want you to, okay?" This time his voice was closer to a roar.

Gracie stopped and stared at him, her arms still raised in her animated gesture of what they were going to do to the shop.

Even Baby Grace stared at him wide-eyed, but at least he didn't send her into tears again.

"I mean"—he lowered his voice and cleared his throat— "I don't want you to feel obligated to take up the business."

But she had a feeling there was more to it than that.

"But we can use the money, *jah*?"

He nodded, though she could see his reluctance.

"Then we should open the shop."

He grunted something, then turned on his heel and stalked out of the building.

Gracie watched him go. Something was up with him. He was a long way from the man she got lost with on a country road just days ago. But she was in this marriage now. For better or worse and everything in between. And she was going to find out exactly what it was.

* * *

She finished her tour of the house and property just in time to cook supper. Baby Grace was happy to be in the playpen as long as she could see Gracie. Once she was out of her line of vision, the baby started to cry. Gracie had yet to figure out what that was all about, but she would. There was still time.

After supper, she put the baby to bed, helped the boys get washed up, and everyone gathered downstairs so Matthew could read from the Bible.

This. This was what she had been waiting for, this family time. So her marriage wasn't conventional. So the boys squirmed and pinched each other as they listened, but somehow managed to stop every time their father looked up. So what if it wasn't exactly picture-perfect. This was her family now, and she loved them.

Yes, that was true. She had already fallen in love with the boys, and Baby Grace could capture anyone's heart in a second.

Just . . . Matthew.

This was day one. And she was expecting too much, but she felt she could love him. Right up until the time he walked into the shop with his angry eyes and dark scowl. It was as if he knew he had the power to scare people and he pulled it out whenever he needed it. But why? Why would he need to scare her? Why was he so adamant about not having the shop open? Most of the farms around there depended on the money brought in from sales to make ends meet. It wasn't like Ohio, and certainly not like what she had seen of Lancaster County, but they did all right. They had their share of Englischers who came out to buy pickles, jam, and sauerkraut as well as the ones who wanted fresh produce or who sent handmade soaps and lotions away to friends who didn't live near an Amish community. She had heard them talk. They all thought it was quaint. Maybe it was, maybe it wasn't. But no one could dispute the fact that it was necessary.

Love him or not, she had promised to be his wife. And yet he seemed to want to take all that away from her. Why?

Matthew closed his Bible, and the boys groaned.

Only then did his words register. Time for bed. She had been so lost in thought that she missed what he read.

The boys dutifully placed a kiss on her cheek and trudged up the stairs.

"Does anyone want to be tucked in tonight?"

"*Jah, danki.*" Benjamin ducked his head as he said the words, bashful and hopeful all at the same time. He was the sensitive one of the bunch, and she suspected he missed his mother most of all.

The other boys waved away her offer, citing reasons like *I'm too big* and *That's for babies*. But not Benjamin.

"All right," she said. "Get changed into your nightclothes and brush your teeth. I'll be up in a moment." She wasn't going to take their rebuff personally. Maybe they did feel too big to be tucked in. Or maybe that hadn't been a part of their previous nighttime routine. She couldn't expect them to accept her as their *mamm* on the first night. All things in time, Eunice always said.

Thinking of Eunice made her a bit homesick, but there was no looking back now. She pushed thoughts of her loved ones away and gathered up the little bits that boys seemed to trail behind them: a sock, a piece of string, a couple of twigs, and half a button.

"You should make them come back and pick all that up." Matthew's voice was quiet, and unreadable.

"No sense being a hardnose straight off."

"It's your call." Matthew shrugged.

At least that was. Everything else was still up for debate.

She gathered up someone's errant shoe. Who knew where the mate was.

"About earlier," he started.

She shook her head. The atmosphere had turned uncomfortable once again. She didn't want to hear him say he was sorry, because she was fairly certain she was going to be dealing with his mood swings for many days, weeks, even months to come.

Lord, give me patience.

"Don't," she said, unwilling to say more, yet thankful nothing else was necessary.

He sat there in silence for a moment, then finally gave a quick nod. But he didn't meet her gaze. And she didn't know what to make of it all. She supposed she needed to be just as patient with him as he would need to be with her. The situation was unusual and uncomfortable from both sides.

She watched him for a moment, trying to figure out what was going through his mind, then she gave up, got herself an oil lamp, and headed for the stairs.

There were three bedrooms upstairs, though the boys only occupied two. The third was used for storage and would come in handy when—*if* more children came along.

She poked her head in the first doorway, finding Stephen and Henry crawling into bed. "Teeth brushed?" she asked.

"*Jah*," they answered in return.

She gave them a nod. "Lights off then. See you in the morning." Then she eased out of the room and closed the door behind her.

Across the hall Thomas was crawling into bed while Benjamin waited patiently for her to come tuck him in. He really was such a sweet child, she thought. All the boys were adorable, lovable, and very entertaining, but only Benjamin could be described as sweet.

"Teeth brushed?" she asked the twins.

They nodded, but opposite each other, as if to prove they were different from one another. Like that wasn't completely evident.

"Come on then, Benjamin, let's get you tucked in."

He hopped onto the bed and squirmed under the covers, his smile wide enough to take away the sting of his brothers' refusals. Once he was down, head on his pillow, he folded his hands over his chest and waited for her, that smile still shining.

Like the older boys' room, the twins' room was set up with two narrow beds side by side, with a small nightstand between them. The bottom of the nightstand held books while the top space was clear except for a kerosene lantern. Gracie noted that it was the tubular kind, which was safer around children. She wouldn't have expected anything else from Matthew.

Gracie nudged their lantern aside and placed hers next to it to have both hands free. Benjamin grinned as she pulled the covers up, then squealed when she didn't stop until they were over his head.

"Gracie, stop, stop." He giggled.

She pulled the covers back down. "Is something wrong?" she asked innocently.

"You aren't supposed to cover up my head."

"Oh." She acted as if she had no idea. "Let me try that again." She pulled the covers up and over his face, only stopping when he giggled and corrected her.

"What?" she asked. She probably shouldn't be getting him wound up before bed, but she couldn't help herself. He was ripe for the teasing.

"You did it again."

"I'm so sorry," she said. "But you know what they say?"

He shook his head, eyes still twinkling.

"Third time is a charm." She held up three fingers. "That means that after three times, I should get it right. Have we had two tries?"

He nodded.

"So this is number three." Her smile was a little wider as she pulled the covers up, over his head, then back in place again, as if she only then remembered to correct herself.

"Charm," Benjamin said.

"Definitely." She leaned over and kissed him on the forehead. "See you in the morning."

Benjamin mumbled something, she wasn't quite sure what, then she turned to find Thomas scrambling out of bed.

"Do me!" he cried. "Do me now."

The smile on her face was almost out of control as she performed the tucking-in ritual on Thomas. It didn't matter that she used the very same technique as with his twin. He lapped up the attention, giggled and laughed, and she felt herself become a little more accepted into the household. And that was worth a lot. More than gold.

Now if she could figure out how to work the same magic on their father.

Chapter Twelve

Gracie stared into the darkness over her bed until her eyes watered. No matter how hard she looked, she could not make out the ceiling. What she was going to do if the baby woke up was anyone's guess. She couldn't see three inches in front of her face.

She would have to talk to Matthew tomorrow about installing some battery-operated touch lights around the room for nighttime changings and feedings. And she wondered what they had done before. She supposed he had left the door open and the small lights spaced down the hallway would have given some illumination. Then again, they were operated by motion-sensor and would only come on if someone walked in front of them. She supposed that they would have stayed on long enough for him to find his way across the room and pick the baby up from the crib. So what had he used to make his way out of the room?

Hmmm . . .

Or maybe he slept with the baby in his bed.

She shook her head at herself. First of all, that was such an Englisch thing to do. She didn't know of any Amish couples who allowed their babies to sleep with them. She supposed there had to be a few, but none that she knew about.

And secondly, she couldn't imagine big ol' grumpy Matthew Byler allowing such a tiny creature to rest next to him. Wouldn't he worry about rolling over on her? And what about all that screaming she did whenever he was around? Gracie couldn't imagine having a nonstop crying baby, much less a nonstop crying baby right next to her in bed.

Maybe that was why he left the room dark: so Baby Grace didn't see him coming. Maybe he used the sneak attack method to console her at night, swooping in and satisfying whatever need she had before she realized it was him and not her mother.

Gracie supposed that was possible and about as logical as any of her other theories.

But truly, all her rambling thoughts were nothing more than means to keep her mind off the fact that she had heard Matthew go to bed nearly half an hour ago, if she was gauging her time right. Half an hour? Forever? What did it matter when she was in this room and he in another? She looked toward where she knew the door to be. There were no hall lights coming on to indicate that he was headed her way.

She hadn't known what to expect on her wedding night, but it certainly wasn't this!

But . . . if she were really being honest with herself, he had warned her. Only here in the cover of darkness did she see his words and actions for what they were.

He had told her that she needed to be close to the baby, so he had stuffed her in here. He had told her that he wanted to get married as soon as possible, while his baby was screaming her head off, inconsolable. He had told her that she didn't have to open the shop this year. Well, she didn't really know what that was about. But there it was. He had told her a lot of things. She had only heard what she wanted to hear.

Her heart sank in her chest and gave a heavy thud. What

had she gotten herself into? She was never going to be able to have a family of her own if she and Matthew had separate rooms.

The thought sent heat flooding into her face and she buried it in her pillow. Like there was anyone around to witness her embarrassment.

Just because they had separate rooms now didn't mean that they would always have separate rooms. Maybe this was just for a time. A trial. Sort of. They got married quickly and out of necessity for him. Perhaps he was just giving her time to adjust. Or himself. After all, he'd only lost his wife a few months ago. Less than four.

Perhaps he wanted the space so he himself could have time to adjust. Their marriage had broken his year of mourning. Maybe he was waiting for that to pass before starting anew.

Now that sounded logical enough. Though it seemed that where Matthew Byler was concerned, logic wasn't always involved.

And truly, unless he came to her and explained, there was only one way for her to know the truth, and that was to ask him. Something she didn't think she could work up the courage to do.

The next few days proved to be the most fulfilling and the most trying that Gracie had experienced in a long while.

She knew Matthew had fields to plant and budding crops to tend to, but she couldn't help the feeling that he was avoiding her. She was usually up before him, having been summoned to the crib by Gimme Grace. At least that's what she had nicknamed the baby in her head. It seemed the more she did for the infant, the more she required. Gracie spent the morning before the sun came up soothing her back to sleep, only to spend the next two hours getting breakfast cooked and children ready for the day. After that, there should have been a little time to rest, but as if on notice that Gracie was about to have five minutes to herself, Baby Grace would cry, awake and needing something else. Each day was different—some combination of food, a dry diaper, a clean dress—and sometimes all three.

After the baby was taken care of and soothed, Gracie would load her into the sling carrier that she had found that first day and head outside to work in the garden plot or in the yard, but usually she was just in time to run some type of interference between the boys—most often Henry versus the twins.

By then it was time to start getting something ready to eat for dinner. Most days, Matthew didn't come in from the field, and it was just her, Baby Grace, and the boys. Clean that up, try to get the baby down for a nap, and then pick up everything the boys had strewn about while she had been trying to get the baby to sleep. About that time Stephen would come in, wanting a snack before chores. The other boys, not to be outdone, wanted one as well. Inevitably, someone would allow the screen door to slam shut behind them—despite all her warnings to close it easy. The baby would wake up screaming at having been disturbed, the boys would head outside, and it was time to cook supper. Sometimes it would be close to dark before Matthew would finally come in. By then, the kids were all fed, washed, and ready for bed, the chores were done, the house picked up, the baby asleep—finally—and his supper waiting for him on the stove. He didn't seem to want any company, so she would wander off to her room to read quietly as she listened to him shuffle around, getting ready for bed. Then she would turn off the light and then the whole thing would start all over again the next day.

The highlight of her day was putting the boys to bed. Ever since that first night when only Benjamin asked for a tuck-in, Thomas, after witnessing the fun, decided that he needed one as well, and then Henry and Stephen had decided that maybe they weren't too big for the activity after all. But since it had become an every night occurrence, she had to come up with new ways to make them laugh. So far, every one of her efforts had been successful.

At least something was going right. She supposed it was all peachy for Matthew. He had managed to get everything he wanted. Someone to take care of his children, clean his house, and cook his meals.

But she supposed she couldn't complain. She had gotten what she wanted . . . sort of. She had gotten a family. Just not in the way she had imagined. What was it Mammi Glick was always saying? *Be careful what you wish for, you just might get it.*

Next time she'd be a little more specific when she said her prayers.

But today was Tuesday, cousins' day, and a bright interruption to what was starting out to be a monotonous week.

After Stephen left for school, Gracie loaded the baby, Henry, the twins, and Pepper into the buggy and headed off.

The boys chatted all the way over to Eunice and Abner's about how they were going to play with Michael and Caleb, Jim and Anna's twins.

"Sorry," she told them. "Only Samuel and Joshua will be home. The twins will be at school."

"Aww," they chorused.

Henry kicked the back of the seat in front of him. Baby Grace frowned.

"Don't kick, Henry. You'll disturb the baby."

"*Jah*, Gracie."

She wished Matthew had made good his threat to install dash mirrors in the buggy so he could see what the kids were doing behind them. Instead she tossed a smile over her shoulder. "If you're lucky, we might be able to talk

Joshua into taking you to the pond fishing. Pepper will like that too, *jah*?"

Despite the many signs they had posted, no one had come by to claim the dog. Gracie had even added the phone number to Leah's store as a contact, but no leads. Secretly Gracie was glad. *Jah*, the dog gave her one more thing to care for, but she enjoyed the pooch. At Matthew's house, Pepper was the one thing that belonged to her. Sort of.

"I can go by myself," Henry boasted.

"I'm not sure that's a good idea," Gracie said. In fact, it was a terrible idea. Had they been her children, she might have let them all go down to the pond together, but they weren't her birth children. She was as good as the baby-sitter these days, and the babysitter shouldn't take chances like that with her charges.

"I wanna go fishing," Thomas said, his voice taking on a whiney edge.

The boys had been working hard with her the last few days, sweeping out the shed, hoeing the rows back into the vegetable garden, hanging laundry, and mopping floors. She supposed they were due for a little fun time. Cousins' day might be put on hold for a couple of hours if Joshua wasn't around. Or perhaps they could move the entire operation down to the pond so they could work and watch the kids fish. Hopefully it wouldn't come to that.

"I was beginning to get worried," Leah called as Gracie pulled the buggy to a stop under the large tree to one side of the barn.

"Baby Grace was not ready to go," Gracie said, with a smile. Grace had been ready, but then she spit up all over her dress and Gracie's. One stain might have been tolerable if Gracie could have wiped it clean with a wet rag, but the spot was roughly the size of a Christmas ham. There would be no spot cleaning today.

Leah and Hannah chuckled, as Gracie had hoped, and

the moment gave her time to unload the kids from the buggy.

"Are we going fishing?" Henry asked as soon as his feet hit the ground.

"Let me see if Joshua is there, okay?"

"I can watch them," he said importantly.

"I know you can," Gracie replied, helping the twins down. "But I would feel better if Joshua went with you."

"But—" he started to protest again.

"Henry," she cut in, effectively stopping his words. "Let me see if Joshua is here first."

"*Jah*, Gracie."

She must have raised her voice louder than she had intended.

"Joshua's gone with Dat to deliver a shed," Hannah said with an apologetic grimace.

Gracie turned back to Henry. He stood next to her, his chin lifted at a stubborn angle. "How about we go inside and see if Eunice has any cake, hmm?"

He seemed to think about it a minute, his little-boy stomach warring with his desire to be in charge for once. "And if there's no cake?"

"We'll figure that out then."

Reluctance slowed his response. "*Jah*, okay."

"Who knows?" she said as she got the baby from the buggy and slung the fabric snuggie carrier across one shoulder. "She might have pie instead."

"Or too." He grinned, then took off toward the house.

Gracie sighed and watched him go. Crisis averted.

"How's it going, cuz?" Hannah asked.

Gracie made her way across the yard where her cousins had already set up their worktables. She was so happy to see them. She had missed them so. But something in her expression had Hannah and Leah watching her carefully.

"What?" Gracie stopped, set the baby carrier down, and

started wrapping the carrier around her. With any luck she would feed the baby and Grace would go to sleep, nestled into the soft carrier.

Hannah and Leah exchanged a look. That was one thing about the two of them that sometimes rubbed Gracie wrong. They could communicate without speaking. Never mind that they had spent so many years apart when they left to go to the *Englisch* world. They had a connection that couldn't be broken. Normally this telepathy—at least that's what Gracie thought it was called—didn't bother her, but today . . .

Gracie propped one hand on her hip and looked from one to the other of them. "What?"

"You look . . ." Leah started, but trailed off and looked back at her sister.

"Tired," Hannah picked up. "Are you sure you're up for today?"

"*Jah*," she said, nodding her head with more force than necessary. She had been looking forward to today since Thursday night. Never mind that it had been her wedding day. She had anticipated getting together with her cousins since then. Tired or not, she was having cousins' day.

Another look passed between Hannah and Leah, but Gracie didn't have time to respond to it. Henry came barreling out of the front door, the screen slamming behind him. At the noise, the baby jumped and started to wail.

"Eunice said I have to eat dinner before I can have cake *or* pie." His tone told her exactly how he felt about that.

"If Eunice said . . ." Gracie trailed off, hating the resigned note she heard in her voice. If she looked as tired as she sounded, no wonder her cousins were concerned.

"How is that fair?" Henry asked. "Joshua's not here, Eunice won't let me have cake or pie, and you won't let me go fishing." He was gearing up for a full-on tantrum.

"It's not fair," Gracie said, unhooking the baby from the

carrier seat. The baby's face had turned red and her legs kicked as if she were warding off anyone who got near. "But sometimes that's just the way it is." She could barely hear her own voice over the baby's crying. "And we have to accept that. Now I suggest you bring down your tone before you lose dessert even after you've eaten."

His eyes widened, but he didn't protest. Maybe he knew he was pushing her past her breaking point. Or maybe he was saving this argument for later. Who knew? He looked around at the three women standing there, then headed back inside. "Baby's crying," he threw over one shoulder, like no one was able to hear her but him. The door slammed behind him, and Baby Grace's wails intensified.

Maybe it was the day, the fact that she was so tired, or that her cousins were there close to her, but Gracie felt tears prick at the back of her eyes.

"Gracie?" Leah asked cautiously.

Gracie blinked furiously to keep those tears from falling. She was not admitting defeat. There was nothing to be defeated from. It was not a game. This was her life, and it was exactly what she wanted.

She bounced Baby Grace to soothe her cries and forced a smile to her lips. "*Jah?*"

"Are you okay?" Hannah asked.

Gracie blew out a quick breath. "Of course." She hoped like everything her tone conveyed her intent. *What could possibly be wrong?* She shifted the baby and patted her on the back. Now if she could stop her own tears as easily.

Leah and Hannah exchanged another one of their looks, then Leah pulled her cellphone from the pocket of her skirt and hit a couple of buttons. That must have been enough to make a call. She put it away and nodded. "Brandon's on his way. He'll take the boys, and you give me the baby."

Gracie looked at her in horror. How could she? Baby

Grace was her responsibility. She couldn't just hand her over to her cousin and allow Leah to take care of her.

"I'm going to take her inside and Mammi's going to watch her. The baby loves Mammi and Mammi will love watching her. Then you can have a break."

Gracie stiffened. The idea sounded like heaven, but at the same time seemed impossible. This was what she wanted: a family. And after all the families she had helped over the years, she was accustomed to being the one in control. The one with the answers, the solution. Now she felt as frayed as a sawed-off rope. She had had such confidence in her abilities and now . . . now she felt like a failure.

"You are not a failure," Hannah said. "So quit thinking that you are."

"How do you know what I'm thinking?" Gracie asked. She didn't want to be belligerent, but she wasn't ready to admit defeat. Er, relinquish control.

"Seriously?" Hannah shot her a look.

Right. They had grown up together. They knew each other almost as well as they knew themselves.

"Gimme." Leah reached out and wagged her fingers at the baby.

Reluctantly, Gracie handed her over.

She watched as Leah cooed at Baby Grace, who looked up at her in wonder. Tears still wet her chubby cheeks, but at least she wasn't crying.

"She'll be fine," Hannah said.

Gracie took a shuddering breath. "I know, it's just . . ."

"Just what?" Hannah asked gently.

"Not easy," Gracie finally said.

Hannah nodded. "It's something else entirely having to care for them on your own instead of just helping out."

Boy, was that the truth!

"And I just had one." Hannah chuckled as if remembering.

"I—" How could she explain? She had married Matthew to get the family she wanted and had ended up with the family he had. She had no idea if or when things would change for them. Plus, walking into a family with five children all still grieving for their *mamm* was harder than she ever imagined.

"She just cries all the time," Gracie admitted. "I can usually get her calmed down, but it's the smallest things that set her off. And it takes forever to stop her tears." Her own tears rose in her eyes once again. "It makes me think she's in mourning. She misses her mother." Gracie wiped the tears from her cheeks. "How do you tell such a tiny person that you're sorry, you understand, and you want to make everything better for them?"

Hannah shook her head. "You don't. You just be there for her. Care for her. For all of them. It'll take time, but they will come to know that you aren't going anywhere, and they can trust you to be their *mamm*."

And that's what she wanted more than anything. Well, almost. More than anything she wanted a baby of her own, but she supposed it was better now to get Baby Grace through these bumps in her path before they introduced another into the mix. And maybe by then, Gracie might have figured out how to talk to Matthew about their separate rooms.

Cousins' day was just what she needed.

Brandon showed up about fifteen minutes after Leah took Baby Grace into the house to sit with Mammi. He took the boys—who had pieces of cake in paper bowls— to the pond to fish. Gracie shuddered, imagining them digging up worms while eating their cake, but she wasn't going to hover. With any luck they would at least wipe their hands on their trouser legs after baiting their hooks, but she knew the chances of that might be slim. Still, a girl could hope.

With Baby Grace with Mammi and the boys with Brandon, Gracie felt as if a great weight had been taken from her. Suddenly she could breathe a little easier, her steps felt lighter, and her mood lifted.

She hadn't realized the heaviness of her responsibilities until they were removed.

To say Matthew hadn't been a help over the last week was an understatement. But she didn't want to complain. Perhaps if she could see that her own dreams would be fulfilled, she might not be quite as resentful of his actions.

There. She admitted it. She resented him. She was tired, worn down, and frustrated. And he was . . . doing whatever he pleased. In Henry's words, *What's fair about that?*

And she had taken today to come over and visit with her cousins and to make products to sell in the shop. The kids were entertained, and she might be able to relax for the first time all week, and she was mixing lotions. Still working.

"Uh-oh," Leah muttered.

Gracie looked at her cousin. "What?"

"Yep," Hannah agreed.

"What?" she asked again, this time a little more impatiently.

"You've got that look."

Gracie braced her hands on her hips and narrowed her eyes. "What look?"

"That one." Hannah laughed. "It doesn't come out often."

"But when it does . . ." Leah shook her head as if that were explanation enough.

Gracie sniffed. "I don't know what you're talking about."

"Probably not. But I saw it that time that Benuel King's little brother chased you around the schoolyard during the annual picnic."

Gracie frowned. "I was ten. No, I was nine. Nine years old. How can you remember that?"

"It's not a look that's easily forgotten," Hannah interjected.

"Not buying it." She was a sweet and gentle person. She knew it to be true. Everyone said so.

Leah shrugged. "Because we left not long after, I suppose. Last memories and all."

The memories stopped everyone, pulled them back to a different time and place, then Hannah laughed. "What about last year when David replaced your soap powder with salt and baking soda? You kept adding it because you didn't think it was sudsing enough."

Gracie tilted her head to one side. "It actually got my clothes pretty clean."

"You never told David that," Hannah said.

"And I never will."

They fell quiet, lost in their own memories, each one still working at bottling the goat-milk lotions and soaps.

"Seriously though," Hannah started. "Is everything okay?"

This would be the perfect time to unload, to ask all the questions chasing around her thoughts. How should she talk to her husband? How *could* she talk to him about things so intimate?

But the words lodged in her throat.

There was not a chance of asking him, if she couldn't bring herself to discuss such matters with her two very best friends in the world. God certainly hadn't given her any answers.

Yet she didn't want to worry her cousins. And they had only been in one marriage each themselves. How would they know what was normal and what not? Who was to say what was normal? Certainly not her.

"Of course," she said, with a small flick of one hand. Surely that was convincing.

But Hannah and Leah shared another one of those twin looks, and she knew they didn't believe her. That was fine. It didn't matter, she told herself. As long as she kept telling herself this was exactly what she wanted, then perhaps one day it would turn into just that.

Just before three, Gracie gathered up the boys and the baby, along with a milk crate full of lotions and soaps all labeled for sale, and headed home.

Despite her churning emotions and the work she had put into their cousins' day, she felt rested. Sort of. That weight had settled nicely around her shoulders the minute she had taken Baby Grace from Mammi Glick, but this time it was more comfortable by far. She felt as if she could carry it for a long while. Who knew how she would feel tomorrow when Matthew left her alone to fend for herself and his children as he went out and planted. If that was really what he was doing.

She hated the doubts that rose into her thoughts. But how long did it take to plant three fields? She had planted the entire vegetable patch before lunch. Gauging size from that, he should have been done yesterday. Yet today he got up and headed for the fields once again, without a by-your-leave or *Thanks for the coffee,* or *I hope you have a good day. See you at supper.*

Still she was a little surprised when she saw him pacing back and forth on the porch as she drove down the lane toward the house.

That was the thing about riding in a buggy, there was plenty of time for people to see you coming, and Matthew stood still as a statue from the moment he caught sight of her until she hopped down. She was halfway there when she got the first glimpse of his eyes. *Blazing* was the adjective she would have chosen if asked. His eyes looked like blue flames, burning hot and bright above the thick black bush of his beard.

Once her feet were on the ground, he moved toward them. He didn't say a word. It was almost as if he didn't trust himself. He fairly hummed with suppressed energy. Or maybe that was simply anger. But why?

She felt it best to wait until the older children were out of earshot before asking. She might be hesitant about asking other questions, but this wasn't one of them. He was mad at her, and she wanted to know why.

Matthew unhooked their horse as the boys hopped down. He handed the reins to Henry without a word. The boy knew what to do.

As if they too knew that their *dat* was teetering, none of them said a word. Henry trudged toward the barn with the twins trailing behind.

He waited until they had disappeared into the dim interior before turning toward her. On her.

"Where have you been?"

The words were electric, crackling and sparking, though he seemed to be in complete control of himself.

"Eunice and Abner's," she answered casually. It should have been a casual question, but the intensity was all around.

She turned from him as if everything were normal and pulled Baby Grace and her carrier seat out of the back of the buggy.

He blew out a breath. Was he trying to keep a hold on his temper?

"What were you doing over there all day?"

How did he know she was there all day if he had been

out in the fields? And the answer was maybe he hadn't been out in the fields. Maybe he had been at home, wondering where she was.

"It's cousins' day. I went over to make some products to sell in the shop." As if sensing the tension around her, Baby Grace started to fuss, kicking her legs and waving her hands in the air around her face. From the explosive expression the munchkin wore, she was about to gear up for one of her famous tirades.

"I thought I told you not to open the shop this year."

"No." She shook her head slowly and used one foot to rock the carrier. Maybe that would hold off any fit that was brewing. "You told me I didn't have to open the shop this year."

"Same thing."

"It's completely different."

"You thought you could go over there all day without leaving a note or anything. Without telling me where you had taken my children. What about Stephen?"

So many of his words struck her like arrows. He was mad because she hadn't left a note and had taken *his* children. But she needed to get control of her own emotions before she said or did something she might regret.

She sucked in a deep breath and blew it out. "I'm home before Stephen. That was the plan all along."

He snorted, and her control slipped. As if backing her up, Baby Grace let out her first new wail as Gracie descended on Matthew.

"I didn't leave a note because you haven't been home before dark since the day we got married. And speaking of which, that makes them my children as well. Not to mention the fact that I care for them while you're out doing whatever it is you do until dark." She didn't add that she didn't believe it had anything to do with field work. She didn't have to.

To her surprise he took two steps back as she charged toward him. Now he held his ground. "Someone has to support this family."

"And someone has to take care of the children. I've got an idea," she said, her gaze never wavering from his. "I don't tell you how to do your job, and you don't tell me how to do mine."

He stood there staring at her, and she stared back, breaths heaving in and out of her chest as if each one took more effort than the last. It was as if her temper, normally calm and hard to rise, was making it difficult to breathe. But she wasn't backing down. He was wrong. The Bible might tell wives to submit to their husbands, but wrong was wrong, no matter how you sliced it. And Matthew Byler was wrong.

But it was a standoff, neither one wavering, neither one daring to blink.

Behind her in the carrier Baby Grace sobbed. Neither one moved for what seemed like forever but couldn't have been more than a handful of seconds, then Henry came out of the barn, twins trailing behind him.

He looked from them to his sister. "Baby's crying," he said before heading into the house.

Chapter Thirteen

"Can I talk to you for a second?"

Gracie stopped washing dishes but didn't turn to face him. Matthew wondered if perhaps he didn't deserve her full attention. He had acted shamefully this afternoon, but worry would do that to a man.

And he had been worried, worried sick, his *mamm* would say. The Bible said a person wasn't supposed to worry, but that's all his life had been for so long . . .

Once Gracie moved in and took over the household duties and taking care of the children, that worry slipped away. Now all he had to concern himself with was whether the blade on his plow was sharp enough to cut the dry Mississippi ground and if he had enough seeds to produce the size crop he wanted this year. He had two more mouths to feed. And baby formula was expensive.

"I just want to apologize for this afternoon. I didn't mean to . . . fuss." It was the best word he could find. It was better by far than *scream at you like a mad man*. But he was shocked when he came home for the noon meal and she wasn't there. The children were gone, the dog was gone, and his mind shut down. All he could imagine was them hurt or dying somewhere. His life flashed before his eyes.

He spent nearly an hour praying for them to come back, praying that they were all right, praying to God to take the terrible images from his mind. He came home, and it was like losing Beth all over again.

Only this time he had lost the sweetest person he had ever met.

But how could he say those words without exposing his heart, his secrets? Secrets that he vowed to carry with him to the grave. He owed Beth that much.

Gracie turned around slowly, so slowly that it was a little frightening. The sweetest person was gone and in her place was someone who was bright, angry, and wary. "Fuss?" she asked. "That's what you're calling it?"

Best not to answer that. Not that he had a response he thought would satisfy her. "I was really worried when I came home in the middle of the day and neither you nor the kids were here. I was afraid something had happened to you."

He saw a flicker of the old Gracie in her expression, then she hardened it once more. But he inwardly smiled. He had gotten to her.

"Even the dog was gone." He had all but checked to see if her suitcases were missing as well. That maybe she had left him, and everything they had started, behind. *And* taken his children and his dog with her. How could he tell her that was his biggest fear without laying himself open for her criticism and censure?

There wasn't a way.

She squeezed out her dishrag and laid it over the bar to dry, then picked up the pan of dishwater and headed for the back door.

It looked heavy and he wanted to take it from her, but he had a feeling that offering would only bring more trouble.

So he watched as she tossed it out the door, shook out the plastic tub, then brought it back into the kitchen.

She plopped it into its place on the wash table, then looked at him, grudgingly. "I didn't mean to worry you. Honestly . . ." She shook her head and bit off her words.

"Honestly what?" he asked.

But she shook her head and wouldn't continue. Aside from grabbing her by the arms and shaking her like a rag doll, he saw no way of making her speak. And truthfully, he didn't think laying hands on her would help his case at all.

He had a case with her? When had that changed? He wasn't sure. He had been avoiding her this first week, pretending he had more work to do than he really had, doing his best to stay out until she was busy with the kids. Coming in when he thought she had already gone to bed. Anything to keep away from her. It was the only way he could keep both his sanity and his promises to himself.

There was something about Gracie Glick. Gracie Byler, he corrected himself. She turned away and started to wipe down the counters, the table, and the stove where she had cooked. He studied her, hoping that she didn't notice, but he drank in the sight of her. Pale blond hair, those big blue eyes that seemed enormous in her heart-shaped face. He wasn't sure how some man hadn't seen it in her before. She was the marrying kind. And not just because she was Amish and raised that way; she was born to be a wife and a mother. She soaked it all in like a thirsty sponge. It suited her, made her glow with a sense of purpose and made him realize just how blind the other men of Pontotoc were. How could no one else have seen this before now?

Or perhaps God had been saving her for him.

The thought was staggering, and he nearly fell backward as it occurred to him. That couldn't be. God wasn't giving him a second chance. He wasn't worthy of one.

She turned to him, cocked her head to one side and looked toward heaven. "I'm going to bed," she stated. Then she brushed past him and down the hall, leaving him standing there like a speechless, lovesick schoolboy.

He wasn't worthy of second chances. God hadn't given him one in Gracie. She was there because she wanted a family; he was there because he needed help with his family. And that was all there was to it. There wasn't some divine plan at work. No angel to save him. No course to forgiveness.

And the sooner he accepted that, the easier it would be on them all.

"Okay, Henry, you take that board outside and stack it with the others, then we'll start putting everything on the shelves."

"*Jah*, Gracie."

He did as she asked, and she dusted her hands against her apron and surveyed the little shop. It was almost ready. Everything was clean, the vegetable bins scrubbed out and the walls sprayed down. They were nothing more than treated lumber, so they had tossed water on them to clear out any spiders or other creepy crawlers, then allowed them to dry. Shelves were slid into place and signs for the vegetables that said *coming soon* were put up. Now all they had to do was stock the shelves with the products they did have and check the cellar for any products that might be left in the pantry. Tomorrow was Sunday, but they would be open Monday for sure, and in a month or so they might even have some fresh produce for sale. It was a shame they had gotten such a late start, but that was just the way it was. And if they had any luck at all on their side, they could have a few pints of strawberries by the end of the week. Barring the birds didn't get to them first.

Gracie peeked out the window toward the large tree just to the west of the shop. It was perfect for blocking the afternoon sun and provided cool shade for Baby Grace's afternoon nap.

In the last four days since her ill-fated cousins' day, Gracie had managed to get the baby on some type of routine. Maybe because once she called Matthew out on his absentee behavior, he started staying closer to the house. He came in for the noon meal, was washing up for supper before she even called him in, and otherwise became the *dat* she thought he had always been.

The boys loved it, beaming up at him from their places at the table even as they ate. The whole atmosphere had changed in their home. That's what it had become: a home. At least more like a home than it had been before.

They were thriving, Baby Grace was settling in to the new norm, but it scared Gracie. This was what she had imagined when she had said she wanted a family: togetherness, working side by side, a mother and a father and children all in harmony with each other and God. Aside from the fact that she and Matthew still had separate rooms, everything was perfect. Too perfect, and she couldn't help but believe that in itself made it a lie.

"And these are made with goat milk?" Henry asked, eyeing one of the bottles of lotion with skepticism.

She turned away from checking on the sleeping baby and back to Henry. "Absolutely." The twins had taken to napping on a blanket nearby, and for that Gracie was grateful. They needed the rest and Henry needed the time to have her all to himself. Pepper snoozed between them as if it was the best place on earth to be.

"Goat milk," Henry muttered, then shook his head as if to say *What will they come up with next?* Then he picked up a bottle of shampoo. "What's a phosphate?" he asked, sounding out the last word a little slower than the others.

"I'm not sure," Gracie said. "But Leah and Hannah assured me that they are bad, and we shouldn't have any in our hair products."

"*Jah,* it says the same thing on the conditioner too."

"Mmm-hmm." She stopped tacking up the price signs she had made to the edges of the shelf and turned back to face Henry. "Did you read that bottle?"

He looked at her and frowned. "I guess. Why?"

She looked around the room for something else for him to read. If indeed that was what he was doing. There was nothing around but lotion bottles and the bags of beads and buttons she had found under one of the lower shelves. She supposed that Beth had been planning on making them into jewelry and keychains to sell to the Englischers. She figured now that was a good family project for her and the twins.

"Here," she said, grabbing a bag of beads. "Can you read this?"

He looked from her to the bag, a small frown on his brow. The twist of his mouth said he thought she had lost her mind, but Gracie didn't care. Could he read? How amazing!

"Beads assorted colors, four mm, nine-ninety-nine." He looked back to her. "What's four mm?"

"The size," she explained with a laugh. She pulled up another bag just to be safe. But he read every word. What was Matthew going to say when she told him Henry could read?

By the time supper rolled around, Gracie was so excited she could barely contain it. She pulled the chicken she had fried earlier out of the icebox along with the bowl of pasta salad and set them on the table. It was starting to get too hot to eat warm meals, and by the time canning season got into full swing, thick ham sandwiches and potato salad, or grilled meats and big salads filled with fresh vegetables from the garden would become the best meals to eat to keep the house from getting so hot. Especially since Matthew's house wasn't set up with a cook house. Some of the Amish homes in the area had a special building separate from the back of the house where they could cook and keep the heat out of the main living space. It was handy in the summertime, but also allowed the family to bend the rules of the Ordnung a bit by having running water to the cook house. Since it wasn't attached to the main house, it got around the rule prohibiting running water in the houses, but anyone who had this setup was careful not to flaunt it too much in front of the bishop lest he rewrite that part to include all outbuildings as well. No one wanted to be the person who ruined it for everyone.

"Boys," she called, but she didn't have to summon them twice. They had grown accustomed to her schedule and headed straight to the water spigot to wash up before supper.

For once, Baby Grace had settled down and was cooing softly from her place in the baby swing Gracie had found in the third bedroom upstairs. The room was primarily used as storage, though there was no rhyme or reason as to what was stored there and where it was put. The good news was she had found some everyday treasures there, including the swing and a stack of books that she had used to entertain Henry for the remainder of the afternoon. She had him reading to the twins and laughing proudly at the new skill he had discovered. Who knew how long he had been able to read and no one had known?

She finished putting the last of the food on the table, a jar of applesauce, the peanut butter spread, and a jar of kudzu jelly to go with the bread she had baked the day before.

The boys came back into the house, water trailing behind as they drip-dried on the way.

"Grab the towel, please."

"You do it, Henry," Stephen said.

"It's not my turn," Henry protested.

"It is too," Stephen countered.

"Gracie," Henry called, looking for backup.

She thought for a second. "It's your turn, Henry."

"Aw, man." He kicked a bare toe at the edge of the linoleum and trudged back toward the door where they kept the towel they used to wipe the floor.

She hid her smile and started to take the bread to the table, nearly jumping out of her skin as she caught sight of Matthew. For a big man he sure moved quietly.

"I didn't hear you come in," she breathed, one hand pressed over her heart.

"Obviously," he drawled, and she thought she saw the twitch of a smile on his lips.

He shouldn't have surprised her. He had come in for supper every night since their argument on Tuesday. It was wonderful and a little unnerving all at the same time. It was his house, what did she expect him to do? But at the same time, she wished he was eating somewhere else so she didn't have to look across the table and see him there. It became entirely too easy to pretend that they were the happy family that she had always dreamed of having.

"Guess what?" Henry said the moment after the prayer. He lifted his head and pinned all his attention on his father.

"What's that?" Matthew asked, picking out a couple of pieces of chicken and passing the platter to Gracie. She stood and gave each of the twins a leg, and a thigh for Henry.

"I can get my own," Stephen said, taking the platter from her to spear his own piece. Then he passed it back to her so she could serve herself.

"I can read." Henry's smile stretched from ear to ear.

"You can not." Stephen rolled his eyes at his brother's words as if they were the dumbest thing he had ever heard.

"Can too," Henry argued.

"Nuh-uh," Stephen tossed back. "You can't read because you haven't been to school."

"He can too," Thomas said.

Benjamin nodded to back up his brother's claim, but Stephen wasn't convinced.

Henry looked crushed.

Gracie nudged Matthew under the table, getting his attention and nodding pointedly at his middle son.

"How about you read me something after supper?" Matthew asked.

Henry beamed. "I can."

"Can not," Stephen countered.

"Can too," the other boys chorused.

"Enough," Matthew said, his voice quiet but firm, and the boys fell silent.

"We got the shop all ready today and Gracie says I can run the cash register." Henry shot his brother a challenging, tell-me-I'm-not look.

"I can too, right?" Stephen asked, looking to Gracie for confirmation.

"Of course," she replied. "After school in the afternoons and this summer."

"There's only a week left of school," Stephen said. "So next week I can run the cash register."

"*Jah*," she replied.

"But I can too," Henry protested. "You said."

Gracie smiled, flashing it to both boys equally. "You'll take turns the way brothers should."

They looked at each other, their looks warring, then they turned to Gracie.

"Okay," Stephen said.

"Fine," Henry grumbled.

Gracie ducked her head to keep them from seeing her grin. They were both so cute and in such competition with one another. But she had a feeling once they hit their late teens, they would be inseparable.

She looked up to find Matthew watching her, his expression unreadable.

She raised one brow in question, but his face never changed. He continued to study her as if he wasn't quite sure what she was and how she had gotten into his house. The look was unnerving, and she found herself having to turn away. It was too intense, too raw and yet guarded. And what did it mean?

She looked back, but Matthew had switched his attention to Thomas, who got a splinter from helping clean the shop and was showing his father his bandage. It was a little larger than necessary. Well, maybe a lot larger, but he had been crying so, and for some reason bandages seemed to make everything better.

They finished their meal, discussing important things like fishing at the Gingeriches' pond next weekend on the off-Sunday from church, crickets, and baseball. Then they had their after-meal prayer, and the boys helped her clear the table, then went into the living room to listen to their father read from the Bible. But tonight Henry had a turn. The words of the King James translation were difficult for him, but he managed to get most of them and prove to his father and his older brother that he could read. Matthew was suitably impressed, though Stephen's response was filled with more resentment than praise.

Gracie listened from the kitchen, wondering where Henry had picked up the skill. It was almost as if he had been born reading, which wasn't possible, but seemed like the only explanation.

After reading, she sent the boys upstairs to get ready for bed while she finished the kitchen and put Baby Grace down for the night. Then she went upstairs for the nightly tucking-in ritual.

She was just entering Stephen and Henry's room when she heard the front door open and knew that Matthew had gone out.

Ever since their argument, he had been more present, but there were times like these when he relied on her to parent and allowed himself . . . what? Time to breathe? He had plenty of that when he was out in the fields. Time to be himself? Again, he was gone most of the day, coming in only for their noon meal and then at supper time. And he was missing so much.

Henry's tooth had come out the day before. Between his broken arm and his snaggle teeth, he looked like one of those Englisch boxers. And there had been other, smaller occurrences like Thomas's splinter and Benjamin's black eye. He'd come around a corner too fast in the shop and run smack into one of the thick wooden display tables. Gracie just knew Matthew would have a fit when he saw, demanding to know why she wasn't watching the boy, but he took his son by the chin and turned his head from side to side to check it out from all angles. He grunted something that sounded like *boys are boys*, then went to wash up for supper.

Church Sunday was always a little frantic when children were involved. There always seemed to be a boy's missing shoe or a girl's missing head-covering, or spit-up where a baby was involved. Today's church Sunday included all three, along with broken suspenders, a loose button, and a tear in the church shirt they had cut the sleeve out of to accommodate Henry's cast.

Only by the grace of God did they all get into the buggy and make it safely on time for church.

Gracie always loved church, loved hearing God's word and about all the love He had for them all. Not every sermon was quite so uplifting, but she knew that all of the Word was equally important.

She received a couple of odd glances when she walked in, Baby Grace asleep and snuggled into the wrap-around carrier that she had found. She supposed no one had seen such a device. She hadn't either until she found this one already among the baby's things. She supposed Beth bought it somewhere, or perhaps received it as a gift from Ohio friends or family. Gracie found it immeasurably useful in allowing her to have the baby close but her hands free to do other things. She knew there would be a time, very soon, when Baby Grace would be too big to be carried in such a way, and until then she planned on using the carrier as much as she needed. Like today.

She could take the baby upstairs and listen to the sermon from up there, but it was so hard to hear with so many babies around and so far away from whoever was preaching, and she was afraid that if she got too comfortable she might just fall asleep, no matter how riveting today's message might turn out to be.

So she filed in with the other ladies of the congregation and took her place between Hannah and her other cousin Abby. She had sat here or between Hannah and Eunice practically her whole life, except for the years when Hannah was gone and Tillie was in church. But always with her aunt and cousins. Yet today she could feel the gazes upon her. Which was ridiculous.

She was just uncomfortable, this first church Sunday since she and Matthew had gotten married. It was normal, she was certain, to feel eyes upon her. It was inevitable. The women were all wondering if she was already pregnant and if she would be able to handle two babies twelve months apart. But they were only wondering that because the baby she now held she hadn't given birth to. Which was unfair. She may have only been taking care of Baby Grace for a few days, and the child might have cried for what seemed like most of it, but she loved the little munchkin. How could she not? Those big blue eyes were filled with such betrayal, such abandonment that Gracie felt a kinship with the other Grace. She too had lost her family. Maybe not in the same way. But she knew that loss. They were soul sisters, meant to be together. Or maybe even brought together by the Lord.

The thought was so enlightening she gasped, drawing several more gazes toward her.

She looked straight ahead, pretending that everything was just as it should be, but only managed to snag Matthew's gaze from across the room. All this time she had thought that she was there for him, or maybe the boys, but perhaps her job was to keep Baby Grace on the Lord's path. The idea was staggering.

From beside her Hannah reached out and touched the back of her hand.

Gracie didn't need any words to know what the gesture meant. *Are you okay?*

She kept her gaze tangled with Matthew's but squeezed her cousin's fingers in response: Jah. *I'm fine.*

But she was more than fine, she was redefining her purpose. And the idea was staggering.

"What was that all about?" Hannah asked, sidling up next to her and nudging her in the ribs.

After the service, while they were setting up the tables and food to eat, Gracie switched Baby Grace from the fabric carrier to the one they used in the buggy, gave her a binky and a rattle, and pitched in to do her part. Now she was finishing up, serving the last of the ladies and the children before she would grab a plate of her own.

"Nothing." She didn't want to share her revelation, not even with Hannah.

"But you are okay?"

Gracie gave her a smile. "Of course. *Jah*."

Hannah studied her a bit longer then took the pitcher of water from her. "Go get yourself a plate, I'll finish up here."

"But—" she started, but Hannah shook her head.

"Every week you are practically the last one to get a plate. I've already had a snack. Now go get something to eat, and I'll pour drinks. You look like you're about to fall over."

Gracie smiled gratefully but shook her head.

"I will not take no for an answer. You can't give so much of yourself that there's nothing left to have for your own."

"Did Eunice say that?"

Hannah frowned at her with a mock seriousness. "No, I did. Just then."

Gracie laughed and reached down to get Baby Grace's carrier.

Hannah moved to stand between her and it. "Nope. Leave the baby here with me."

Gracie opened her mouth to protest again, but Hannah cut her off with a shake of her head. "I will not take no for an answer."

"Okay. *Danki*," Gracie said and moved to get a plate. But first she needed to use the outhouse and wash her hands. She hadn't gone since before she left the house, and that was over four hours ago.

Remarkably enough there wasn't a line at the outhouse and she pulled in a deep breath before plunging inside. Outhouses were never particularly pleasant, but on a church Sunday they were particularly fragrant. Gracie always found it best to get in, get her business done, and get out in as little time as possible. And that had been her plan until she heard the voices outside the wooden walls.

"There's something strange about the whole thing," a woman's voice was saying. It sounded a lot like Mary Ann Hostetler, but she wasn't certain.

"I think you were just hoping for a chance with him yourself," the other woman replied. If the first woman was Mary Ann, then that would have to be Freda Esh, because they were inseparable.

"Me?" Mary Ann squeaked. "Not a chance. He's just too . . . big, and dark, and moody."

There was only one person with that description: Matthew Byler. They were talking about her and Matthew!

As much as a part of her wanted to stay inside the outhouse and eavesdrop, she knew it was wrong. And even if she had been tempted, the smell alone would discourage such behavior. But if she left now, they would know that she knew that they had been talking about her and Matthew.

Did she care?

For some reason she did. She didn't want people analyzing her marriage. Not when she hadn't gotten it figured out yet. And especially not when she thought it might have a greater purpose than any of them knew. But she couldn't continue to hold her breath and she wasn't sure how long she could stand breathing in . . . outhouse air.

She had no choice.

"There's something weird about his wife's death too," Mary Ann was saying. "Don't you think?"

"Maybe Gracie should take a little more care—"

Gracie couldn't take it any longer. She burst from the outhouse, the door slamming to one side as she gulped for fresh air.

Granted, it was still tainted by proximity, but it was a sight better than the closed-up air inside the bathroom box.

The two women whirled around, more than shocked to see her standing there. After all, what were the odds that she would be in the outhouse at the exact time that they snuck around back to gossip about her without being heard?

Somewhere on the spectrum of slim to divine intervention.

"Hi." Gracie smiled, unwilling to cause a scene. She just wanted to clean her hands and get a plate and forget this ever happened.

"Hi," Freda returned. "We didn't know you were back here."

Obviously. "Well, when you have to go, you have to go." Her smile began to waver. And she wasn't sure how much longer she could keep up this charade.

How could someone feel they were doing the right thing for themselves and another person or persons, while others only saw it as fodder for the gossip mill?

Mary Ann and Freda exchanged an *I don't know, how much do you think she heard?* look, then forced their own smiles.

"I guess I'll go check on my baby. I mean, Matthew's baby." Why did she say that? She was already beginning to think of Baby Grace as her own. Especially since Matthew didn't seem to want to have anything to do with her. Not that he did much more with the boys, but some.

She moved to go around them, and they let her. She could feel their gazes on her as she walked away. Her legs wobbled, and it seemed as if she had half forgotten how to walk. She stumbled once and managed to catch herself but didn't look back to see if they were still watching. She knew they were.

Gracie rounded the house and went over to the water spigot to wash her hands, out of sheer habit. It wasn't like she had any kind of appetite now. Even if she hadn't had an extended stay inside the outhouse, the conversation she had overheard would surely have taken away any desire she had for food.

It was one thing for her to analyze her marriage and quite another for the people of her church to do so. But what had she expected to happen? Truly.

Without a second thought she moved over to the table where Hannah and Baby Grace waited.

"Where's your plate?" Hannah asked.

Gracie shook her head. "I decided I'm not hungry after all."

Hannah eyed her shrewdly. "What happened?"

"Happened? Nothing happened. What makes you think something happened?"

"Well, because when something does happen and you want to hide it, you overcompensate."

Gracie blinked. "Me?"

Hannah shot her a pointed look.

"I really don't want to talk about it." It was the best she could do. And it was the truth. She didn't want to talk about it. It was still new and raw. She wanted to examine it first, hold it close for a little bit before she shared.

"All right," Hannah said, but Gracie knew she wasn't letting it go entirely. Cousins' day she would have to answer for it all, she knew. But until then she had a day and a half to come up with the answers, try to figure out why the gossip bothered her. She already knew why she said that about Matthew's baby. She might be his wife, and she might be caregiver to his children, but she was nowhere near their mother. So why did it hurt so much that others knew that her marriage was as much of a farce as it truly was? It didn't change one detail. But somehow it hurt more.

Chapter Fourteen

"Did you get a driver for tomorrow?" Gracie looked at Matthew across the supper table.

They had to go to the doctor and have Henry's arm looked at, and most probably a new cast put on. Hopefully. The one he had now was such a light color that it had picked up dirt from everywhere he went. Gracie shuddered every time she looked at it.

"*Jah*." Matthew nodded and swallowed. "He'll be here at ten to pick up the two of you."

The two of—"You're coming too, *jah*?"

He shook his head. "I have too much work to do. I got so far behind . . . before the wedding."

She was thankful that he didn't bring up Beth. The children were doing their best to adjust, and they didn't need any reminders. "But I thought—" She stopped.

"You thought what?"

Gracie could feel the children's eyes on them. They were paying close attention to every word, soaking it in, gauging the atmosphere according to body language and tone, whether they realized it or not. She measured her words carefully. "I thought you were coming too." After all, Henry was his son. She might be his mother now, but the time had been short. They still thought of her as Gracie. Not *mamm*. Her taking him to the doctor was akin to sending him with a distant aunt. Or the babysitter.

"I'm sorry if you got the wrong impression." But he didn't sound very sorry. He sounded . . . bored, as if matters of the doctor and appointments fell onto her side of the chores list. She supposed the Englisch sent their children all over with a nanny; this was about the same thing. And most of them turned out all right. Didn't they?

Matthew watched Gracie from across the table under lowered lids. He didn't want her to know that he was watching her. She had been acting strange ever since . . . Sunday at church. That was when it all started. She seemed distant, almost preoccupied, but he couldn't say why. She seemed extra attentive with the children, especially the baby, and for that he was grateful. They needed a woman around, a mother's touch. And Gracie was as fine a mother as he could have wished for them.

So why did he resent her?

Jah. He admitted it. He resented her. She had won his family over in a matter of weeks. They all depended on her for food, clean clothes, a bandage when they got hurt.

And during all this she managed to clean out the shop, get it stocked and ready with the products that were currently available, and even open for business. She never missed a cousins' day at Abner and Eunice's, and through it all she had a smile on her face.

So what had he done? He had shoved a little more onto her plate. Sure, tomorrow there was an auction in New Albany. Danny Yoder had already hired a driver and a couple of them were going over and splitting the costs. He could cancel that. It wasn't like it would affect much. But why? His children preferred to be with Gracie.

That was the way with mothers, was it? He couldn't remember. It had been such a long time since Beth had been what he would have called a regular mother that he had forgotten about all the things she had done for Stephen and Henry when they were babies. But after the twins were born, everything shifted, and they started to follow him, spend more time with him.

"Is that all right with you?" he asked.

She nodded, a little more enthusiastically than necessary. "*Jah*, of course. Are you okay taking care of the baby?"

He prayed the horror didn't show on his face. He couldn't take care of the baby. She hated him. If Gracie left her with him . . . she would cry all day and make herself sick. He didn't think either one of them deserved that. "I thought you would take her with you."

She thought about it a moment. "And the twins will stay here with you?"

He told her about the auction, leaving out the part that he could cancel. Fact was, he didn't want to cancel. There were a few things listed that he needed if he could get them at a fair price, and since he had gotten such a late start farming this year, he needed all the fair prices he could get.

"I don't think I can handle all four of them and take care of Henry."

"Maybe Eunice can keep them for the afternoon."

"Maybe." But the tone of her voice was doubtful. "Or Anna."

A stab of conscience seared him. He could forgo the auction. Any other time that was exactly what he would do. He had done so many times for Beth, when they had forgotten about one thing or another and double scheduled on the same day. So why wouldn't he do the same for Gracie?

He had no idea.

* * *

Thankfully, Eunice was more than happy to watch the twins and Baby Grace while Gracie took Henry in for a checkup. As expected he came out of the casting room boasting an eye-watering orange cast despite her best efforts to talk him into a staid blue one that in two days wouldn't look like it had been thrown into the pigpen. But she had learned one true thing where Henry was concerned: pick the battles. And frankly, she admired his spunk. She wished she had a little more of that ability to say what was on her mind and accept what people said back to her. Right now she had neither.

Henry, on the other hand, was always into one thing or another. If she corrected him on every little infraction, she would never stop speaking his name. That wouldn't be healthy for either one of them. And if it meant that he had an orange cast that might literally glow in the dark, so be it.

The doctor said his arm was healing right on schedule, and he should only have to wear the cast another three weeks. That was good news. The bad news was that meant three more weeks of having to stay on him to keep it dry, three weeks of no swimming, and going to the end-of-the-school-year picnic in a cast. She knew he was disappointed that he wouldn't be able to play in the sprinkler and some of the other fun activities that involved water, so she had promised herself to take him swimming the day the cast came off. Even if for fifteen minutes.

The driver took them by Eunice and Abner's so they could pick up Baby Grace and the twins. The group of them made it home just in time to pick Stephen up on the road as he walked home from school. The driver was good-natured about all the extra passengers and laughed along with them as they piled into the back seat and started down the road once more.

Of course when they pulled into the lane that led to their house, Matthew was nowhere to be seen. Gracie tried not to be disappointed. She paid the driver in cash, then gave him a couple of bottles of lotion for his wife and a jar of persimmon pie filling. He was a good driver and she vowed to call him when they went back to take Henry's cast off. She hoped he would be available.

"Okay, everybody in the house. Let's see what needs to be done."

They all grumbled but trudged up the steps and across the porch. "You know there's lemon cake in the kitchen."

Their steps hurried until they practically raced to the table to get their afternoon snack.

Stephen got down plates and cups while Gracie unbuckled the baby from her carrier seat and placed her in the infant swing. She hoped that would keep Baby Grace occupied for a bit while she got the cake served and the milk poured. Then she would mix up some formula and feed her as well. Gracie's snack would have to wait a little longer. But wasn't that the way of motherhood? She had watched Eunice eat last at every meal, making sure that her husband and children were settled and fed before she got her own food. Some would say that it was a sacrifice, and she supposed it was a little. But it was more of a calling. That's what motherhood was. It was a calling to care for another, to keep the family going, to put these tiny people above yourself, no matter what.

She had thought fatherhood was the same, but after Matthew's attitude yesterday over her and Henry going to the doctor without him, she wasn't so sure.

Gracie pushed that thought away and heated a bit of water to mix the formula. Baby Grace seemed to be able to keep it down better if it was warm and not straight from the fridge. Behind her the other children chattered. Suddenly she felt sorry for Beth. Not because she died, but because she was missing out on her children's lives.

If you're up there watching, she prayed, *I hope I do right by you. Your kids are precious. And I promise to always treat them as my very own.*

"Gracie," Stephen called.

She turned to him, her thoughts centering on the here and the now.

"Grace needs you, Gracie." Stephen made a face. "That's kind of hard to say."

"It is," Gracie agreed. "I've been calling your sister Baby Grace."

He nodded. "Baby Grace. I like that."

"Me too," the other boys chorused.

"And," she said, plunging ahead with something she had been wanting to say to all the children, but she hadn't had the opportunity. It seemed every time all four boys were in the same room together there was a scuffle of some sort, or a disagreement, and there hadn't been any time for talking about other things. "You can call me Mamm if you like."

They seemed to think about it, but no one said anything one way or the other.

Gracie let the matter drop. No sense running it into the ground. They either would or they wouldn't, and only time would tell.

It was almost dark by the time the driver dropped him off at the house. All in all it had been a good day. He needed it, just a day to not worry about anything other than whether or not to bid on a saw blade or have sweet tea with lunch. How long had it been since he had been able to drop his worries? So long ago that he almost felt guilty staying out so late. But it wasn't entirely his fault. The plow that Danny Yoder wanted to bid on was one of the last items to go up on the auction block. Since it was his main reason for the trip, no one wanted to tell him they needed to leave. But the kicker was Danny didn't win the plow. In fact none of them bought anything other than a hot dog at the concession stand. But he wasn't going to call the day a failure. It was a roaring success, if only to take a little more of the weight off his shoulders.

But now he was ready to be at home. Ready to see his boys, see if there were any supper leftovers that he could eat and . . . ignore Gracie.

He stopped on the porch, not going inside. Not moving at all. Ignoring Gracie. That was exactly what he had been doing lately. Ignoring her, all the while coexisting with her, talking with her about matters in their household, but otherwise pretending that she wasn't there. Why?

Because if he didn't she would consume his every thought. And he had no idea why. Maybe because she was a bit larger than life. She was perfect. Everyone loved her. She helped out every time she was needed and whoever needed it. She rescued lost dogs and gave them a home and carted the baby around in that glorified bedsheet she had found somewhere. And he found himself wanting to know more about her. Favorite color, how it had been when she went to the coast to help the hurricane victims. Had she done that more than once? Was she enjoying the family? Was she happy?

He wanted her to be happy, and the thought terrified him. If he wanted her happy then it meant he cared, and he didn't want to care about her. He was afraid to care for her. Afraid that if he did, one thing would lead to another and he would lose her just like he had Beth. So it was better that he ignored her. He kept his distance and he avoided her at every turn.

He sucked in a fortifying breath, then opened the door to his own house, feeling a little like a stranger.

There was a lamp lit on the living room table and a faint glow coming from the kitchen. He figured the lamp there was lit too, showing the way and waiting for him to come home.

It was late. Later than he had thought. The boys were in bed. Gracie had surely already put the baby down. And she herself could have already called it a day. The house was quiet, but welcoming. And he basked in the warmth he felt. It truly was a home now, and all because of Gracie Glick Byler. Just thinking the words sent shafts of fear spearing through him. It was what he wanted and what petrified him all at the same time.

As quietly as possible he made his way to the kitchen. As he suspected, a lamp was there, illuminating his way. And a note lying in the place where he usually sat.

Please wake me up when you get home.
I have something I need to talk to you about.

Gracie

The words sent anxiety coursing through him. Something had happened while he had been playing hooky from being a father, something terrible had happened. Heart pounding, he made his way to the room she shared with the baby.

He knocked lightly on her door and opened it before she said anything.

She was sitting on her bed, book in hand. The soft light from the oil lamp cast a golden glow around her, but not enough to pierce all the darkness. Her hair was down, pulled back in a ponytail at the nape of her neck and covered with a faded pink bandana. He glanced over to the crib where the baby slept. At least she was okay. She might not like him, but he would die a thousand deaths if anything happened to her.

"I got your note," he said quietly. "What's happened?" He hated asking, knowing that he wasn't going to like the answer. Why had he stayed out so late? He should have been here with her, for her.

Gracie, beautiful Gracie, frowned. "Nothing's happened."

He returned her look, trying to figure out what she was talking about. Nothing had happened? Why the note? "What? Henry?" He had his doctor's appointment this morning, a checkup and a new cast.

"Fine. He got to get the orange cast this time." He opened his mouth to ask why she hadn't talked him into something more . . . Amish, but she cut him off before he could utter a single word. "I tried. But you know how stubborn he can be."

Matthew could only nod. "If Henry's fine . . ." And the baby was fine. "Why the note?"

She placed one finger in her book to hold her place. From where he stood he couldn't see what she was reading. *Martyrs Mirror* or some book she picked up somewhere. It was all the same to him. "I wanted to remind you that the end-of-the-school-year picnic is tomorrow."

"Tomorrow?" When had he lost track of the time? He didn't think that was for another week or so. And why did she have to give him a heart attack with that note of hers when she could have told him that on paper?

"I know it will mean a lot to Stephen to have you there. He could talk of nothing else when he got home today."

Matthew shook his head. His heart rate had returned to normal, as did his sense of responsibility. "I can't make it tomorrow." He had been gone all day. He needed to stay at home and catch up on chores, not picnic. Besides, there would be other picnics, *jah*?

"Matthew." Her voice was soft, nearly chastising, but not quite. That wasn't Gracie's style.

"It's simply not possible. I have all the work I didn't get done today, plus tomorrow's work waiting for me."

She pressed her lips together but didn't say anything.

She simply stared at him, then shook her head. "Okay." Her expression went from disappointed to unreadable.

"I'm sorry," he said. He wasn't sure why he thought he needed to add that. He just did.

"*Jah.*" The one word was a bit clipped. She gave him one last cool look, then opened her book once again.

She might not have chastised him, but she certainly knew how to dismiss a man.

And suddenly he found himself wanting to stay. Just to talk, just to be near her. How crazy was that? And what good would it do? So he would know exactly what he was missing when he went back to his own room? No, *danki*. He would pass on that one.

"Uh, good night," he said and ducked out of her room. He closed the door behind him but held on to the knob as if he wanted to open it again, walk inside and be with her. Regardless of consequences.

Even stranger, he wanted to kiss those thinned lips and see if he could get them to relax into a smile. Have her tell him all her secrets.

But if she told hers he would be obliged to tell his own, and that was something he wasn't prepared to do.

With one last look at the door, Matthew turned and made his way down the hall to his own room.

Disappointment didn't quite cover how she felt the next morning as she got the kids ready to go to the picnic. Stephen was crushed that his *dat* had already left for the day before he even got up. But he tried not to let it show. The other boys didn't notice, but Gracie could tell.

It felt like nothing short of a miracle that she could get them up, dressed, and into the buggy *and* be on time for the picnic, but it happened. She was still a little surprised as she spread their quilt out on the grass in the schoolyard.

Children were playing, running with each other, coming up to their parents, laughing and having a wonderful time just being together.

Strangely enough it made her think about the time that she and Matthew had gotten lost on a back-country road. That time seemed a million years ago and yet the memories were still so sweet. She had thought then that everything would be different than it was now—the same as it was then, him laughing, smiling, and enjoying himself—but once they got married everything changed. Why?

"Gracie! Gracie!" Stephen came running up, his smile as wide as the horizon. "We're going to have a three-legged sack race. Have you ever been in a three-legged sack race?"

She bit back her laughter. "Not recently, no."

"Henry's going to race with me, okay?"

There was a split second when she wanted to tell him no, but she couldn't bring herself to. Henry deserved a little fun and if this brought the boys closer together . . .

"Tell him to be careful if he falls. He doesn't need to be banging that cast against the ground."

Stephen beamed at her. "I will, Gracie. But don't worry. We're not going to fall."

Surprisingly enough, they didn't. And Henry even managed to join in the softball game. Though it was a little hard for him to hit the ball with one arm in a cast. All in all, everyone seemed to have an enjoyable time. But Gracie felt . . . isolated. She had never felt this way before. She was used to being part of the action, among the families even if she wasn't a part of them. But that wasn't the case today. She loved these children, but they weren't solely her responsibility and yet that is exactly what had happened.

She was roused from her disturbing thoughts as Stephen trudged to their quilt and plopped down next to her and crossed his arms. His bottom lip protruded slightly, and she could see a storm brewing in his eyes.

"What happened?" she asked.

He shook his head.

But then Henry came up and flopped down beside him. "There's a *dat* and son race."

"And my *dat* isn't here." The words couldn't have sounded more heartbroken unless he had taken a page from Baby Grace's book and squalled while he said them.

"Can someone else—" she started, but he shook his head.

"What good is a father-son race if it's not a father and son? Plus, Amanda said it would only be fair if everyone did it the same."

Amanda was right, but Gracie couldn't get past her anger with Matthew. There was something inherently off about the whole situation. Why couldn't he be there today? Why he had stayed gone all day yesterday? Why did he sleep in the room down the hall?

"It's just a silly old race." Gracie waved one hand as if to show just how silly and pulled the towel from atop their picnic basket. "Don't tell anyone, but I have three slices of cherry pie left. I sure wouldn't want them to go to waste. And it looks like the picnic is about to wrap up." She allowed her gaze to roam around the play yard, but the picnic festivities were still in full swing. Yet Henry and Stephen didn't know that. How easily the mind of a young boy could be swayed if food was involved.

"We can help you eat it, Gracie," Henry boasted. He stuck his chest out importantly and jerked a thumb toward himself. "I'm one of the best pie eaters there is."

"Are," she corrected, then she frowned. Was it *is* or *are*? Now they both sounded wrong. "It doesn't matter." She pulled the pie pan from the basket and grabbed a couple of paper plates. She knew she shouldn't bribe them with food to forget their disappointment, but she couldn't stand to see the heartbreak on their faces. And if a piece of cherry pie could correct that, then so be it.

But she had more than cherry pie on her mind as she pulled her buggy to a stop and unloaded the kids later that afternoon.

"Can we check the money jar?" Henry asked as he jumped down from the buggy.

Gracie winced as he hit the ground. Honestly, the boy was so rambunctious she was surprised he didn't go around with two broken arms all the time. Only by the grace of God.

"Stephen, go with him."

Stephen nodded but his footsteps were heavy as he followed his brother to the little shop to see if anyone had stopped at their store and bought something while they were gone. Most everyone in their community had a shop in front of their house and it was impossible to man it at all times. So the honor system was put into place. As far as she knew, Eunice never had any problems. Gracie supposed if you expected people to follow the rules and respect another's property that the reverence could fall into place on those expectations alone.

She helped the twins down and as she knew would happen, they followed their brothers to the shop.

Then Gracie pulled Baby Grace's carrier seat from the back of the buggy. As was her custom when she arrived alone back at the house, she would place the baby in the shade of the porch, unhitch the horse, hand him over to Stephen and Henry, then get the baby and the twins into the house. And like so many other times since she had married Matthew, she was alone.

Because he was gone.

The thought kept playing over and over in her head. She just didn't understand it. He had seemed like such a good father before. What had happened?

She had happened. She was pretty sure that his marriage to her and realizing that the crushing responsibility could be shifted to another was enough. He knew he was free to do and act in any way that he liked.

Well, Gracie didn't like it. Not one bit. Especially when it disappointed Stephen or any of the children.

She wanted to unload everything and wait at the kitchen table for him to return. She imagined laying into him the minute she saw him, telling him the what-for and how the cow ate the cabbage, and all those other things that Mammi Glick said. But Mammi also said that you catch more flies with honey than vinegar and that was exactly what she planned on doing.

"Look!" Henry ran toward her, a fistful of money in his good hand. "We made like a hundred dollars."

Stephen hurried behind him, rolling his eyes and pushing his glasses up as he skipped in his brother's wake. "You might be able to read, but you can't count worth a darn. There's not more than twenty dollars there."

"Is too!" Henry didn't stop until he was standing directly in front of Gracie. "Tell him." He waved the money around so erratically that she couldn't even begin to guess how much was there. She saw a twenty in the mix, so there was at least that much, but the rest was impossible to see until she got the bills away from him.

"Give it here," she coaxed. "You can help me count it." It was the perfect learning opportunity. It was true that Henry was a whiz at reading and all things that had to do with the written word, but his math skills had yet to be developed. But that was expected. She had read somewhere that the two different sides of the brain controlled a person's love or acceptance of certain things like art and math. Henry had certainly gotten the love of Englisch stories and art. But math would need some work before he started to school in the fall.

The thought of him being gone from the house until three every day made her want to cry. How was it possible to wish someone would slow down and stop growing, but at the same time wanting all the best for them? She wanted Henry to grow up, be a strong man someday, but at the same time she wished he could remain small and innocent forever.

They counted it out loud, all five of them. Stephen was the only one to get all the numbers correct. Henry, not willing to be wrong, hesitated before each number, waiting until Stephen said it before saying it himself. The twins shouted random numbers and Gracie couldn't decide if they were trying to count or sabotage their brothers' concentration.

"Sixty-three dollars," Henry exclaimed. "How close is that to a million?"

"Not very." Gracie smiled.

"What do you know about a million dollars?" Stephen challenged.

Henry shrugged. "I know I would like to have a million dollars one day."

That was a surprise. "Why?" Gracie asked. "What would you do with it?"

"Bury it in a coffee can behind the shed," Stephen teased.

"Spend it on toys," Thomas shouted.

"*Jah*," Benjamin agreed.

"Just keep it, I guess." Henry's frown seemed to indicate that he hadn't thought about it that far.

"What good is it, if you just keep it?" Stephen asked.

"*Jah*," Thomas agreed. "You should spend it."

Henry shook his head. "I would keep it," he said decidedly. "That way if I ever wanted anything I would have all the money I needed to buy it."

Except for love, she thought. Nothing in the world could bring a person love but a little luck and the grace of God. Right now she seemed to have neither.

"Can I talk to you for a moment?" Gracie stopped in front of the chair where Matthew sat, and waited for his response. Supper had been eaten, the boys washed and put to bed, and Baby Grace was already asleep in her crib. The supper dishes had been cleaned and put away and all the evening chores complete.

Matthew had been sitting in his favorite chair reading *The Budget* and basically ignoring everything that was going on around him.

He hadn't read to them from the Bible since that first night, and she missed that ritual. She wanted to ask him to bring it back, for the children's sake if not for their own, but not tonight. Tonight she had something else to talk to him about.

"*Jah*," he said, though his voice sounded exasperated and wary all at the same time.

"There's a couples' night tomorrow at Aaron Zook's. I thought it would be fun to go. What do you think?" Why was her heart pounding so? It was a simple invitation, but somehow it meant a lot for him to accept.

"What kind of couples' night?"

She shrugged. "Potluck supper and games." Why did it sound so boring when just a few minutes ago it was the most fun she could think of?

"I don't think so." He shook out his paper as if he was about to open it once again and dismiss her for the night.

White-hot anger surged through her, intense and unfamiliar. She couldn't ever remember being this angry before, and she couldn't contain the feeling. "You're embarrassing me."

He looked up from his paper, his eyes narrowed in confusion. At least she hoped that's what it was. "What are you talking about?"

She could say never mind and walk away, but what would that accomplish? Their marriage might be unusual, it might even be unorthodox, but it was the one they had. Surely they could find some common ground where they could meet. Right now they were living separate lives, only intersecting for supper and church. And she was tired of it. She knew people were talking about them, and it bothered her. No matter how many times she told herself to forget it, not worry about it, it always came back to poke at her.

"I'm talking about everybody we know is talking about us and how we don't do things together and how our marriage is suspicious."

"Suspicious?"

She waved away the word. Maybe that wasn't exactly what the women had said, but it didn't matter. The fact that they were wondering about them was enough. "You and I never go anywhere together and people are noticing. How can I pretend that this is a normal marriage if you won't even go to the end-of-school-year picnic with me? Or to your son's doctor appointment?"

"That's what you're doing? Pretending we have a conventional relationship?"

"What else am I supposed to do?" A new embarrassment was creeping up on her. "I thought that it would be a little . . . different than this." She couldn't come right out and say it. Married or not, it was too personal by far.

"It?" he asked.

Was he really not following the conversation or was he playing dumb in order to stall her out and hope she dropped the whole thing? Maybe it was a little bit of both.

"I—" Could she do this? Could she talk to him about such personal matters? She supposed if she was going to get what she came into this marriage for, she was going to have to. "I told you when we got married that I wanted a family."

He nodded. "You have a family."

"A baby," she clarified.

He stopped nodding to frown. "You have a baby."

"My own baby." She laid a hand over her heart, not quite believing she said the words.

"But I asked you," he said.

"You asked me if I wanted more children."

"I did—would you please sit down?" He had to crane his neck back to look her in the face. And she supposed it was uncomfortable to continually look up at a person you were almost arguing with.

She eased down onto the couch on the end opposite him. This conversation had taken an unexpected turn and was lasting a lot longer than she had expected.

"You asked me *What about more children?*" If her memory served her right, those were his exact words.

"And you said you would take what God gave you." His voice took on a musing quality.

"He has a plan for me. For us."

Matthew shook his head, almost sadly. "I thought you meant that you were happy with the children you would have coming into this marriage."

"I love your kids, *our* kids," she stressed. "But I've

always wanted to be a mother in my own right." Why it was so important to her she couldn't say. It was just one of those things, those life dreams that she had carried with her as long as she could remember.

"I don't want any more children."

Chapter Fifteen

His confession stabbed through her.

"What?" The word was more of a shocked exhale. Was he really telling the truth, or had she slipped into some horrible dream?

"I don't—"

"Don't repeat it." She held up one hand, though her gaze was firmly on her lap. She couldn't look at him. She was angry, yes. And hurt. But it wasn't directed at him. She wanted it to be. She wanted to yell and rant and pace back and forth, but the whole thing had been a misunderstanding. She had married him with false expectations, and he her. They were both victims of a situation of their own creation. She had asked him to marry her first. She had told him that she knew he needed help with his children. He had asked her what she would get out of the deal. *A family* was all she said. Not *a baby of my very own*. Those were the words she should have told him. Now, after all the words had been tossed around, she had practically asked him to fulfill the intimate side of their marriage. And it was never his intention. The embarrassment was staggering. Much more than Mary Ann Hostetler and Freda Esh talking about them. So much more.

"I'm sorry," she said. She rose to her feet and tears sprang to her eyes. She had been an utter fool. A complete and utter idiot. "So sorry." She turned and crossed to the hallway, intent on going to her room.

"Gracie." Her name was a soft whisper on his lips. But she wouldn't stop. She needed time. Time to work all this out and make peace with the decisions and mistakes that she had made. "Gracie," he called again.

"Not now, Matthew." She tossed the words over one shoulder and ducked into her room. She closed the door quietly as to not disturb Baby Grace and prayed that he didn't come after her. She needed to be alone, to work through it all. And maybe then this marriage wouldn't feel like the biggest mistake of her life.

He called her name again, but she either didn't hear or she ignored him. He was pretty certain it was the latter.

Some emotion he didn't understand churned inside of him. He should jump up and run after her. But she had told him not in so many words to leave her alone. *Not now, Matthew* meant *I'm not ready to hear your explanation.*

Or to her they would be excuses. That's how it went in such important differences of opinion.

But to think of it like that made it seem small. And it was huge.

And even if he did go after her, what would he say? That he was sorry? That he hadn't meant for her to misunderstand his intentions?

But she had apologized to him. What did she have to be sorry for, other than calling him on his reluctance to do things with her?

He didn't quite understand all that himself, except that the more time he spent with her, the more he liked her as a person and that was a bit terrifying. She took care of his children and watched over them better than their own mother had. She hadn't complained once about the baby and how much she cried. It was as if Gracie knew what was in the baby's heart and only time and love would correct the wrongs that had been dealt her. Gracie had brought in a goodly amount of money from the shop and handed it over with only a small allowance to help pay for the supplies needed for the lotions and soaps. She had supper on the table every night, the clothes cleaned and put away. She had his entire house running like a well-bred horse—smoothly, steadily, and beautifully.

And she was sorry because she wanted a baby of her own. That was something he just didn't think he could give her. He knew he couldn't. She thought she knew what she wanted, but she didn't understand all the risks, all the terrible things that could go wrong. Children were a blessing, that much was true. And he was content with the blessings the Lord had given him. Maybe with time she would be too.

But he had seen the hurt in her eyes, the embarrassment, what it had cost her to talk to him about such matters. And he wanted to take that away. His only hope was to give her all that she wanted and asked for. Everything but a baby.

Dear God in heaven . . .

She started the prayer but lost the words. How had she been such a fool? It was all right there if she had just seen what was really in front of her instead of what she wanted to see and hear.

Before the wedding she thought he had been asking if she was willing to have another baby. She was, and she was willing to try and see what blessings God would bestow on them. Yet that wasn't what he had been asking her at all. And then after the wedding, when he brought her to her room. That should have been enough to warn her right there, but she thought he was just giving her time to adjust to their new arrangement. It wasn't like they had to jump in. They were married for life and had all the time in the world, God willing. Baby Grace was only a few months old. They could wait a bit. Maybe court after marriage and get to know one another better. But he hadn't wanted to go anywhere with her but church, and she spent most of her time caring for the baby and making sure the boys stayed out of mischief, which completely made it nothing like courting.

Lord, forgive me for thinking of Your holy church that way. Amen.

That wasn't really how she meant it. She just meant that the one time she did go somewhere with Matthew it was to church, and that wasn't courting at all. That should have been a warning to her. Yet once again she had seen only what she wanted to see and heard only the things that fit into her own reality. He hadn't wanted to go to any events with her. He hadn't even wanted to go to the doctor with her.

Or had he been using her to take care of things so he didn't have to?

The idea was staggering. She was nothing more than a nanny and a housekeeper. No wonder she stayed in the room off the kitchen like some Amish Cinderella. He had tried to tell her and she hadn't listened. She had no one to blame but herself.

But today, things were going to change.

She checked the mirror to make sure her appearance was as perfect as possible. Not one hair out of place, prayer *kapp* set in the proper way. Dress clean, apron clean, and ready to face the day.

Well, maybe not that last part. And she was really stretching it, wearing a clean dress in the middle of the week when she hadn't fallen into a cow patty. But she needed her pride today more than she had ever needed it before. She needed to be able to hold her head up and say, *Look at me. I'm worthy even if you don't think I am.*

But she knew those words weren't fair. He hadn't said she wasn't worthy, only that he didn't want any more children. And it was the one thing she wanted most in this world.

She pressed at the dark bags under her eyes. She wished she knew how to get rid of them. She bet the Englisch girls had a trick for it, but she had no idea what that might be. Those puffy, discolored half-moons told the tale of her sleepless night.

But the good news was she had come to terms with a lot of this mistake that had become her life.

First, she was going to stop pretending that she and Matthew had something more than a business-type relationship. It was no one's business why they had gotten married and what it gave to each of them. Their personal relationship was no one's business but their own. But she had to stop kidding herself. There were no more children in her future.

It wasn't her dream, but she knew she would eventually come to accept it. She couldn't be greedy with God's blessings. She had five beautiful children. They might not have been born to her, but this misunderstanding had made them hers all the same. And she was going to keep her vow to Beth Byler and love those five as if they were her own, always and forever.

Second, she was moving out of the tiny little room off the kitchen. Sure, it shared a hallway with Matthew's room, but it was still a little too much like servants' quarters and she was no servant. She may not have a true wife's standing in the house, but she would never have it if she allowed him to dictate every facet of her life. He might have set up the furniture in that room, but she was moving into the third bedroom upstairs. With Baby Grace. Matthew could have the lower level all to himself. Something he seemed to enjoy.

And third, she was going to make today and every day from this one forward the best day she could possibly have. She knew the deal now. She knew the truth. She had nothing else holding her back. She had these great children, a husband who loved them and cared for them all, including her. She wouldn't complain about not having more. Some people had even less. Today was the day to have an attitude of gratitude just like that poster she had seen at Walmart in town. Come to think if it, next time she was there, she might buy one to hang on the wall of her new space. A reminder that she didn't hurt anymore.

She checked over her appearance one last time, then turned on her heel and confidently made her way to the kitchen. It was time to start breakfast and get this day started. After all, this was the day. The first day of the rest of her life.

She plucked the baby from the crib, changed her diaper, blew little raspberries in the crook of her neck and rubbed their noses together in sweet Eskimo kisses. Gracie tucked Baby Grace onto her hip and breezed into the kitchen to get breakfast ready for them all.

She had placed the baby in her playpen and had the bacon frying when Matthew came into the kitchen still pulling his suspenders over his shoulders.

"Good morning." She tossed the greeting to him and flashed him a big smile as if this was the way they greeted each other every morning.

He scowled, but she was used to the look. She turned back to her frying pan, resolve still firmly in place. Today was going to be a fantastic day. She wouldn't allow it to be anything else.

Matthew mumbled something that sounded a little like

a greeting, then reached around her to the coffeepot still sitting on the stove eye.

She nodded toward the counter to their left. "There's a mug out there for you."

His look went from grumpy to confused then back to grumpy again. He really was cute when he scowled like that. Or maybe she thought that because she knew what was behind it.

"Gracie, I—" he started as he poured himself a cup of coffee.

"Say no more. There's nothing else to talk about." She gave him another of her biggest smiles. "Can you wake up the boys for me, please?" she asked sweetly, then shook her head. "Never mind." She turned off the fire under the bacon, then made her way to the stairs without once looking him full in the face. She might have a plan for how to get through this rough patch, but that didn't mean it was easy.

She got the boys up and fed without breaking her stride. Or her smile.

But she was determined. She had made a mistake, but she was going to make sure this was the best mistake she had ever made.

All the while, she could feel Matthew watching her. She knew he couldn't figure out what she was up to, but it was simpler than he could ever imagine and because of that, he would never realize the truth. She was just making the best of it all.

She could tell that he wanted to hang around until he figured out what had changed for her during the night, but he had to leave and take care of his work. There were barn chores to be done and fields to be worked. She thought he had said something about re-shoeing their buggy horse. So as reluctant as he was, he left the house looking back twice before he got to the barn.

Let him wonder, she thought to herself. She still had changes to make.

Matthew looked back toward the house and wondered once again what had happened to Gracie during the night. He felt terrible about their misunderstanding. Terrible didn't even cover it. He was almost as devastated as she had been, but this morning . . .

She acted as if nothing had happened.

Well, that wasn't exactly the truth. She was acting so contented, bright and cheerful. She hadn't been this happy the entire time since he had married her. And on the heels of what had to be the worst news that she had received in a long while. She wanted a baby and he didn't want any more children.

Actually, that wasn't the truth. He could handle more children. He himself had come from a large family. The Amish were known for their large families. He would love to have more children. But the risks involved . . . He couldn't get past the dangers. They just weren't worth it. And if he gave his heart to another, how could he ask her to risk all for one more addition to their household?

But this is what she wants.

He pushed that voice away. This was what she *thought* she wanted. She had no idea. She hadn't been down that road. She didn't know what all it entailed. And telling her would do no good. She had her heart set on a baby. The one thing he wasn't willing to give her.

But this morning . . . she acted as if the night before had never happened. As if he hadn't dashed all her dreams.

And he felt like dirt. Lower than dirt. How could she even look at him? How could he even stand himself?

He couldn't give her what she wanted and keep the

promises he had made to himself. And to Beth. He owed Gracie that much.

With one last glance at the house, he turned back to oiling the bridle. He could wonder until the good Lord came back and he would never figure out the heart or the mind of a woman.

"What do you think, little girl?" Gracie looked at the baby, but tiny Grace had no opinion. At least none she was willing to voice.

Gracie had to admit, it seemed like a bigger task in person than it had in her mind last night.

She had sent the boys out to the garden to pull weeds. She wasn't sure why anyone said it that way. There were no weeds in the plot the four of them had turned, hoed, and planted. It was grass, pure and simple. But *grassing* didn't have the same ring to it as *weeding*.

With the boys occupied, she and Baby Grace had come upstairs to claim their new space. She wondered if they really needed some of the things in the room or if they could be tossed out. Then she reminded herself that all the items currently in her way belonged to her husband, not her. Even if she wanted to, she couldn't just pitch out things that weren't hers. Which meant everything would have to be moved. All the furniture from her bedroom downstairs would have to be moved into this room, and all the furniture and forgotten items in this room would need to be hauled downstairs. But she could do this.

Plan in place, Gracie kissed the top of the baby's head, dusted her hands, and got down to work.

"How was your day?" Matthew casually glanced toward Gracie across the supper table.

Gracie passed him the bowl of green beans and gave him another one of those beautiful and annoying smiles. "Great. And yours?"

I could think of nothing but you and how you've changed. Did I do this to you? Why don't I like it?

"Fine. *Jah*, uh, fine." He scooped out some green beans for Henry, who groaned.

"Da-at."

Matthew ignored him.

"Go ahead and eat," Gracie said. "I'll fix the kids' plates."

"I don't mind," he said, but he no sooner got the words out of his mouth than she jumped up from the table and started filling plates.

"I wouldn't hear of it," she chirped in that over-bright voice, that over-bright smile still gracing her lips. He hated them both. What had happened to his Gracie?

He felt like a heel, eating while she bustled around filling plates and cups and otherwise doing everything for everyone.

He wanted to yell at her to sit down and eat, but he had a feeling it wouldn't do any good. This was all part of whatever game she was playing. Or maybe it was his punishment for misleading her, however unintentional.

You could change your mind.

He pushed the voice away. Now was not the time.

"There." She finished getting everyone something to eat and returned to her chair.

At least now he could eat in peace. Which meant he could eat without having her rushing here and there trying to see to everyone's needs.

She jumped up and snatched his water glass from in front of him. "Let me get you some water. Hold on a second."

Before he could protest, she rushed into the kitchen. She

returned only a few seconds later with his refilled glass in one hand and the pitcher in the other, just in case.

"There you are." She set his glass in front of him and settled back into her seat.

He just stared at her, watched her, and she pretended not to notice. He wasn't sure when everything would go back to normal, but that day couldn't come soon enough.

It was amazing what a person could accomplish when they kept a positive attitude. Now that Stephen was out of school, she enlisted his help as well. He and Henry watched the shop and the twins while she and the baby carved out their new space in the upstairs bedroom.

She had found some furniture movers she was certain Beth had used to clean for church and placed them under the furniture to drag it to the staircase. Whether the piece was going up or down, she cushioned the stairs with the same quilt they had used at the end-of-year picnic at school and pushed the furniture to its new place. It wasn't easy, but it felt good to accomplish it by herself. She didn't need anyone's help. She could do everything she needed all by herself.

Except for the crib.

She propped her hands on her hips and studied the spindly thing. It didn't have a flat enough side that she could turn it on to push it up the stairs. And she certainly couldn't pull it up by the legs. It had casters, so it was no problem getting it *to* the staircase, but *up* was another matter altogether.

"What do you think, Baby Grace?" she asked the infant.

On hearing her name, the baby flapped her hands, waving them in the air in front of her while kicking her feet to show her joy. Otherwise she had no opinion on the matter. Or so it seemed.

"You should have an opinion," Gracie said. "After all, it's your bed."

"Who are you talking to?"

Gracie whirled around to find Matthew standing behind her, that usual scowl wrinkling his brow. "I didn't hear you come in."

"Obviously."

She stopped, giving her heart time to return to its normal rhythm.

"Well?" he asked.

"Hmmm?"

"Who were you talking to?"

She laughed nervously. She hadn't been prepared to see him so soon, and her happy, Proverbs 31 wife demeanor had slipped a notch or two. "The baby."

He looked from her to Baby Grace, then back again. "*Jah*. Okay." His tone seemed to suggest she might be losing it.

"Well, you know. They say it improves language skills. To talk to babies. That's why younger children in a family usually speak clearer than their older siblings did at the same age. Because they hear the older kids talking. And the older kids didn't have anyone but their parents. And . . ." She trailed off. She was babbling and that didn't make her appear confident and happy. *Time to shut up, Gracie.*

He just studied her for a moment, looking, watching. As if whatever ailed her would manifest itself while he stared.

"*Jah*. So . . . what are you doing here?" she asked.

His frown deepened. "I live here."

Another nervous laugh. "What are you doing home at this time of day?"

"It's almost noon. I came in to eat."

Almost noon? Where had all the time gone? "*Jah*. Of course." She gave yet another forced laugh. "I was just about to go make us all something."

He looked around. "Where are the boys?"

"Minding the shop. Which means sitting outside the shed playing marbles."

"I didn't see them when I came in."

Her heart gave a stutter. "That's where I told them to be." She rushed over to the window and looked toward the shed that served as their little home store. The boys were nowhere to be seen.

"Watch the baby," she said. Then she rushed out of the house, calling their names as she ran.

No answer.

She wasn't going to panic. Panicking would not help anything. She needed to keep a clear head. She would find them. She had to. And they had to all be okay.

Clear head, she reminded herself.

Pepper. The name rose into her thoughts like a shooting star. Pepper was always with the boys. If she wasn't around, then she was wherever they were.

Gracie gave a shrill whistle and called her name. "Pepper! Pepper!" If they had gone so far away that they couldn't hear, then maybe Pepper would. A dog's hearing was so much better than a person's. And with any luck she would come running, and the boys would take off after her.

"Where are they?" Matthew came out onto the porch, looking this way and that as he spoke.

"I don't know," she said, exasperation tainting her voice. How had this happened? How had she gotten so involved with moving her things into the spare upstairs bedroom that she had forgotten to watch out for four little boys?

She whirled on Matthew. "Aren't you supposed to be watching the baby?" How could he leave her all alone in the house?

"She's fine," he said.

And that's exactly what she'd thought about the boys

too. Now where were they? No one knew. "Pepper!" she called again. "Pepper!"

One day of trying to be the best wife a man could ask for regardless of the sham that was their marriage, and she couldn't maintain. She couldn't manage more than twenty-four hours. How pathetic was that?

Then she saw them. Four straw hats lying in the dust. The boys were gone, but their hats were still there.

"Stephen!" she cried. "Henry! Benjamin! Thomas! Stephen! Pepper!"

"Mamm," Stephen said. "Why are you hollering at us?"

She whirled around, so many emotions zinging through her. Had he just called her Mamm? Where had he been? Where were the other boys? Why was he so dusty?

"Stephen." She pulled him to her, the gratitude of having him safe winning over all else. Tears rose into her eyes. He was fine, and he had called her Mamm. "Where are Henry and the twins?"

He pointed toward the crawl space cover that had been moved aside. "Still under the house."

"Under the—" she started. "Why are they under the house?"

"We thought we heard kittens."

She laughed a bit, even though her tears still threatened. "Kittens." She ran a hand down his dusty hair and cheek. "Go tell them to get out from under there. If the mama kitten picked that place to have her babies, she thought it was safe. Let her have that. If they're under there, they'll be out soon enough."

"*Jah*, Mamm." He smiled at her, then ran back to the crawl space entrance. He disappeared in an instant and she could hear their muffled voices as Stephen relayed her message.

Now back to Baby Grace.

She heard her screams the minute she walked in the door. Not hurt or hungry, but angry. Sheer lividness.

"Oh, baby," she crooned, picking up Baby Grace and cradling her close. She braced one arm behind her head and the other under her bottom, but Baby Grace was beyond consolation. At least easy consolation.

She kicked her feet and arched her back, fighting Gracie with all her strength. She didn't know something so small could be so strong. And a quote came to mind. *Though she be but little she is fierce.* Some Englisch writer said it a long time ago. She only remembered it because of a girl on her hurricane relief team. She was short in stature but worked twice as hard as any man. She had that saying on a T-shirt, as if to remind them all of who she was.

Baby Grace was little. But she was fierce.

Gracie struggled to keep her hold on the baby and had almost succeeded in getting a good solid grip on the child when a scream sounded from outside.

She pressed the baby to her and rushed from the house.

Henry was crying, holding his leg with one hand as he clung to his father with the other.

Matthew. She had almost forgotten he was there. He was trying to get a look at the injury, but Henry was having none of it. Gracie could see the blood seeping between his fingers.

"Mamm," he cried. He turned loose of his father, then rushed to her.

She didn't even have time to relish in the fact that he had called her Mamm when he hit her full force, grabbing her around the hips and slamming into her.

She stumbled backward from the force of his embrace but managed to stay on her feet. But he needed consoling, and doctoring if the amount of blood staining his pants was any indication.

"Here." She thrust Baby Grace at Matthew in much the

same way he had to her that first day, when she had come over to ask him to marry her.

And just as she had, he grabbed the crying baby, shock and surprise overtaking his features.

Baby Grace screamed even louder. Gracie wasn't sure her hearing would recover. But she couldn't worry about that now.

"Let me see your leg," Gracie said. Her voice was loud, near a shout in order to be heard above the cries of both children.

She cast a quick glance at Matthew, who was struggling with Baby Grace, trying to calm her even as her cries escalated. He would have to figure out something on his own. Just one more chip out of her perfect-wife-and-mother façade.

"Henry." She pulled his arms from around her and plopped onto the ground. She urged him down next to her and braced his leg on her lap.

"What happened?"

"I don't know." He stopped crying long enough to answer, then decided to quit altogether with a sniff and a wipe of his nose on the back of his sleeve. "Something bit me."

Gracie pulled apart the ragged and bloody edges of his pants to examine the wound. It was long and jagged. Not a bite at all, but a scratch, most probably from a nail.

"I don't think it needs stitches," she said, "but when was the last time he had a tetanus shot?"

"Tetanus shot?" Matthew repeated. At least she thought that was what he said.

"We had to get them when we went to help the hurricane victims. In case we stepped on a rusty nail or something. It keeps a person from getting sick from it."

He frowned as if he had never thought about getting sick from a nail. "Never, I guess."

"Well, he needs one," she said flatly, then realized her mistake.

"A shot?" Henry whined. "I don't want to get a shot." He shook his head. "No-no-no-no-no-no-no. I had to get a shot when I hurt my arm," he wailed.

"It's okay," she promised. "This is a good shot." But she remembered how much it hurt and how her arm ached for a day or two afterward. She was certain chicken and ducklings were in their future. It might be the only thing that would overcome this betrayal.

"Can you take him?" she asked Matthew. She couldn't imagine leaving him and the baby alone together with three other boys to watch after. The thought was ridiculous, seeing as how he was Grace's father and she had been living with him her entire life.

"Nooooooo," Henry whined. "I want you to take me."

Gracie met Matthew's gaze over the top of Henry's head. *I'm sorry*, she mouthed.

He scowled and gave her a stern nod. He understood, but he wasn't happy about it.

"You boys go play outside," he told Stephen and the twins. Grace was still squalling, inconsolable since Gracie and Henry had left. Well, Gracie.

"*Jah*, Dat," Stephen said, gabbing each twin by the shoulder and turning them toward the door.

"And no more crawling under the house."

"*Jah*, Dat," they chorused and disappeared out the door.

Just add that to the collection of rules along with no jumping out of the barn loft onto a wagon full of hay.

What was it his mother used to say? Boys will be boys?

But she didn't have any saying for girls other than sugar and spice.

The baby might be sweet on the inside, somewhere, but it wasn't a side she showed him.

"Shhhh . . ." He bounced her and rubbed her back, walked around the room, singing "Jesus Loves the Little Children," but nothing.

And the continued crying was wearing him down. It broke his heart and made him feel like so much less of a father, of a *person*, that he could hardly stand it. But she knew what he had done. She knew that he was responsible for her mother's death. He could have done something. He could have saved her, but he'd been too far away. And now she was dead.

After what seemed like hours, the baby finally fell asleep in his arms. He was afraid to put her down and risk waking her, so he checked on the boys, who were throwing a baseball around. Well, Stephen was tossing the ball to the twins, who were chasing after it, then kicking it back like it was a soccer ball. He could tell that Stephen was about at the end of his patience. And then he would toss down his glove and storm away, not able to handle when things weren't in perfect order. In some ways that was exactly like Matthew. But everything that had happened this year had almost cured him of that trait. He knew all too well that he could make all the plans he wanted, but God was in charge of all his steps.

He should see if Gracie would stitch that Bible verse on a pillow for him. A cute reminder might be a good thing for them all. Proverbs, he thought, if his memory served him.

A man's heart deviseth his way: but the Lord directeth his steps.

With one last look at the boys, he took Grace over to the rocking chair and sat down with her.

Her weight was warm and solid in his arms, and she

smelled like baby lotion and the special detergent that Gracie used to wash her clothes. How could he love someone so much even when they hated the very ground he walked on? And he did . . . love this baby. She was the last piece of Beth. It was only fitting that she looked just like her. Beth had wanted a girl so badly. Had asked, almost begged Matthew to have one more baby after the twins. All boys, she used to say as she made a face like she had smelled something bad. If they didn't have a sister, they wouldn't grow up knowing how to treat women. They needed a sister, she had told him, and convinced him to try one more time.

And that last time she had gotten her girl and never had a chance to enjoy her. Two weeks wasn't any time at all.

In a way, he had only had two weeks with her as well. For once Beth died, the baby changed. Now she cried all the time.

Not when she's with Mammi Glick. Or Eunice. Or Gracie.

Maybe it was men that she had an aversion to. Or his beard. He had heard of that; a baby not taking to her father's beard and crying every time she saw him.

But he knew that wasn't the reason, no matter how badly he wished it so.

"I'm sorry," he whispered against the blond curls coming out from under the fabric of her head covering. He kissed her there, softly, enjoying the feel of her fine, silky hair against his lips. His little girl. He loved her so much. "So sorry," he said. "I know it doesn't mean much, but I'll spend my life trying to make it up to you. You deserve a good and sweet *mamm*. I got you one. I love you and I will always take care of you."

As he said the words he realized how true they were. He would always love her, always care for her. She could cry all she wanted, and he might get frustrated and a little frazzled, but it didn't change his love for her.

"I miss her sometimes too," he said. "But I miss her how she used to be. You didn't know her then. But she was a wonderful woman. And she loved you very much. And I know, no matter what, she's looking down from heaven watching you grow and loving you still."

Tears rose into his eyes and he pressed his cheek against her head and let them fall. He did miss Beth. He missed her how she was, and how she ended up. He had loved her, but their love wasn't meant to be. Now he was in a marriage with a dynamo of a woman who seemed to make sunshine light her footsteps and rainbows trail behind her. She was perfect, beautiful and sweet. And he almost hated her for that, even as he was starting to fall for her.

His thought came to a screeching halt. He didn't want to fall for Gracie Glick. Falling in love would bring a host of problems that he didn't want to face. Couldn't face, not yet. So he took that little thought and locked it away. Then he kissed the top of the baby's head again and fell asleep.

Chapter Sixteen

"Matthew." Gracie laid one hand on his shoulder, afraid to startle him when he was holding the baby. They looked so content there, dozing together, that she really didn't want to wake them. But when she took inventory of the angle of Matthew's head, she decided that waking him would be better than him having to deal with a sore neck tomorrow. Besides, it was almost time for supper. "Matthew." She shook him gently and he finally responded, stirring slightly, opening his eyes and focusing on her.

"Gracie?" He blinked at her a couple of times, then pushed himself up a little straighter in his chair. He ran one hand down Baby Grace's back as if assuring himself she was still there, still okay, and still asleep.

She stirred just a bit, turned her face the other direction, then smacked her tiny bow-shaped lips, never once opening her eyes.

"I must have fallen asleep," he muttered, obviously still trying to get his bearings.

"While we were at the medical center."

That woke him up. He sputtered a bit, looking from her to Henry, who stood beside her. "Everything okay?" he asked.

"It is not," Henry said emphatically. "Gracie said it wasn't going to hurt and it did. Real bad."

So she was back to Gracie now.

"It?" he asked.

"The shot," Henry grumbled.

"I'm sure Gracie thought she was telling you the right thing."

Henry shook his head, unconvinced. "She has to make me chicken and ducklings tonight for supper."

"Henry," Matthew started, his voice a clear warning. He didn't even bother to correct him on dumplings. "That's not how we get the things we would like from people."

Henry frowned, obviously hurt. "She promised."

Matthew looked at her, and Gracie nodded.

"All right, but next time, even if you are hurt, you may not talk to people that way, understand?"

"*Jah*, Dat."

"Is everything else okay?" he asked, nodding at Henry.

She nodded. "The doctor said the cut was deeper than it looked, but the place on his leg was bad for stitches. Though I think he meant bad for stitches when you're five and like Henry."

"What does that mean?" Henry asked.

She continued without responding. "He had the nurse put some of those strips on it to hold it shut. And the shot."

"I hated that part," Henry told them as if they didn't already know.

Matthew nodded and started to stand.

It all was good news and he seemed satisfied. Henry would be fine, though he had a gash on his leg to match the cast on his arm. And the doctors didn't overly question her about the incident. Thank heavens.

Gracie moved closer. "Want me to take her?" she asked, holding out her arms.

But to her surprise, Matthew shook his head and headed toward the bedroom where her crib had been.

"Matthew," she called as he started down the hallway. The crib wasn't there. It was still sitting at the foot of the stairs, waiting for someone to take it to its new place on the second floor.

He stopped, turned around.

"Her bed is not in that room any longer."

He frowned, that look she knew so well. And she knew that scowl of his would deepen when he heard what else she had to say. "Where is it?" he asked.

"At the foot of the stairs."

"And why is it there?"

"Henry . . . it's time to go out and get your barn chores done," she said. "Get your brothers to go with you." Stephen and the twins had been outside playing when they returned from the doctor.

He opened his mouth to protest, remind her that he had a cast and a cut leg, but she stopped his words with a sharp shake of her head.

Henry groaned, then trudged outside. For once he didn't let the door slam behind him. Baby Grace slept on.

"Why, Gracie?" Matthew asked again.

"Because I was moving it up to the second floor."

"Why?"

She blew out a breath. She had known that this moment would come, she just wished she'd had more time to prepare. But with the boys crawling under the house, Henry's cut leg, and a trip to the medical center, there hadn't been any time. "Because I was moving it into my room." Not the best answer, but the best one she had right then.

"And your room is upstairs?"

"It is now."

Matthew shifted Baby Grace's position ever so gently to

adjust her but not wake her. Thankfully she slept on. "Stop talking in riddles," he growled. "Why is your room now on the second floor?"

"Because I want to move up there." It was all he needed to know, and yet it was nothing at all.

Still, it seemed to satisfy him. "And the crib?"

"I was trying to get it up the stairs when you came in and then Henry and the boys . . ." She trailed off. He'd been here for that entire exchange. But he'd been caught up with other things and missed the fact that she had been moving furniture.

"I see." The shadows of his churning thoughts moved across his face. He didn't tell her what he was thinking, but she could see that he was, and he was making his mind up about everything, and she had no say in it at all.

Because she refused to give him details.

"Take her." He moved toward her and gently handed the baby over. The soft action was a direct contrast with his hard expression.

Gracie took the baby and followed Matthew into the foyer. With a grunt he lifted the crib and hoisted it up the stairs. In a second, he had disappeared into the room that she had claimed as her own.

"You've been busy," he called.

She didn't respond. She could use the fact that she still held the sleeping baby as an excuse not to answer. But really she didn't have anything to say back. Yes, she had been busy cleaning out closets, rearranging furniture, moving all the stored items from that room to the room down off the kitchen. There were a few pieces of furniture that she couldn't move. There was a dresser in there and a cedar chest she hadn't looked in but supposed contained an heirloom quilt or two. It was a specific assumption, but it seemed to fit what she had known of Beth Byler.

Matthew came back down the stairs a few moments

later, his gaze focused on his feet. Finally, when he came nearer he raised his eyes to hers. "You can take her up to bed now."

She swallowed hard and nodded. This was supposed to have been a good decision. She was supposed to have been set free by claiming her own space and not letting this sham of a marriage push her around. So why did her heart break a little as she looked into his soft blue eyes?

Because despite everything—his scowl and booming voice, the fact that they had married under false pretenses and that he seemed to treat her more like a housekeeper-nanny combo than a wife—she was starting to have feelings for him. Stronger than sympathy that he had lost his wife. These feelings had to do with the way he treated his children. The way he scratched Pepper behind the ears, the way he would do little things for her that branded him a gentleman. Helping her hang the sheets after she washed them so they didn't drag in the red Mississippi dirt. Helping her down from the buggy when they went to church. Meeting her gaze over the dinner table and smiling just for her when Henry said something particularly funny. All those things and more rolled into one and made her realize he wasn't the man everyone thought he was. He had a soft heart, a kind spirit, a loving hand, even though that hand was almost the size of a dinner plate. He was, as they said, a gentle giant. And the scowl he wore most of the time wasn't anger, but thoughtfulness. And she couldn't find fault in that.

She wanted to apologize for moving rooms. For disrupting the balance they were working so hard to achieve, but she bit back the words. Now wasn't the time to kowtow. She needed to stand up and be strong.

Though she be but little, she is fierce.

She might not be little like Baby Grace, but she was

innocent in her own ways, young on knowing how to stand up for herself. And now was the time to be fierce.

She lifted her chin and stiffened her resolve. "Thank you." Then she moved past him and up the stairs to place Baby Grace in her newly moved crib.

Matthew watched his wife move up the stairs with a grace that befitted her name.

She had moved her things into the other bedroom. There hadn't been a bed in there since he moved it down into the baby's room. But it was up there now. She must have moved it. Along with the rest of her things. Some of the furniture was the same, but the rest she had switched out. All but the crib. Why hadn't she asked him for help?

Would he have helped her?

Most probably, though he didn't understand her desire to move rooms. He wanted to ask her but didn't. What difference did it make to him where she slept?

It didn't. It shouldn't. And that wasn't exactly what was bothering him. It was that she didn't say anything to him about it until now. Why was it a secret? Was it a secret? He had no idea. And that's what bothered him. He thought he'd gotten her all figured out and then bam! She hit him with a part of herself that he hadn't known about. Had it been there all along? Or had she just developed it because of their marriage?

He wouldn't ask. He couldn't.

He watched her come out of the room she had claimed and back down the stairs. She stopped when she got to him and lifted her chin to a new angle. Another something he hadn't seen before.

"I guess I need to start supper if I'm going to have dumplings ready in time."

"Ducklings," he said, trying to draw a laugh from her.

He got only a smile. "You don't have to make that for him," Matthew continued. "He was being disrespectful."

"Have you ever had a tetanus shot?" she asked.

"Not that I can recall."

She gave a quick nod. "If you had, you'd have wanted chicken and ducklings too."

The next few days fell into a pattern of complacency. It was strange to Matthew. After Henry's run-in with the rusty nail, Gracie had seemed to change a bit. She had lost that overly happy smile and too bright voice. They were replaced by her normal smile and her normal voice. And that was something Matthew could live with.

But was it Henry's accident that caused the change, or her moving into the upstairs bedroom?

Then again, why would either of those events bring about such a shift in attitude? It didn't make sense. But he had learned long ago that women had their own definition of logic.

Yet that change still nagged at him. He just couldn't wrap his mind around it. Was trying still as he sat at the table and watched her move around the kitchen.

The baby was starting to sit up a bit. But mostly Gracie propped some fancy pillow around her that allowed her to sit in the highchair and bang against the tray for what seemed like hours on end. Gracie seemed unaware of the noise as she moved around the kitchen, getting an early start on supper. It was hotter cooking in the early afternoon, but they had discovered that it was easier to eat when the temperature in the house had time to cool off before suppertime.

"Are you enjoying your new room?" he asked.

She half turned to face him as if she only needed a glance and turned back to slicing chicken. "*Jah*."

But the word held no hidden meaning, nothing to tell him why she had moved and why she was acting the way she had been these days.

It wasn't that he didn't like it; he simply didn't understand. He hadn't understood Beth. Why did he suppose he would know more about Gracie?

"Henry gets his cast off tomorrow, *jah*?" he asked.

She nodded but didn't turn from her chore.

"I'll take him."

This time she did spin around, gaping at him as if he had just declared he was becoming Englisch and running for president. "You'll take him?"

"*Jah*. Of course." Henry was his son, after all. "I'll take Henry, and you can stay with the baby and the twins." Otherwise he would be home with them and he wasn't sure he could handle another fit like the one the baby had had the other day.

"Eunice already said she would watch them." She dunked her hands in the dishpan full of soapy water, then rinsed them in the other. When she turned to fully face him, she was wiping her hands on her apron. The same way he had seen his *mamm* do, and Beth, and every one of his sisters. "I can take him."

Not after what she had said to him after the last appointment. He had been lax as a father. Not because he didn't love his children. He loved them so much. He had made a mistake, foisting all their care onto Gracie's shoulders, and she had called him on it. She was right.

He'd been thinking about this a lot, and she was absolutely right. They never went anywhere but church together. He didn't know if people were really talking, but women were more prone to that than men, so he would have to take her word for it. He hadn't wanted that responsibility of caring for his children, being a husband, doing all the normal things. He had needed a break from what his reality had become.

He wasn't proud of it. But there it was all the same. But since she had pointed out how he had been acting, he could see the error of his ways. Now it was time to do something about it.

"I'll take him," he said, shifting his tone to "no argument." She must have heard it for she gave him a quick nod. And before she could turn away from him and back toward the counter again, he gave her the other news.

"Danny Yoder is having a couples' get-together tomorrow night. I think we should go."

She frowned at him, a dark look that was as ominous as it was unreadable. He knew she wasn't happy, but that was all he could see. Then as quickly as it came, the look disappeared. "I don't think so. But *danki* for thinking of me."

Was she serious?

First, who else would he think about other than his wife, and secondly, why was she turning down his invitation when just a couple of weeks ago she had issued one of her own just the same? That didn't make any sense at all.

"I thought it would be fun. Everyone's bringing drinks and snack foods. I thought we might take that dip you made for the wedding." He wasn't sure what all was in it, but it did have water chestnuts. He had discovered that afternoon that he loved them.

He hadn't even finished speaking when she started shaking her head. "No." This time she didn't even say thanks. She merely turned back to the counter and stared out the window over the worktable.

One could see the whole of the backyard from that window. The tire swing he had hung for the boys, the line of trees that marked the creek where Beth had drowned. The garden where she and the younger children were growing vegetables. It was a happy backyard despite some of the tragedies it had seen. To the outsider, it might even look perfect. Like the family inside the house had the best life, the best love, the best of all those things that God provides. But it was all a lie.

And that bothered him. When had it changed? When had he gone from not caring what everyone thought to not liking the lie he lived with this remarkable woman? Better still, what was he going to do about it?

He rose to his feet and went over to stand next to her, viewing the yard he had just recreated in his thoughts. He couldn't give her all that she wanted. Something in him wanted to, but he knew it could never be. There was simply too much at stake. No matter how much he wanted to give her everything that she desired and more, a baby was not something he could go back on. But he could give her the other things that she wanted.

"I really want to go to Danny's," he said softly.

She didn't turn, just continued to stare out the window as if the answer she needed lay somewhere out there. "You don't have to," she finally said. Her voice was barely above a whisper. From behind them the baby pounded on her tray and gurgled something no one save her could understand, but Matthew was only concerned with the female in front of him.

"What if I want to?" he asked.

She shook her head. "How can that be?"

He shrugged. "I don't know. Maybe you got to me the other day."

She continued to look out the window as if she were afraid to look at him directly. "See, that's the thing. I don't want to get to you. I want you to want to."

Strangely enough he understood all that. "But you do get to me." He reached up a hand and trailed his fingers down the edge of her prayer *kapp*. And he moved a little closer to her.

"I—I get to you."

"Uh-hmm." Just like now. What had gotten into him? One minute he had been sitting at the table talking about things like doctors' appointments and couples' game nights. How had it gotten to him standing so close to her, breathing in her scent and wanting a bit more? Like a kiss.

The word zinged through his mind like a crazed arrow. That was what he wanted and, surprisingly enough, he had wanted that for a long time. Ever since they had found Pepper on the road, the horse had played games with her as they walked, and they had ridden back home with a funny old man named Eugene Dover. And that had been so long ago. A month. An eternity.

Just a taste, nothing more. Something to satisfy his curiosity. Were her lips as sweet as her disposition? He had to know.

He took her by the shoulders and turned her around. Then before she could even protest, he pressed his lips to hers.

At first the kiss was chaste, sweet and innocent. Not much different than a kiss between friends. If kissing friends sent fire running through one's veins. But after that first taste he wanted more.

He pulled her a little closer still. Just one more kiss, a deeper kiss to satisfy the new questions springing into his mind. Would she kiss him back? Would she push him away?

She braced her hands on his chest, but she didn't apply any pressure. She simply laid them there as if she needed to feel the warmth of him.

He took that as a good sign and wrapped his arms around her, dragging her close enough that their kiss flared a little more.

What was happening? He knew. It was unmistakable.

He had been down this road once before, but not like this. Never like this.

How easy it would be to just keep kissing her and kissing her until—

"Ew, Dat is kissing Mamm."

Chapter Seventeen

Henry!

Gracie pulled herself away from Matthew and hoped she didn't look as dazed as she felt. She knew she was colored pink with embarrassment. She didn't remember ever being this mortified. Not even when her cousins were teasing her, pretending to pick blackberries while she and Jamie Stoltzfus sat on the back porch, almost courting.

"Ew," the twins echoed.

Stephen pushed his glasses a little further up on the bridge of his nose and studied them. "*Mamm*s and *dat*s are supposed to kiss," he said importantly. "Everybody knows that."

Baby Grace pounded on her tray as if in league with her eldest brother. One hand was fisted around a plastic rattle shaped like an Englisch telephone. Who made such things? And why was she even worried about it?

Because it's easier by far to think of those things rather than Matthew's kiss.

And the boys walking in on them. At least they were back to calling her Mamm, though she wasn't in the proper mood to enjoy it.

"Ew," Henry said again, his nose wrinkled as if he had

smelled something bad. "And double ew, Baby Grace has a dirty diaper."

As if reminded of the state of her underpants, the baby started to fuss. Gracie considered it a lifeline from heaven to move away from Matthew and scoop up the baby. Gracie blew a raspberry in that little crook of her neck that she loved so much and got a good whiff of the offending diaper.

"Whew," she said, breathing out her nose. "Let's get you changed."

She breezed them up the stairs as if nothing was amiss, yet so aware of the five sets of male eyes that followed their progress. She breathed a little sigh of relief that she almost regretted and ducked into their room where she had everything stored.

She needed to make a little changing station downstairs next to the couch, but she had been so bent on moving up into the room, lock, stock, and barrel, she hadn't left anything that belonged to either of them downstairs. Having other people's things in their room, like the cedar chest and the rocking chair, was a different matter altogether. She— *they*—had to be in there wholly even if they shared the space with the possessions of others.

She heard him on the stairs before he peeked into her room. The third stair from the top creaked when anyone stepped on it. She wasn't sure anyone else had noticed but her.

"Can we talk?" he asked, hesitantly. His head was in the room, but his feet were on the other side of the threshold, as if he were afraid to enter for some reason. Maybe because this was her space, a room that she had carved out for herself without any say-so from him.

She folded the diaper under Baby Grace's bottom and reached for the wet wipes. "That's not necessary."

"I think it is."

Instead of looking at him, she made herself busy changing the diaper. It was something she probably could have done in her sleep, but she focused on it like it was her first time without supervision. "Really, Matthew." She gave a forced laugh. "There's nothing to talk about."

It was just a kiss. Say that. It was just a kiss.

She opened her mouth to say the words, but they stuck in her throat. It wasn't just a kiss. It was the best kiss of her entire life. True, she hadn't had many to compare it to, but that kiss was like one of the kisses she had read about in those paperback romances she had devoured during her *rumspringa.* Her parents wouldn't have approved. It was the one thing she hid from them. The books weren't the sweet kind, where people went to church and shared a chaste kiss or two. Of course they weren't too risqué. But risqué enough for a young Amish girl. She slipped the books under her mattress and never told a soul. They might not have been something her family would have approved of, but she did learn a lot about kissing. And Matthew's toe-curling kiss was just like one of those in the Englisch books.

"You don't have to explain," she said instead.

"There's nothing to explain. I kissed you," he said simply.

"Why? I mean, you don't have to explain why."

"Because I wanted to."

The heat in his gaze was so intense she had to look away. That was just Matthew. Everything was intense, larger than life, just like he himself was.

She wrapped the diaper in a plastic shopping bag. She needed something to do. She'd pulled her gaze from his, but she hadn't wanted him to think she was weak. Weak in the knees maybe, but she wasn't weak. She was smart. And she was terribly close to losing her heart to Matthew Byler. It was one thing to be trapped in a loveless marriage and quite another to be trapped in a marriage where only one held love for their partner.

"Can I come in?"

She wanted to tell him no, that he couldn't. Because if he came in then he would really want to talk, and she wasn't ready for all that. She needed a little time to get her mushy brain back together, to sort through all the details of his kiss and find the pieces that told her he wasn't serious about her. She might be his wife, but that was it. He'd all but told her that they wouldn't have any sort of intimate relationship.

So why is he going around kissing you?

She didn't have an answer for that. And she sort of wanted one. No. She *really* wanted one. And the only person who could give it to her was hovering just outside her door.

With an exasperated sigh, she motioned him into the room.

He came in hesitantly, looking around as if he hadn't seen every inch from where he was standing two seconds ago.

"I can take that out for you, if you want." He gestured toward the cedar chest sitting at the end of the bed.

She shook her head. "It's fine right there. No sense in moving it." In fact she kind of liked the chest. Maybe later she would try to get one of her own. Perhaps see if Abner could make her one. She had never seen anyone who could take a piece of wood and turn it into a masterpiece like Abner Gingerich. She supposed other master woodworkers were out there, but she had never met any of them.

"If you change your mind . . ." He trailed off, leaving the rest understood but unsaid.

He ventured a little farther into the room, stopping only when he got to the rocking chair. He eased down into it, and she wondered if it was a gesture to make her more comfortable. He couldn't very well grab her up and kiss her silly if he was sitting down while she stood.

But to be on the safe side, she thrust the baby at him. "Here," she said without ceremony. "Hold Baby Grace."

Given no other choice, he took the infant from her. "Baby Grace?"

She gave a small shrug. "That's what we've taken to calling her—me and the boys. It can get confusing having two Graces in the house, even if one is a Gracie."

"That's cute," he said.

"I figured it was easier that way." She wouldn't tell him that she had started dropping the Grace and just calling her Baby. With those turquoise eyes and blond hair, she should have called her Angel, but Baby was just fine for now.

"Of course." He gave a nod. Of approval? Maybe, but if he didn't agree, it wouldn't change anything about what she called the precious little bundle. She was Baby Grace, or Baby for short.

Then the strangest thought occurred to her. "I've never heard you say her name."

"I have." But his tone was slightly defensive.

"I've never heard you." She took the challenge right back to him.

"Of course, I have. She's my daughter." He kissed the top of her head as if to prove his words to be true.

"Then say it now," Gracie dared him.

He shook his head. "I will not. This is ridiculous."

"Because you don't want to say it. Or because you can't say it?"

"I'm not even going to answer that," he said. "It's beyond ridiculous. It's . . . batty."

"If it's no big deal, then why won't you say it?"

He stuttered for a moment, as if trying to get a handle on it all. Then he exhaled like air leaking from a holey balloon. "She hates me," he finally said.

"She doesn't hate you." The very thought was the saddest thing Gracie had ever heard. How could he believe that a child as young as Baby would have any ill feelings for anyone?

"She cries every time I hold her."

"You're holding her now."

"She hasn't figured out yet that it's me back here. Once she does, she'll start crying again."

Gracie shook her head. That just wasn't possible.

"And it's only me."

Now that she refused to believe. "She cries when other people hold her."

"That's not what I mean. Even when Aaron was over here. She stopped crying when he held her."

Gracie thought about it a moment. She could see in his eyes that he was telling the truth, at least his version of it. "You did okay with her when I took Henry in for his leg."

"She cried herself to sleep. I did everything I knew to do. I held her and sang to her. I even apologized to her, but still." He stopped with a sad shake of his head.

"You apologized to her? For what?"

"Nothing." He was holding something back and she wasn't sure if she should press him or let it drop. He took the choice from her by continuing. "She hates me."

"Stop saying that. Why would she hate you?"

"Because she knows the truth about me."

"The truth?"

"Never mind." He turned away.

"No." Gracie shook her head. "That's not how this works. You can't say something like that and just expect me not to ask a couple of questions."

"Fine," he said. "Two questions."

"Why would she hate you?"

"Next question."

"You didn't answer that one," she pointed out.

"I said you could ask. I didn't say I was going to answer."

He was trying to make her laugh, get her off task. Charm her in that way he was so good at.

"I'm not going to accept that."

What had happened to sweet, sweet Gracie who was always so accommodating? Who always wanted to help?

Maybe he had mistaken compliance for weakness. He had been wrong. She was not backing down. There might have been a time when she would have, but no longer.

His expression was a war of emotions she couldn't name. Then there was a flash of shame, another of hurt, then pride, and finally resignation.

She watched as he took a deep breath and raised a hand to his head as if making sure everything there was intact. She waited and waited, but his words when they came took her completely by surprise.

"Beth didn't just drown," he said slowly. "She killed herself."

Chapter Eighteen

Once the words were out, he thought he'd feel better, but the sickened look on Gracie's face was enough to bring all the shame back to him.

"She what?" Gracie whispered. Then she shook her head. "You're wrong. You have to be mistaken."

"I wish I was." *More now than ever before.* "And it's all my fault."

"That can't be."

How he wished he had her ability to deny the truth. But he knew what he had seen with his own eyes.

"It was an accident," she said. "Everyone said so. She fell in the creek and drowned."

"She walked into the creek and drowned herself. She left the twins and Henry alone in the house. She left the baby bundled up on the bank."

Gracie's expression was one of pained surprise. "No one ever said any of these things."

The Amish gossiped, that much was true. But not like the Englisch for the entertainment value alone. Gossiping to the Amish was about sharing the stories of community, spreading the word, and helping others. Talking about one another got benefits started, relief funds organized, and supper schedules lined out. It was as much a part of the community as buggies and wash lines.

"I've never told anyone else." His voice was so quiet, he barely heard it himself.

"Not even the bishop?" Her own tone matched his.

"Especially not the bishop."

"But you—" She stopped. "How could you not tell anyone? Somebody may have seen something differently."

"There was nothing different to see. She set the baby on the ground and walked into the water." In the February cold.

"I find that hard to believe. Impossible," she said. "She had just had a baby. Why would she do something to jeopardize her life?"

In that moment he understood why Gracie was having such a difficult time understanding. She wanted a baby more than she wanted anything in the world. Beth had had everything that Gracie dreamed of. How could she have been anything but over the moon with her life and the way things turned out?

"She was depressed," he said quietly. "A deep sort of sadness." He paused, trying to gather all the words that he needed to tell this story. He hadn't thought he'd ever tell it and didn't have them collected already. "It started after the twins were born." He shook his head. He was making a mess of this.

"It was before that. All the pregnancies. Except for Stephen. She was happy after Stephen was born. But after Henry . . . she was so down that she had a hard time caring for him. I thought it was the stress of having to deal with two children, both of them babies really. But she said she was fine. She would give me a smile and promise me that everything was all right. But after the twins were born . . ." He wagged his head from side to side at the sad memories.

"She was just so melancholy. That was the word she used. It didn't sound quite so bad. And I knew that having them was hard on her. Stephen was barely four and Henry just two. Now she had two more to care for. But I was so blind. I talked to people—well, a couple of people: my mother and my oldest sister—and I asked them if there was anything I could do to help. They told me to just be there for her. Help when she needed it and be supportive when she didn't."

He shot Gracie an apologetic smile. He had been so intent on telling his story that he had almost forgotten he had an audience. And she sat there so quiet, barely making any sound at all as he spoke.

"By this time we had the opportunity presented to us to buy this farm. I thought it would be good for her, a change. She would be in a new place, able to meet new people, kind of start over. But when we got here, being away from her family and everything that was familiar was almost more than she could handle. I tried everything I could to make her comfortable, make her happy. But she hated it here. Not the place, but being away from her family.

"So I did anything and everything I could think of to make her happy."

He paused then, thinking back to the decision. Had he sealed their fate as he had tried to give her something to bring back that happiness from before? "She wanted another baby."

A squeak came from Gracie and the noise, though quick and soft, startled him all the same. She reached out a hand and squeezed his fingers. He didn't pull away from her touch, just kissed the baby on top of the head and continued with his tale.

"She wanted a girl. That was all she talked about. What

she would name a girl if she had one. How much fun it would be to have a girl to teach. She wanted to share recipes, teach her how to cook, how to fix her hair, how to sew, crochet, and knit. All those things that women do.

"At first I didn't want to, but as time went on I thought maybe it wasn't such a bad idea. Maybe one more baby would make her happy." But one more baby had taken her over the edge.

"Baby Grace," Gracie whispered.

He nodded, swallowed hard. His voice had turned hoarse and there was a lump in his throat. But for the most part his story had come to an end.

"See?" he finally said. "I killed her. If I had only told her no more babies, she wouldn't have died."

Gracie stared at Matthew, hardly able to believe what she was hearing. He thought he was responsible for Beth's drowning? He thought that she had intentionally died in the water? It was beyond her comprehension. She had never heard of such a thing as a woman getting so sad after having a baby that she felt the need to take her own life. What despair! What tragedy!

What a terrible idea that Matthew believed Beth would do such a thing. What a terrible notion that he believed he was somehow responsible for it.

She didn't doubt that he believed the story he told her. He felt every word was honest and true. He had somehow made the real facts fit his own need to take the blame. She may have only been married to him for just a few weeks, but she knew enough of him to know, he would want to take the blame from his wife. He would want to lay it on himself. He was the one left to care for the children. So it had to be his fault.

"It was God's will," she said, squeezing his fingers once again.

Baby Grace reached in and tangled her own fingers with theirs. It was a sweet moment, quickly shattered when Matthew pulled away from her touch. He thrust Baby Grace toward her as if he couldn't bear to hold her any longer.

Gracie took her and held her close for a moment, kissed her chubby baby cheek, then put her in her crib to play with the mobile of fat yellow stars with a rainbow, a sun, and a smiling moon. She couldn't help but wonder where it had come from. Was it a thoughtful shower gift, or maybe handed down from baby to baby? But the image that really stuck in her mind was a pregnant Beth strolling the aisles at Walmart or some other store, looking at the mobiles and picking out the brightest, happiest one for the baby on the way. She couldn't have known if it was a boy or a girl, and she wanted the best for it whatever the gender. But she had secretly prayed for a girl, then apologized for taking up God's time with a silly prayer. She should be praying about the health of the baby and nothing else. Someone who would do all that wouldn't do something as tragic as drown herself in a stream while her children waited in the house and her newborn was exposed to the cold February air. It simply wasn't possible.

He sighed and stood. "I knew this would happen."

"What?" She turned from the crib in time to see him stalk to the door. "Matthew?"

He stopped just before leaving, turning slowly to face her.

"What would happen?" she asked again.

"You think I'm a monster."

She shook her head. She had seen him with his children, he cared for them, loved them, wanted everything in the world for them. He even loved and held the squalling bundle he believed was somehow blaming him for her mother's death. An utterly ridiculous idea. "I don't believe you're a monster. Not even for a second."

"Then—"

"I even believe that you believe that what you say is the absolute truth."

He scratched his head, then gave a short nod, her words having finally made sense. "What I told you is really what happened."

"I know you believe that. But I believe in God's will."

He seemed to grow two feet across and two more feet up as he stood there. Anger rose into his features, a livid, raw emotion she had never seen from him before. She held her ground, refusing to even step back an inch as he came toward her.

"You believe in God's will?" he asked softly, the tone in direct contrast with his red-faced anger. "So it was God's will that she drowned herself? She left three little children alone and a two-week-old baby outside to freeze to death. You think that's what God wanted?"

"It was God's will that Beth died. How she died . . ." She shook her head. "I don't know. It must just be part of the tragedy of life. But it is not your fault that she drowned."

"Herself," he corrected. "She drowned herself."

"Matthew."

"You don't believe me," he said quietly.

"I believe you think it's the truth."

His gaze bored into hers as if drilling holes straight through to the other side. "That's not enough."

He wanted to hit something, maybe hammer a nail, reshape a horseshoe. Strike something with his fists or a tool, it didn't matter. He had felt this way only one other time, and he had never expected to feel such a need for violent release again.

Instead he climbed up into the hayloft and threw down bales of hay until the sweat ran into his eyes and stained his shirt at the armpits and down the middle of his back. By then half the hay was on the main floor of the barn. He would have to move most of it back, but he still had enough energy from his anger to take care of it without a problem.

She didn't believe him. He told her things he had never told another living soul. Not his brother, his mother, the bishop, not even Beth's grieving family. He'd told Gracie and she hadn't believed him. Even worse, she wanted to spout about God's will. How he hated those two words. He'd heard them his entire life, believed them even, until his wife walked into ice-cold water and ended her life. How could he believe God had a hand in anything? There were even days when he sometimes wondered if God had simply left them all alone to the devil's follies.

Those days bothered him. He hadn't been raised to lose his faith, but how could he keep his beliefs intact when so much was trying to kill them? It was a battle he faced every day. His struggle was real, almost tangible. And he hated it.

Hated even more that Gracie didn't believe him.

He wanted her to believe him. No, he *needed* it. He had bared his soul to her. She was his wife. Maybe not in every sense of the word, but in enough that he was starting to depend on her. Not just to take care of the children, but to help guide him and their household. He valued her opinion. She knew things that other Amish women didn't know. And not because she had left and become Englisch, but because she had remained Amish and gone out into the world to help others. There was no more noble cause. And he admired her for that. The Amish were always talking about helping your neighbor and they did, but sometimes only in their community. They kept so closely to themselves that they couldn't see others, on the outside, might need help as well. But not Gracie. She had seen it and answered the call. And he loved her for it.

He stopped, hay bale raised halfway into throwing position. He loved Gracie.

How had that happened?

He couldn't love her. She didn't believe in him.

But that wasn't true. She did believe in him. She had told him as much. She just didn't believe that he had told the truth about Beth's drowning. She wouldn't believe that he had any part of it. But he knew what happened. He could have stopped Beth. He should have stopped her. He should have seen the signs, or at least had her mother come down to be with Beth after the baby was born. If he had been paying attention, if he had been watching, he would have seen. And Beth would be with them still today.

And Gracie would still be living with the Gingeriches.

Somehow, that didn't sound right. She was supposed to be here with him and the kids. Supposed to be a part of their family. They were calling her Mamm and depending on her for things kids depend on their *mamm* for. They loved her. Especially the baby.

He tossed the hay bale and reached for another. And she was wrong about that too. He had said her name. The baby hated him, but he'd said her name. Why wouldn't he? He was her father. But yet he couldn't remember a time when her name had been on his lips. Since Beth had died she had been "the baby" even in his thoughts.

How had that happened? He shook his head. He had no idea, but he wasn't about to try and analyze it. He'd done enough soul searching for one afternoon.

And no matter what thoughts he turned over in his head,

he couldn't help but remember: Gracie hadn't believed him, and that's what hurt the most.

By the time supper rolled around, Gracie still hadn't seen Matthew, and she wondered if they would get a repeat of those earlier days of their marriage where he would come home late and eat whatever supper she had left for him in a pie plate on the stove. Or if he would come home at all.

The hurt look in his eyes was heartbreaking. And she hated that she was the one who put it there. But couldn't he see?

Everything was God's will. They didn't have to understand it, they didn't have to like it, but to question it would surely drive a person crazy.

Had God willed the hurricane that had devastated the Gulf Coast? Had He wanted all those people to die? She didn't know for certain, but she had to accept that He had a plan and it was up to them to follow.

She did know that it was God's will for her to go help. It was God's will that she and Matthew got married, and it was God's will that he didn't want to have any more children even though that was her biggest dream in life.

Maybe she couldn't have children of her own and God was sparing her that pain and heartache. She didn't know. Might not ever know. But she had to trust Him and that trust was something Matthew had lost. She ached for him, prayed that he would somehow get that trust back. For without trust in God's will, what did they have? Nothing. Chaos. Heartbreak.

She leaned out the front door. "Come to supper!" There were a few whoops and hollers and four dusty boys came scrambling toward the porch. She shook her head. "Wash up first."

"Is it chicken and ducklings?" Henry asked.

Gracie didn't bother to correct him. They had tried so many times, but he was convinced ducklings was the proper term and couldn't be persuaded to call them anything else. "Not tonight," she said.

He stuck out his lower lip.

"It's fried chicken," she said, hoping that would smooth it over. She had made it special for Matthew, hoping to extend it as an olive branch. *I'm sorry I hurt you, but I still care about you.* It was a weak offering, but the only one she had right then.

"Where's Dat?" Stephen asked as he ducked into the house.

Somewhere. "He'll be in in a bit." She hoped anyway.

"He loves fried chicken," Henry said, grinning at her as he followed his brother into the house.

The twins were right behind but their hands, now wet, looked worse than before, like muddy little tentacles.

"Let's try that again, boys." She turned them around and, careful not to let the screen door slam behind her, marched them back to the water spigot. She turned it on and showed them how to rub their hands together to help the water remove the dirt.

She might not be getting a baby all her own, but she had five wonderful children who were calling her Mamm. She shouldn't ask for any more than that.

"Mamm, Baby Grace needs you," Henry called from the doorway. He ducked back inside, letting the screen door slam. She could hear Baby's wails from where she stood in the yard. Gracie was needed. Matthew might not need her, but the children did. She loved them, and they loved her. God's will had surely been fulfilled. She smiled a little to herself.

"Come on, boys. Let's go see about your sister."

Baby's tragedy turned out to be a dropped binky that had rolled under the table. She had been propped up in her highchair waiting patiently for her supper and gnawing on her pacifier, something she seemed to be doing a lot lately. Gracie knew it was early, but she had a feeling that Baby might already be cutting teeth. It was exciting and a little sad at the same time. Gracie had only been there a few weeks, but she could already see the change in the baby. She was growing up so fast. Too fast. But wasn't that what all mothers thought?

She retrieved the binky, got her bottle ready, and gathered the boys around the table.

But Matthew was still not there. She thought she had seen him in the barn when she was helping the twins wash their hands.

"Can we eat?" Henry asked. He had his hands in his lap as if he didn't trust himself to grab the food and start devouring it. He was swinging his legs with enough enthusiasm to rock himself back and forth.

"Not yet." She gave them a quick smile to let them know that everything was okay—even if it really wasn't—and started toward the door. "He must not have heard me call him."

She hurried outside and over to the barn.

"Matthew?" she called, easing inside. She thought she had seen him, but she wasn't positive. She might be searching in an empty barn. "Are you in here?"

The space seemed a little messy. Hay was strewn around in places that didn't normally have hay. Maybe she was mistaken, and he wasn't in there. If he had been, the barn would surely look better, neater, than it did. He would have swept any loose hay into one of the horse stalls, or over into the pigpen. Not left it on the floor.

"Matthew?" She rounded the corner on the side where the hayloft was located. *Mess* was not a strong enough word for what she encountered. It looked ransacked, as if vandals had broken in, busted hay bales, thrown the loose hay about, then run out the back.

But Matthew stood in the middle of the mess, sweat nearly turning his shirt a darker shade of blue. Only a few patches around his belly and next to his collar told its true color.

"What are you doing?" she asked.

"I decided to, uh, rearrange the hayloft."

She looked up at the jumble of bales that made up the loft. "Uh-huh." What else could she say? It was all a mess. Not at all like Matthew. She wasn't sure what was going on, just that he wasn't hurt. It seemed like he was trying to work through whatever was bothering him using the hay as a means to figure it out.

"Supper's ready."

"I'm not hungry."

He had to be, with the amount of "work" he had done in the barn. It looked as if he had tossed all the stored hay onto the main floor of the barn, then had thrown it back into the loft from where he stood now. She wasn't sure why he would perform such an act. But it certainly seemed that was what he had been doing.

"It's fried chicken," she said, using her most enticing tone. She sounded ridiculous and was not surprised when he shook his head.

"Save me a plate." He turned back to whatever it was he was doing. Except he simply stood there until she agreed and left the barn.

Save him a plate, she fumed all the way back to the house. She would save him a plate, but she didn't want to. She wanted to let the boys eat their fill of the chicken, not correct them when they left too much meat on the bone, and throw the rest of it out for Pepper.

But she wouldn't. It might annoy her that he wasn't accepting her offer. After all, how could she make amends when she couldn't get him in the same room? That didn't mean she was giving up though.

She went back into the house, sat down at the table, and smiled at the children. "Let's pray."

"Dat's not eating?" Henry asked.

"He asked me to make him a plate." She could tell the children were a little disappointed. After having their mother gone, and now their father gone, they craved the normalcy they had once before: two parents sitting with them around the table, eating in harmony.

She placed Baby's hands together on her highchair tray and bowed her own head. She prayed as she always did that God would bless the food and nourish her body in his service. But she wanted to pray for guidance on how to make amends with Matthew and get their marriage back on its unique track. It might not be a normal marriage, but it was the one she had and she wanted to save it. But she was afraid that if she started praying about her and Matthew, they might all miss supper.

She released Baby's hands and lifted her head, then shuffled in place enough to let the other children know that prayer time was over.

"Now," she said, shifting a little more. Then she rose and started doling out food. She fixed Matthew something to eat in the tin pie plate she used when she knew he was going to be late, served the children, made her own plate, then lifted Baby from her highchair.

"You always feed her first," Stephen said, his mouth full of bread and applesauce.

"*Jah*," she agreed. "But don't talk with your mouth full."

He swallowed. "Sorry, Mamm."

"Why?" Henry asked. His mouth was full too, and Gracie could only assume that he wanted the same attention his brother had received.

"I feed her first because I'm her *mamm*," she said. It was

the only reason she could come up with. "That's just what *mamm*s do. Like reminding their children not to talk when they have food in their mouths."

As far as answers go it wasn't very informative, but it was exactly right on. *Mamm*s took care of their children. They made sure they weren't hungry or cold. That they had a place to sleep and a roof over their heads. Why? Because that was just what *mamm*s did.

Thoughts of Beth flooded in on her. *Mamm*s took care of the children. That was their job. It was something she had known since she was a little girl, playing with dolls. *Mamm*s never wanted to leave their children, would never do anything to hurt their children. But she knew that last statement to be naïve. She had heard enough on the news, even seen some in her own community. There were parents who were rough with their children. Too rough.

She remembered the doctor questioning them about Henry's arm. How he broke it, what he was doing, who was around, and where his parents were at the time.

And if that statement wasn't true—if not all *mamm*s took care of their children—then how could she believe that the other ones were? That was more than naive; that was plain ol' stupid.

"Gracie!" From the tone of his voice, she suspected that it wasn't the first time Henry had called her name.

"*Jah*. Sorry."

She popped the bottle from the baby's mouth. While she had been daydreaming, Baby had fallen asleep and was using the nipple as a pacifier.

Gracie lifted her as gently as she could and propped her on her shoulder. Maybe a burp or two would sneak out without waking her. She should have been paying more attention instead of trying to figure out the mystery of Beth's drowning.

There was no mystery, she reminded herself. Beth had

fallen into the creek, possibly hit her head, and drowned, facedown in the water. And that's all there was to it.

"Gracie," Henry started again. "When's Dat coming in?"

"When he gets his work done." It was a lame answer. So lame, if it had been a horse they would have had to shoot it. But it was all she could think of. She rubbed Baby's back, still hoping to work a little gas out before she laid her down for the night.

With any luck Baby would sleep through the night, but Gracie wasn't counting on it. She was going to sleep really early and would probably wake up hungry just after two.

"Do we have to wait dessert on him?" Stephen asked.

"I want to eat dessert now," Benjamin said. "Please." *Sweet child.*

"Finish your green beans."

He made a face and she returned a stern *mamm* look. He grabbed the remaining green beans on his plate and shoved them all into his mouth at once.

"Benjamin," she scolded. She had thought too soon. He was mostly a sweet child. But he had his times. "We don't eat with our hands."

"We eat bread with our hands," Henry said.

"That's different."

"Why?" he asked, though they all seemed to be waiting for an answer.

And this was what Eunice would call a *mamm* conundrum. How to explain and still get her point across? "We do eat bread with our hands," she patiently explained. "There are a great many foods we can eat with our hands. But the rest must be eaten with a fork or a spoon. You boys are old enough to know which is which and remember to do it. Green beans are one of those fork foods."

"Is french fries a fork food?" Thomas asked.

"They can be. I know a lot of people who eat their french fries with a fork."

"What about chicken nuggets?" Benjamin asked.

"I suppose they can be either." And this was another conundrum.

"Mashed potatoes and chicken fried steak?" Henry doubled over in a fit of giggles.

"Silly boy." She waggled one finger at him. "You know the answer to that already."

He laughed harder.

"Do we get to eat dessert now or not?" Stephen was serious about his sweets.

"*Jah*." She stood, careful not to disturb Baby Grace and rubbed her back to soothe her. "Let me put Baby to bed."

Surprisingly enough, no one grumbled over the delay.

"And while I'm gone, clean your plates so you'll grow up big and strong."

These words did prompt a few protests, but she didn't acknowledge them. She had found that it was better not to engage.

And the exchange had given her an idea. She needed to find out Matthew's favorite dessert. She would make him whatever it was as a peace offering. It wouldn't be enough to undo whatever pain she had caused him, however unintentional, but it would be a step in the right direction and that was all she could hope for.

Matthew moved out of the hall and into the shadows as Gracie crossed to the staircase. He had heard the entire exchange between her and his children. She was strict on them but somehow managed to get everyone to like her, accept her. And for that he was grateful. She was good with them. She was a good mother. And he felt a stab of guilt that she wouldn't have a baby of her own. But she didn't understand what he was saving her from—pain, heartbreak, possibly death. She should be grateful, but she was spouting off about God's will. And the whole thing had him tied up in knots.

She was incredible and yet so horribly wrong. And she didn't believe him.

That in itself had him doubting everything he believed, then building the argument back up even stronger. He knew what he knew. Gracie hadn't been there. She hadn't seen. She had only seen the face Beth had shown everyone at church. Beth had done her best to hide her own pain and sadness, but he had seen it, simmering there just below the surface. And just as he allowed her, she pretended that everything was fine. Perhaps she even believed that if she continued to pretend it would somehow make it so. He should have seen. He should have done something. He had failed Beth. He wouldn't fail Gracie, even if it meant breaking her heart in the process.

"Matthew?"

He whirled around, caught lurking in the shadows of his own house. "*Jah*," he said stupidly.

"Come in." Her tone was inviting even as she frowned at him. "Supper's still on the table. We were just about to have dessert."

"*Jah*," he said again. How dumb could one man sound?

"Are you okay?" she asked softly.

He nodded to keep from sounding like a complete and utter idiot, then gestured toward his clothes. "I need to clean up."

"Do you want me to bring you some water?"

Why was she being so nice to him when he was ruining all her dreams? "No, *danki*. I'll get it. You go on back in there with the kids."

She nodded, albeit a tad reluctantly. "Food's waiting on you."

"Okay." He nodded, then turned away, unable to look into those caring blue eyes, knowing that he was going to break her heart every day for the rest of her life.

Chapter Nineteen

The politeness in the house was beginning to get on her nerves. It had been days since Matthew had confessed all to her. Days since they had worked hard to figure out where they stood with each other. And still not knowing, they had fallen into a pattern of polite remoteness.

They greeted each other in the morning, ate breakfast together, then began the day's work. Most days Matthew came home to eat with the family at noon, then left again to see to the crops and other chores that had to be done. He was always home by suppertime, once again eating with them like they were the perfect little family. The children loved it. Once more their life was as it should be. They had a mother and a father who loved them, even if they didn't love each other.

But one thing this whole ordeal had shown her was how much she truly cared for Matthew. She had thought she was falling for him before. Maybe she had been a little infatuated with him. He was her husband, after all. But now she truly loved him.

She hated it. Wished she could take it back. But she loved the way he was with his children, even Baby, who still cried, no matter what he did to soothe her. He took care of his farm, took care of her, even though she saw betrayal in his eyes every time he looked at her. What she wouldn't give to make those feelings go away. But she knew he didn't want to hear any more of what she had to say about God's will and plan for their lives.

And she really didn't want to hear again all his theories about Beth's drowning. She couldn't comprehend the actions he was describing, and she had begun to believe that the stories he was telling her were simply interpretations on how a man looked at things.

She might not be worldly like Leah and Hannah, but she knew a couple of things, and one of those was that men and women were different in more ways than just physical. When she was on her mission trip she had a tent mate who was reading a book called something like *Men Are from Mars*. Gracie had thought the title was interesting, like some kind of science fiction story, but when she asked, the girl had laughed and told her it was about the different ways men and women respond to their world. And how men and women will react differently just because they are men and women.

The concept was intriguing to Gracie and she had spent the remainder of the trip covertly studying different people around her to see if those gender theories were correct. And for all her observations, they were. And that would completely explain why Matthew was seeing something that wasn't there. That he believed that Beth had done the unthinkable.

Another thing she had learned was that the old adage was true: The way to a man's heart was through his stomach. Or in this case the way to peace in her house. And not a pretend peace, but an honest-to-goodness harmony that she had been working toward from the start. That was going to start with a homemade chess pie. She had found out from Eunice that Matthew's favorite pie was an old-time Southern favorite, rich, yummy chess pie. Remarkably enough, Eunice seemed to be the pie directory of their district. Somehow she knew everyone's favorite pie and could recall it at a moment's notice. So tonight when Gracie got home, she was going to make him a chess pie and see if she could bring back the harmony that had been missing before the children realized that it was gone.

But for now, it was cousins' day. And she had lotions and soaps to make. Once the boys were settled inside with Eunice and a slice of pie each and Baby was in with Mammi Glick, Gracie joined Hannah and Leah in front of the house where they usually worked. It was almost too much to work indoors with all the scented oils and such that they used. The smell could get overwhelming real quick. So unless it was raining, they were out front every Tuesday, mixing and talking.

"Okay," Leah said, pulling a pencil from behind one ear to underline something on the list she held. "We have thirty-five special orders. No wait, thirty-six."

"Wow!" Hannah looked over at Gracie with a happy nod.

"That's amazing," Gracie agreed. "Why so many?" They had never had this many before.

"Graduation," Hannah guessed.

"And Father's Day," Leah added.

"Father's Day?" Gracie was surprised. She didn't know any man who wanted to smell like vanilla and orange blossoms.

"I put a sign up about more manly scents coming soon, and the women seemed to love it."

Gracie peeked over one of Leah's shoulders. "That's great, but how are we going to make cedar eucalyptus?"

"With cedar and eucalyptus oils, of course." She held up a set of bottles of essential oils that Gracie had never seen before. "Voilà," she said with a great flourish. "Let me introduce you to the men's line of goat-milk skin care."

Hannah and Leah were so excited that Gracie felt the need to pretend to be, as well. But she didn't understand this men's line that Leah had dreamt up. It made no sense to her at all. Men didn't use lotions and milky soaps meant to moisturize the skin instead of scrubbing the dirt out from under their fingernails. But her cousins seemed to think it was a sure bet. She supposed with thirty-six orders that they could possibly be right. And perhaps the right lotion after shaving would be a welcome item for men who shaved every day. And not just their upper lips.

Then she tried to imagine Matthew using any of the products they were about to make. The image wouldn't come. She tried the same for Jamie, Leah's husband, and Aaron, Hannah's soon-to-be. Aaron was the only one she could imagine possibly using the lotion, but even that was a stretch.

But she was going to trust her cousins to know more about this sort of thing than she did. And maybe she would take a little sample home to Matthew. He might laugh her out of the house. Then again, he might actually like it.

They made their regular items first, then started experimenting with the men's scents. After a couple of missteps, Hannah finally got down the first formula and from there they were off. And they were still there an hour later when Jamie, Leah's husband, came walking down the lane, their son Peter at his side.

"Hi!" Leah waved when they got close enough to hear. Peter started to run ahead, but since he had injured one of his legs in the fire that had killed his family the year before, he wasn't too far ahead of Jamie as he walked toward them.

A round of greetings went up, but the cheery atmosphere didn't last long.

"What's wrong?" Leah asked.

"Peter, go on in the house. We'll be in there in a minute. Go ahead and tell Mammi, okay?"

"*Jah*, Dat," Peter said, and hopped up the steps and into the house.

"Spill it," Leah demanded. But instead of speaking, Jamie handed her an envelope. "Oh my," she breathed, and turned it so Gracie and Hannah could see.

Gracie would have known that handwriting anywhere. "Tillie?"

Leah nodded but continued to stare at the envelope.

From what Gracie could see, there was a return address, but it was from somewhere in Tennessee. The letter was postmarked in Memphis so Tillie couldn't have gone too far. The thought that she was out there and close comforted Gracie on some level. It made her feel like Tillie was safe somehow and maybe even happy. But that could all be wishful thinking on her part.

"Are you going to open it?" Jamie asked.

It was addressed to Leah and had been delivered to her shop in town. But surely the rest of them were mentioned.

"Uh, yeah," Leah said, but her fingers trembled as she turned it over and tore at the glued seam.

After what seemed like forever, the envelope was opened, the letter out and unfolded. Then Leah started to read.

Hannah nudged her in the ribs. "Out loud, sister."

> *"Dear Leah,*
>
> *"I so hope this letter finds you well. Things here are good. Melvin is still enjoying his job at the garage. All he has ever wanted was to fix engines and he says he's really good at it. I'm glad he's seeing his dreams come true.*
>
> *"I have been working at a day-care center down the street from where we live. It's not the best job—*

pay wise—but they are good to me and don't seem to mind that I only went to school until I was fourteen. The director said I am smart and a quick learner. I suppose that counts for something. I enjoy working with the children. They are a joy every day. I don't know what I would do without them there to make me laugh.

"We're still living in the same apartment as we were the last time I wrote, though we may have to move soon. The landlord wants to raise our rent at the end of next month. The place isn't worth the money he wants for it, but there aren't many places here in our price range. Not sure what we're going to do. Stay put for a while, I suppose, and see what God provides.

"It's amazing how many things are different here in the real Englisch world from the world we always imagined. There seems to be too much color and light here, way too much of everything, which has me longing for the green pastures butting up to a blue sky dotted with fluffy white clouds.

"And Mamm's cherry spice pie. I've tried to make it three times, and even though I can remember the recipe by heart, it doesn't come out like Mamm's. I wonder why that is.

"I suppose I should sign off for now and get some sleep. Tomorrow is the first day of summer vacation and we will have more children than we normally do. Lord, please give me strength, insight, and wisdom.

"Please tell everyone that I miss them and pray every night for their health and well-being. Mamm, Dat, Gracie, Hannah, Brandon, everyone. And please tell them I love them too.

> *"Until we see each other again,*
> *"Tillie"*

As Gracie and the others watched, Leah stared at the letter, then quietly folded it to rights.

"Wow." Hannah rocked back on her heels, but Gracie couldn't tell if it was from shock or if the motion was somehow helping her assimilate the words.

"Wow is right," Leah agreed.

Jamie backed up a couple of steps. "I think I'll go in and save Mamm from Peter. He talks so much these days she may be missing a limb or two if I leave them together for too long." He gave a small chuckle that held very little mirth, then headed toward the house.

"Don't tell Mamm," Leah called.

He gave a flicking wave of his hand and let himself inside.

"Not yet," she continued.

Hannah shook her head. "We can't keep this from her for long."

"I know, but . . ." She trailed off, not saying what they were all thinking: Was Tillie in some sort of trouble?

"Do you think the return address is correct?" Hannah asked. "We could go there and make sure she's all right."

"You could drive," Gracie said.

Leah pulled her smartphone from the pocket of her long denim skirt and started thumbing in commands. "That town is almost four hours from here. We could get up early and make a day of it. Maybe even be back before Mamm realizes we all left together."

"Are we going to tell her about the letter before or after?" Hannah asked.

"Before," Gracie said.

"After," Leah answered at the same time.

"Hold on," Hannah said. "Let's talk about this a minute. We shouldn't go off half-cocked."

"Agreed," Leah said with a quick nod.

"She doesn't say that anything is wrong," Hannah continued.

"She doesn't have to," Leah reminded her.

"It's what she doesn't say. But are those things worth going after her? I mean, maybe if we leave it she'll come to her senses and come home on her own," Gracie said. "If they can't find a place to live."

Hannah and Leah thought about it a moment.

"I don't think that will be what brings her home."

"Melvin," Leah said with a wrinkle in her nose. "He's not good enough for her."

Gracie smiled. "Is anyone?"

"We found your match." Leah playfully bumped shoulders with her.

Gracie did her best to maintain her pleased look.

"What?" Hannah asked.

Evidently she failed. "Nothing." She tried that smile on again.

"Really?" Leah threw her hands in the air. "It's not enough that we're worried sick about Tillie, now we have to worry even more for you?"

"You don't need to concern yourself," Gracie said. Finally she had managed to pull her lips into something that at least felt like a normal smile. "Everything is fine."

"Translation: I'm not going to talk about it," Leah said.

Gracie shook her head. "It's very personal." She dropped her gaze to the table in front of her. They had packaged up about half the products they needed to, but she had a feeling no one was in the mood to make lotions anymore.

"Uh, as close as sisters," Leah scoffed, pointing a finger at each of them in turn.

"What my eloquent twin means to say is we're here for you if you need us. You know that, right?"

"I do," Gracie said.

"Eloquent?" Leah asked. "What kind of Amish woman uses the word *eloquent*?"

"The kind that will also chase you around with a switch if you don't behave."

Leah stuck out her tongue. "I'm just trying to take care of my peeps."

"What kind of Mennonite woman uses the word *peeps*?" Hannah countered.

"Really great ones," Leah answered.

Gracie had no idea what marshmallow candy had to do with anything they had been talking about.

By some miracle they managed to finish mixing and packaging the bottles of lotion and soaps that they needed for the special orders and to replenish both Leah's store and Gracie's tiny shop. Eunice had taken to carrying a few in her own little store, but not much. The idea was to get the customer interested and send them on to Leah's store for a better selection.

And it was unanimously decided to tell Eunice about Tillie's letter after they finished their work. It was hard enough for them to concentrate knowing that Tillie had reached out to them, but when her mother found out, nothing else would be accomplished that day. Gracie remembered how it was when Tillie had first left. Eunice had been a mess. She had lost two daughters, then gained them back, only to lose another.

"Are you ready?" Leah asked.

They nodded and headed into the house.

"Mamm," Hannah called.

Then they all exchanged encouraging looks. This wasn't going to be easy.

Eunice bustled out of the kitchen wiping her hands on her apron. "*Jah*?"

Leah extended the letter to her.

She looked at it, then back to the three of them. "What is it?" she asked, not touching it and eyeing it like it could turn rabid any minute.

"A letter," Leah said.

"I can see that," Eunice said. "Who's it from?"

"Tillie," Hannah said.

Time seemed to stop for a moment.

"I don't understand," Eunice said. She reached for the letter with trembling hands. "Why is it open?"

"Tillie sent it to Leah," Gracie said as gently as possible. "To her shop."

Eunice turned the letter over in her hands and walked stiffly over to the dining room table. She collapsed into one of the chairs and continued to stare at the envelope in her hands.

"Aren't you going to read it?" Leah asked.

Eunice looked at her blankly, then nodded. "*Jah*," she replied, then took out the paper from inside.

Not wanting to hover, Gracie pulled out a chair and sat. Leah and Hannah followed suit. They watched as Eunice read and reread the letter.

"Why did she send it to you?" Eunice asked.

Leah shrugged. "I don't know. Maybe because I came back."

"You came back Mennonite," Hannah pointed out.

"Not everyone has the same epiphany," Leah retorted. Hannah hadn't planned on returning to the Amish church, but love and home can do that to a person, make them want things they had before.

"Is she happy?" Eunice asked.

Leah shrugged. "It's hard to say, but I don't think so."

"I think she feels out of place." Gracie had become an expert in that lately.

"What does that mean for us?" Eunice asked.

"She'll either figure it out or return to what's comfortable—home," Hannah said.

But going back wasn't really an option for Gracie. She had to figure it out, was still trying to figure out what to do about Matthew and his cockamamie ideas concerning his wife's death. Maybe if she prayed about it some more, the answer would come to her. She hoped, anyway.

It was after suppertime when Gracie pulled the buggy onto the dirt lane that led to Matthew's house. Her house. She needed to start seeing it as her own home as well as his. They were married for life, and that wasn't going to change anytime soon.

She stopped for a moment and righted the sign that pointed down their lane declaring goat-milk lotions and soaps were available along with strawberries, seasonal vegetables, and candles.

She had just added that last part. But she figured making candles would be a good chore for the boys over the summer when they weren't helping Matthew. They were still too young for heavy work, and candle making was fun and profitable if managed correctly. Plus it might keep Henry out of trouble. For an hour or two.

She straightened the sign and found a big enough stick to brace it from the back. It seemed that the sign was down almost every time she came past. She wasn't sure if it was not put up properly or if Englisch pranksters were knocking it down in their own version of a joke.

She gave it one last shove into the ground, dusted her hands, and climbed back into the buggy.

She hadn't meant to stay so long at the Gingeriches, but after the letter, Eunice had so many questions, most of which they couldn't answer. But they agreed that Tillie seemed to be dodging the issue. She said that Melvin was happy, and she was happy for him, but not that she was happy for herself. She liked her job, but they were struggling and didn't have enough money to be able to handle a rent increase. She didn't say how much, but they all had the feeling that any amount would have been over their budget.

Leah and Hannah convinced Eunice to give Tillie more time, and she would come home on her own. Gracie hoped they were right.

"Don't you think so, Mamm?"

In the back of the buggy, Henry was chattering on about Eunice and pies. He was convinced his new "aunt" was the best pie maker in the whole entire county.

Pie. She had been going to make Matthew a pie this afternoon, but that time was gone. It was past supper. Maybe tomorrow.

"If you think her pies are good, you should have some of her cake," Gracie answered, still basking in the glow of being called Mamm.

"We did!" he exclaimed. "At the wedding. It was good and all, but pie is better."

"Not all pie is better than cake," Stephen protested.

"I like apples pie," Thomas said.

"Me too," Benjamin added, not one to be left out of the conversation.

"It is so," Henry countered. "Even the yuckiest pie is better than cake."

"It's apple pie," Stephen corrected in that grown-up way of his. He pushed his glasses up on his nose and gave a little nod. They slid right back down again.

"That's what I said," Thomas countered. "Apples pie."

"Me too." Benjamin echoed his earlier words.

"Name one yucky pie," Gracie demanded with a laugh.

Henry tapped his chin thoughtfully as he contemplated her request.

These boys were the light of her life these days. Like

Tillie with her children at the day care where she worked, Gracie wouldn't know what to do without them. There had been a time when she couldn't imagine starting a marriage with an instant family, but now she wouldn't have had it any other way.

God's will, see?

"There are no yucky pies," Henry finally declared.

"Exactly." Gracie laughed.

"But that chocolate cake that Mamm used to make." Stephen's gaze took on a dreamy look.

"The one with the globs of white stuff on the top?" he asked.

When he put it like that . . .

Stephen nodded. "A hurricane-something cake. I think. Dat loved it."

"Yummy," Henry said, rubbing his tummy as he licked his lips.

"Better than pie?" Gracie asked.

Henry didn't hesitate. "Almost."

Gracie laughed, then turned her attention back to the lane. The house was in plain view now. The thought that she would have to see if she could find Beth's recipes and make this hurricane cake for the boys withered as she caught sight of Matthew on the porch. His expression mirrored a hurricane.

"Where have you been?" The storm in his eyes was nothing compared to the one in his voice.

She stopped the buggy in the usual spot and hopped down as if nothing was wrong. Truly nothing.

"How about we let the kids go wash up for supper, and I'll explain what's going on."

Her calm tone seemed to take a little of that wild wind from him, but not all. "*Jah*," he said, his voice gruff and rusty.

Gracie tried to figure out what his problem was as she got all the kids unloaded and on to getting ready for supper.

It would have to be a sandwich night. Was he angry about that? Sometimes he was so hard to figure out. And they said women were complicated!

Once the last boy had rounded the corner of the house and Baby's carrier had been lifted from the buggy and set on the porch, Matthew lunged toward her. Her first instinct was to take a step back, but she knew he wouldn't hurt her. He was big and strong, but a teddy bear with marshmallow-cream filling.

His arms came around her and pulled her close. "I was so worried." He rocked them back and forth, running his hands along the edge of her spine as he did so. Gracie wanted to close her eyes and melt into his embrace. She relished the warmth of him, his strength and size, but she knew the truth. She knew how he felt about her, and if she let herself fall in with his worry, she might not ever find her way back out. *Keep thy heart with all diligence.*

"You were worried about the children." She tried to pull free. She loved being this close to him, but it was not good for her heart, which was too fond of him by far.

But he kept her close. "I was worried about you," he promised. "So worried about you."

"Worried. It's Tuesday. Cousins' day."

"You've never stayed over there this long before."

"We got a letter from Tillie." This time when she tried to move away, he let her.

"Eunice's youngest?"

Gracie nodded. "I don't think she's very happy. I think she might leave Melvin and come back."

"Leave him? Aren't they married?"

She shook her head. "It'll be hard on her, having to come back and confess everything." It would be more than hard, and the backlash would be tremendous. The Amish forgave, but not all forget. Gracie was worried that once Tillie returned—and she was certain she would—

that she might not ever marry. It was hard to say how the eligible males in the community would react to her . . . indiscretion. So hard to say.

"Don't do that again," he said, using the same voice he had earlier.

"I have to go to cousins' day." He might be the head of the household, but he couldn't dictate every minute of her life. She needed cousins' day. They needed the money it produced.

"Don't stay over there that long."

He really had been worried, but she wasn't sure she believed that he had all that worry for her; she would like to think that he was beside himself that she wasn't home, but she knew that he was really beside himself because she wasn't home with his children. Buggies on winding country roads could be a very dangerous thing.

"I won't," she promised. "Today was a special day."

He nodded. "Fine then. What's for supper?"

Gracie plopped down on the floor of her room and opened the big cedar chest there. She had peeked in it before, noting that it had at least one quilt and a few books along with a treasure box. She assumed that they all belonged to Beth and had left them as they were. But now that she had searched the kitchen and all the downstairs for a recipe book, or a box, or some kind of notebook or zip baggie that contained Beth's recipes, she was going out on a limb. Maybe they were in the cedar chest. It was worth a look. She wanted to surprise the boys and make the hurricane cake for them. Matthew too, since the chess pie idea had fallen flat.

She removed the quilts and placed them at the foot of her bed. They were beautiful. One was Beth's wedding quilt, something that she herself had been denied. She hadn't thought about it at the time, but her mother was gone, and her wedding was rushed, so there had been no time for that tradition to be upheld.

Gracie ran her fingers over the beautiful white material, imagining Beth's mother sewing it for her with love and care. There were hearts stitched around the edge and a few sets of doves, beaks closed and wings spread. It took Gracie a moment, then she saw the true pattern. The quilt was all white according to the wedding-quilt tradition, but the pattern of Beth's quilt was a double wedding ring. Gracie could only imagine the talented fingers that had quilted the beautiful piece. Maybe when Baby was older she would give it to her as her own wedding quilt.

Wiping away a tear, she removed the second quilt, a four-patch made with reds, yellows, and blues. Gracie would never have thought to put the prints and colors together, but it was interestingly beautiful. She wondered if Beth made it. If so, Henry definitely got his creative side from her.

Below the quilts she found a stack of thin hardback books. Maybe one would contain recipes. She lifted them out and set them to one side, opening the first one to a random page to see what it contained.

Words. Just lots and lots of hand-written words. But they didn't seem to be recipes. She thumbed through it a little more, but the writing all remained the same. Neat, dainty, and she wondered if it was an indication of the woman herself. She would save these for the children. They might call Gracie Mamm now, but there was another woman responsible for them being there, and she wanted to make sure they didn't forget her.

Gracie set the first book aside and picked up the next one in the stack. She flipped it open to the same thing, lots of words, probably Beth's feelings on this and that. It was good that she had written stuff down. A lot of women wrote daily about how they felt, how a Bible verse affected them, things their children did, both funny and momentous. The very thought made Gracie smile. With a child like Henry, she was bound to be very busy.

Then her gaze snagged on one word. *Samuel.*

She couldn't say why she saw it, it was just there, as if it had jumped off the page to get her attention.

2 Samuel.

A Bible verse.

Beth had written down a Bible verse. Perhaps it meant something special to her. Gracie, feeling a little like a sneaky thief, read on.

> *For we must needs die, and are as water spilt on the ground, which cannot be gathered up again.*
>
> *I feel a little like water that has been spilt. I am spread out, too thin, and no one is able to make me whole again. I pray and pray, but God doesn't answer. Or perhaps His answer is no. This is something I have to bear alone.*
>
> *I try my best not to let the children see it. Or Matthew, but I can tell he knows something is wrong. I know something is wrong. I just don't know what to do about it. Why am I so sad? Why does everything have to be so hard? Every footstep I take, every chore, every meal I must prepare, diapers to change, mouths to clean, bottoms to wipe. This should be a joyous time. My family is budding, and I have the baby girl I have always dreamed of having since I was little, learning at my mother's side. But I'm not happy. I'm tired. I'm weary. Sometimes I just want to lie down and die.*

Gracie dropped the book into her lap and covered her mouth with her hands. Beth had been depressed. She hadn't wanted to burden Matthew with the extent of her sadness. She hadn't known what to do. But none of that meant she did actually walk into the water and drown herself on purpose.

But it certainly fit. Gracie couldn't deny it any longer. She couldn't pretend that Matthew had been mistaken. No, it wasn't clear proof, but it was awfully close.

She pushed herself from the floor, then she placed the quilts back into the chest. She checked on Baby to make sure she was still sleeping soundly, then she picked up the books and headed down the stairs.

Chapter Twenty

He hadn't gotten the hay all cleaned up, and he thought perhaps he had left a little as a warning to himself. A reminder of that time. Gracie was a woman. And women were fickle, strange creatures. Sometimes he wondered what God was thinking when He decided that Adam needed a helpmeet. Maybe He thought Adam needed to be a little crazy. Not that Matthew would ever tell a soul about his musings.

But driving him out of his mind seemed to be Gracie's goal in life. She was the most amazing cook, she was so good with his children, and just as he thought he might fall in love with her she started talking about God's will. How could that be anything less than a means to shove things aside and not deal with them? Mule got sick? God's will. Buggy wheel broke? God's will. Wife walks into the creek and drowns herself?

He had to put a stop to his own thoughts. God didn't will Beth to die. He didn't will him to marry Gracie, and He certainly didn't will for them to fall in love.

Mainly because Matthew was the only one who had.

Yesterday his heart had nearly stopped when he came in

just before supper and found her and the children gone. His first thought was that she had left him. The Amish might not be able to divorce, but that didn't mean they had to live in the same house. But he shook the thought away. She hadn't left him. He only thought that because it was his biggest fear—that he lose her and the children. Any of them. He couldn't stand the thought. So when no one was home at a time when supper was usually almost on the table, he sort of went a little crazy. He had lost Beth; he couldn't lose Gracie and the kids too.

But if she hadn't left, why wasn't she home? It was late and getting later by the minute. And with every second that passed he created worse and worse scenarios in his head of all the things that could have happened to them in a buggy on the back roads of the community. And what if this time there was no friendly Eugene Dover to help her?

He'd almost passed out when he saw the buggy coming down the lane. Gracie was in the driver's seat, Stephen next to her as usual. She had turned around a little on the bench and was looking behind her, laughing at something someone had said, probably Henry.

The anger took over for a moment until she spoke in that sweet voice of hers. From that moment on he simply wanted to hold her close. His children were fine and ran off to get ready to eat. He wanted to grab them and hug them, but he let them go. But Gracie, he could hold her close.

So he had scooped her up into his arms and pulled her to him. He felt her surprise in the stiffness with which she held herself. It took great effort to let her go, and he knew in that moment he had done the worst thing he could possibly do. He truly had fallen in love with his wife!

To say the words was ridiculous.

He loved her. And it broke his heart. How could he keep the promises to himself and give her the life that she had dreamed of? His heart and his mind warred with each other. He loved her. How was he ever going to have any peace?

"Matthew?"

He whirled around. Gracie stood there behind him, a stack of books in her arms. Her cheeks were wet with tears and more continued to fall.

"Gracie." He rushed to her, wanting to take her into his arms, stopping himself just in time. "What's happened? What's the matter?"

His heart sank as he realized something could be wrong with one of the children. Someone hurt or worse.

"Gracie?"

She took a shuddering breath and tried to smile.

His heart's pounding slowed a bit.

"I found these." She held out a stack of books he had never seen before. "They belonged to Beth."

He took the books from her. They felt heavy in his hands, though they weren't that large. Weighty and warm, as if they held an energy all their own.

"Maybe you should read them," she said.

"Did you?" he asked.

"A bit, but . . . I'm not sure it's my place to see it first. Maybe not even at all."

He looked down at the books, unsure if he wanted to see what they contained.

"And I owe you sort of an apology. I didn't read much, but I saw enough to know that you were telling the truth about Beth's state of mind after she had the baby."

"So you believe me?" he asked.

"I believe that she may have harmed herself. That it's possible. But I also know that you have no proof."

He scoffed. "I don't need proof."

She closed her eyes, shook her head, then opened them again as if she had realigned everything in her mind. She gave him that sweet, gentle smile. "I know that you don't believe her death was part of God's will, but it can't be anything else. And until you understand that you had no part in it, we can never be a true family."

Fickle and strange didn't even begin to cover it.

Matthew stored the books in his room, contemplating whether he should even read the words or not. *Not* was winning. Reading Beth's feelings from her last days wouldn't change anything except to maybe make him feel that much worse, that much guiltier for the role he had played in her death. Reading them wouldn't bring her back. Some things were best left alone. But he stored them in case he wanted to read them a little later. Who knew? He just might. But for now he was better not knowing.

Then something overcame him. He picked up the book on the very top of the stack and opened it to a random page. Inside was a sketch. A small drawing of the baby's face. Below it Beth had written *Grace Ellen Byler* and under that the words *I love you.*

I love you so much, she had written. *More than you will ever be able to understand. That's why this is so hard for me. I love you and yet I can hardly bring myself to hold you. I want to, but you feel unnatural in my arms as if you belong to someone else. As if you truly are someone else's baby. But I look into your tiny face and I know that you came from my body. Even with those blue baby eyes, the resemblance is there. You are my child. And yet I feel you hate me.*

    You always seem to cry when I'm near. This breaks my heart and drives me further away until I want to take you to the house of someone you can

*love and leave you there so you'll be happy. But
then I will be unhappy. Oh, what is the solution
here? How can I live if you hate me so? How did I
become so unworthy?*

Matthew dashed the tears off his cheeks and continued
to read. Her words and thoughts were like a train wreck,
tragic and sad, but as horrific as they were, he was unable
to look away. He continued to read the jumbled message
she tried to leave for them all.

*I think perhaps you know. Somewhere in your
baby wisdom, your instincts that God gave you
when He sent you down to earth, you know that I'm
not going to be able to take care of you. You can
feel it when I hold you and my hands tremble. When
I try to love you, but it comes out all wrong. You're a
baby, but you are smart. You know when someone's
no good. How can I ever be good enough for you?*

He snapped the book closed, unable to read any more.
He knew those feelings, those very ones that Beth was talking about. He felt the same thing when he held the baby. He
wanted to hold her and have her not cry, not try to get away
from him. He wanted just once for her to accept him as her
father. She had taken to Gracie well enough; what was
wrong with him?

He put the book back on top of the stack and left them
there on the floor by his bed. He wasn't sure what he was
going to do with them, but it was as good a place as any for
now. Then he made his way back down the stairs.

The house was strangely empty. No twins running in
and out. No Stephen telling them to stop, no Henry egging
them on. No beautiful fussy baby. No unorthodox wife,

also lovely, and more than he could have ever hoped for. Where was everybody?

He went out onto the back porch, but no one was hanging clothes on the line. Someone had been, for they still flapped in the breeze. But these days there was always a load hanging out to dry. With two adults and five children the laundry never seemed to stop.

Matthew came back through the house and out onto the front porch. The front yard was quiet as well. Well, relatively speaking. A gentle breeze blew the leaves in the trees, creating a soft rustle that soothed the frayed ends of his soul. Birds chirped merrily from their branches.

He regretted reading what he had of Beth's journal and at the same time, he had no regrets at all. Maybe one day he could sit down and read them all and maybe he would truly understand what she had been going through and why she felt the need to end her life. *Jah*, he still thought she ended her life. But in all honesty, did it make a difference? She was gone. And she wasn't coming back.

"Hey, Pepper." He reached down to scratch the dog behind the ears. She let out a soft *ruff*, then raced off the porch and over to the shade tree on one side of the house. Under the tree in one of those bright plastic contraptions the baby sat, once again propped up with that weird pillow and gnawing on her fist. Gracie had told him that she thought the baby was teething, but he hadn't taken her seriously. It was too early for all that. Wasn't it? Not according to the amount of saliva the child was producing.

"What are you doing out here all alone?" he asked.

Her head wobbled as she struggled to turn and get a good look at him, and when she did her lower lip thrust out and the crying began.

What had he done now? Nothing. But that wasn't what he was going to do now.

He marched forward and lifted her from the contraption.

Her feet got tangled up and the cloth of the seat caught on her diaper, but somehow he managed to pull the squalling baby free.

"Shhh . . ." he soothed. He cradled her close. Lifted her until she was lying next to his shoulder. She pulled back, kicked her feet and otherwise fought him as if he were a known kidnapper come to get her.

She's four months old, he told himself. She doesn't even know colors yet. Some said babies couldn't even see colors at this age. He didn't know where he heard that, and he wondered if it was true. And how would anyone know? It sounded like one of those things Gracie was always talking about. He would ask her later, but for now he had a crying baby to attend to.

He patted her back as he walked to and fro, pacing with her as he did his best to soothe her.

She cried on, but he wasn't dissuaded.

"It's time to stop crying." He paused. Had he really not said her name since her mother died, as Gracie claimed? That couldn't be, that just couldn't be, but he tried to remember a time in the last four months when he had said her name. There were none. Ever since Beth had died she had become "the baby." But no more.

"It's time to stop crying, Grace. Baby Grace. You have a wonderful, beautiful life. You have a *mamm* and a *dat*, four brothers who love you—though I will admit, you're going to probably hate them in about fifteen years. But we can talk more about that when the time comes. You have a great dog. Just don't tell her I said so. And you have no reason to cry. I love you," he said. "I love you so very, very much, and I'm going to do everything in my power to make you happy. You got that?"

Sometime during his speech, her sobbing stopped, trickled away and now all that was left were a few stray tears wetting her chubby baby cheeks.

"That's better." He kissed those remaining tears away, then blew little raspberries in the crook of her neck like he had seen Gracie do.

She made a strangled noise, and he pulled away, trying to discover what was wrong with her. But it was nothing. She was smiling at him, reaching out to touch his face with her slobbery fingers. He laughed and she made that same noise again. She was laughing at him and he swore he had never heard a sweeter sound.

"What's going on?"

He turned as Gracie came around the house. The bottom half of her skirt was wet and the boys followed behind her. Each one of them was wet in varying degrees. Henry seemed to bear the most water and mud. No surprise there. And he held a dirty rag underneath his chin. He and Thomas wore identical impish smiles, though Gracie didn't appear as charmed by whatever had just transpired. Stephen and Benjamin looked outright annoyed. Matthew had never been happier to see them in his life. They were beautiful and now he had a deeper appreciation for them all.

Gracie said they couldn't be a family until he understood God's will. This moment in time was all he needed. This moment. His entire life had been building toward this moment. Everything that happened had led to this moment, standing in the side yard. His baby girl, for once not crying at the sight of him. His boys, wet, dirty, some annoyed, others happy with whatever mischief they had caused. His wife, his beautiful, wise wife leading the way.

"What happened?" he called.

Her eyes widened when she saw that he was holding a gurgling, laughing Baby Grace. "Not anything as interesting as what happened up here."

"Just making peace," he said with a smile. She was smart and would figure out the rest. He was just glad that he had broken free from whatever was holding him back from having a normal relationship with his daughter. Something had shifted for them today. For him even. The sky seemed bluer. The sun brighter and everything a little sweeter. Maybe because of Beth's journal. Who knew? Whatever the reason he was grateful. He settled Grace into the crook of his arm and turned his attention to his wife. "You?"

"Henry decided that it would be fun to set some crawdad traps at the creek."

He frowned. "We don't have any crawdad traps."

"Right. So he and Thomas decided to make some. Don't look at the screen door."

"Henry." His voice was both a warning and a chastisement.

"Sorry, Dat." Henry said the words without removing the rag. There was a story there, but Matthew knew they would get to it in time.

"But when they got down to the creek, they got their feet stuck in the mud. And they called for help," Gracie continued.

"You went down to the creek by yourselves?"

"Sorry, Dat," Henry said.

"Me too," Thomas said.

"So Stephen and Benjamin went down to help them and—"

"Wait. Let me guess. They got stuck in the mud too."

"Right. Then I had to go down."

"But you didn't get stuck?" he asked.

She shook her head. "Grace of God."

He chuckled lightly, then stopped himself. It really wasn't funny. They had broken the rules, but he was grateful that they had all come out of it okay. "I guess we need to go inside and talk about this screen door and boys going down to the creek without an adult."

"Aww, Dat," Stephen protested. "Me and Benjamin

wouldn't have gone down there if Henry and Thomas hadn't already been there. We were trying to help."

"Noted," he said and Stephen breathed a sigh of relief.

"And that talk may have to wait until we get back from the doctor," Gracie said.

Alarm ran through him like a jolt of lightning. But he pushed that anxiety aside. If something were terribly wrong, Gracie wouldn't have stood there chatting about crawdads and screen doors, she would have taken whoever it was immediately to the doctor. He took a breath. His family was there, fine and whole. "What now?"

"After I got everyone unstuck, Henry decided to check his traps and fell in. He cut his chin on a piece of glass or something. He's going to need stitches."

It was well after dark by the time Gracie and Henry made it back to the house. Henry, normally so energetic, had fallen asleep on the way home, his head in her lap. She watched the miles go by, running her fingers through his fine blond hair.

Something had happened today. Something with Matthew, and she needed to know what it was. She was hopeful, but couldn't allow herself to overshoot what it all meant.

She woke Henry up when they pulled up to the house. She paid the driver in cash and threw in a couple of bottles of goat-milk lotion to sweeten the deal.

Then the two of them made their way inside.

The entire time they had been at the medical clinic waiting for a nurse to come clean the mud and creek water out of his scraped leg and cut chin, she had been thinking about Matthew, the shift she had seen in him when she had come back from the creek.

She had meant what she said. They could never be a true family if he couldn't accept God's will for what it was. But she knew that it was possible that it might never come to pass. And she was prepared to accept that. They would always be two parents with five children between them and nothing more. She couldn't say that was the way she had imagined her life would be, but she was willing to accept it as part of God's plan for her. God's will. And if Matthew couldn't see that for what it was . . .

There are none so blind as those who will not see.

But she was home now and there was a glimmer of hope that Matthew had had a change of heart. She knew she was reaching, but after seeing him with Baby this afternoon, that hope had flared. Then he had offered to take Henry to the doctor so she could clean up instead of riding to the medical center and waiting for hours for Henry to get treated. That hope grew bigger. Big enough that she was having to keep it contained. And still it swelled like yeast bread rising.

"Pull your shoes off by the door," Gracie told him. It was summertime and if she allowed him to take them to his room she would never see them again.

"*Jah*, Mamm," he mumbled sleepily.

"Then go on upstairs to bed. I'll be there in a minute to tuck you in."

"*Jah*," he said, then dragged his way up the stairs. The house was quiet, so quiet, and she hadn't realized just how late it had gotten until that moment. Everyone was in bed. She wondered if Matthew had had any problems with Baby. Then she saw them. Matthew was stretched out on the couch, Baby sleeping happily on his chest. They looked so sweet she didn't want to wake them, but knew that if she didn't, Matthew would have a sore neck in the morning.

"Matthew?" She gently shook his shoulder, needing to wake him but not wanting to startle him.

"*Jah*," he mumbled. He started to turn over then realized

that he had a baby on his chest. "Can you take her?" he quietly asked.

Gracie plucked the sleeping baby from atop Matthew and carefully cradled her close. Thankfully she opened her eyes for only a moment before closing them again as if one quick glance at her was all she needed to know that things were right with the world. How Gracie wished she had the same confidence.

"Henry?" Matthew asked, pushing himself to his feet.

"He's fine," she assured him.

"*Jah*," Matthew mumbled. "God's will."

Gracie's heart skipped a beat, then started back up in double time. God's will? Was he just saying that or was he really prepared to let God be in charge? And if they let Him control things, where would that take them? The possibilities were endless.

"Time for bed," Gracie told him, willing her heart to beat a little slower. There was no sense getting worked up this late for what could essentially be Matthew talking in his sleep.

"*Jah*." He smacked his lips together, then leaned in and gave her a small buss at the corner of the mouth. Not a real kiss, but a sweet peck. But he kissed her as if he had been doing it for years instead of this being the first time for a good-night kiss and the second time for an any-reason kiss.

He started toward his room, then turned back for a moment. His blue eyes weary yet happy. "Tomorrow we're going to talk," he said.

"*Jah*?"

He nodded, then swayed on his feet as if about to fall asleep standing there. "*Jah*," he said. "We have a lot to talk about."

* * *

Gracie barely slept that night. She kept turning Matthew's words over in her mind, trying to figure out what he meant and what they were going to talk about.

She would not get her hopes up, she told herself. She couldn't afford to. Her heart would be broken into a thousand pieces if she allowed herself to believe that things between her and Matthew were about to change, only to find out not the way she had hoped.

Family. That had been the most important thing. And having a baby of her own. But she had learned something being married to Matthew: Having a family was about much more than giving birth. It was about broken arms and stitches, lost toys, getting stuck in the creek mud, and loving each other despite everything else. She knew that she loved Matthew, though she wasn't sure how it happened. One day she was nearly scared of him and the next she knew that he was a lot of bark with little bite to ruin the effect.

She was willing to accept the family that she had been given. She had prayed for a family and God had provided. She was grateful even if her family came in a different form than she had anticipated. But she couldn't allow Matthew to go around thinking that somehow he was responsible for his wife's death. He had to understand God's will. He had to know that God was in charge, that God had a plan and he and the rest of them were part of that plan whether they wanted to be or not. Denial was not going to help him.

But he wasn't anywhere to be seen when she got up the following morning. And there was no note. She supposed that there had been a reason why he had gone out so early, but right at the moment she couldn't imagine what it was, and she dare not speculate. She would have to wait and see when he returned.

It seemed like hours she had to wait, and she found herself pulling all the stuff out of the kitchen cabinets, rearranging it, wiping everything down, laying new contact paper, then putting everything away again.

By noon she had just about given up any hope of talking to him during the day. He was a farmer, after all, and it was the growing season. She couldn't expect too much from him.

Then the terrible thought occurred to her that maybe the night before was a fluke thing. He had been talking in his sleep and didn't remember a word of it. It was all nothing.

Deflated was the best way to describe her feelings when Matthew came in the door for the noon meal.

"How's everything today?" he asked after they had prayed and as she fixed them all a plate.

She settled back in her chair and smiled at him. She hoped it seemed natural and not expectant, but it was hard to tell from where she was. "Fine, fine."

He nodded and listened as his children told him about their morning. Gracie ate and tried not to be disappointed.

Then lunch was over and she was clearing the table when he came up behind her.

"Can I talk to you for a minute?"

She whirled around, pasting on a smile as she faced him. "Of course."

"I went into town this morning to get a new screen door," he told her. "I thought I would hang it here in a bit."

"That sounds fine," she said, nodding and smiling and feeling a little like a fool. Perhaps she had imagined everything from the night before. Maybe she dreamt it. But she knew. The late night. Henry's stitches. Matthew's kiss.

All that only reinforced that some things that happened last night had been real. But she couldn't say about the others. Why did it have to be that they were the most important ones?

"I, uh . . ." he started, then shifted from foot to foot. "I don't know how to do this." He ran a hand across the back of his neck and shook his head. "I . . ." He tried again. "I want to talk to you about last night, but . . ."

"You don't know how to start?"

"*Jah*. I mean. There are some things we need to talk about."

She swallowed hard but tried to keep her hopes in check. "Like?"

He took her hand and led her toward the living room. He sat on the couch and pulled her down next to him.

"Yesterday," he started, turning her hand over in his and studying each finger in great detail. "I learned a lot about myself. Things that I had never known. And God's will."

"You don't have to do this." She started to pull her hands from his. She wanted to hear what he had to say and yet she didn't. She wasn't sure how any of this was going to turn out and it scared her. Maybe it would be better if she didn't know. Things between them were fine just the way they were. No sense rocking the boat, as they said, and overturning things that were better left alone.

But you can't make an omelet without breaking a few eggs.

She wasn't one hundred percent certain that the adage applied, but it seemed to fit and it had popped into her thoughts.

"Yes, I do. Because I decided that I do want to have a family with you. A real family."

"We have a family," she said, her heart beginning to pound.

"I want all of it. I want to know that you are my wife and you are taking care of our children while I am making a living for us all."

She nodded.

"I know that I didn't have anything to do with Beth's drowning."

She shook her head. "Please don't say this if you don't mean it."

"I do. I read part of one of her journals. She was a lot more depressed than she ever let on to me. And the more I read, the more I realized that things happen the way they're supposed to."

"Please don't tell me this."

"I've never had anyone try to talk me out of telling them the truth before."

"I want it to be the truth and not just what you think I want to hear."

"It is the truth."

"Matthew."

"I love you." The words were close to a shout.

"What?"

"I said—"

"I heard what you said. But I don't want you to say it if you don't mean it."

"Gracie."

"Matthew."

He did the only thing he knew that he could do. He grabbed her by the arms and pulled her to him. Then he pressed his lips to hers and he felt her melt under his touch.

"I love you," he repeated.

"You do?" she asked.

"We share a kiss like that and you are going to ask me if I really love you?"

"It's not just me?" she asked.

He laughed. "No. It's not just you. It's me. It's us. I love you, Gracie Byler, and I'm so glad you're my wife. And

I've changed my mind. I do want to have more children. If it's God's will. And I want us to be a true family. That's something I'm pretty sure God wants from us. From there I'm hoping that everything will fall into place."

And as long as they put their trust in God, he was certain it would.

Epilogue

"What's this?" Henry looked at the cake on the plate as if it might jump up and run away any second.

"It's an Alabama Earthquake Cake," Gracie answered.

"But we don't live in Alabama," Stephen said.

Matthew ducked his head, and she knew he was hiding his laughter.

"That doesn't mean we can't eat a cake with Alabama in the name," Gracie said. "The cake you said you liked so much. See the big white globs?"

"Are you sure it's not called a Mississippi Hurricane?" Henry turned his head from one side to the other as if that would somehow fix whatever problem he had invented in his mind.

How she loved these boys. She had realized a lot of things reading what little she had of Beth's journals. She had learned to look at things from another's point of view. She couldn't imagine herself not being happy after having a baby, but seeing Beth's words, every sentence filled with such pain, she understood that there were things out there she didn't understand. Might not ever understand. And as long as she did her best to keep her mind open, she would be able to learn from those things even if she didn't completely agree.

"Pretty sure," she said. "I found this recipe in a box behind the salt and the extra-large container of cinnamon up in the cabinet over the refrigerator."

She winked at her husband. In the last couple of months she had learned a lot about Matthew, more than just how wonderful he was with his children, how he had a soft spot for all dogs, and how he made good on his promise to show her every day how much he loved her and was happy they were together. She had also learned that he loved anything made with cinnamon: cinnamon toast, cinnamon rolls, cinnamon biscuits, snickerdoodles, cinnamon cake, the list went on and on.

Gracie turned her attention back to the children and showed them the recipe box she had found.

"That's Mamm's," Stephen cried. His voice was a cracked mixture of joy and sadness.

"I figured," Gracie said. "And that means this is her recipe for the cake with the big white globs on it. But for certain, it's called an Alabama Earthquake Cake."

"I think we should rename it," Henry said as she doled out slices of the cake for them as an afternoon snack.

This was a special treat and she had already explained to them that cake wasn't going to happen every afternoon of the summer. And neither was pie, she continued before Henry could ask. But they had been thankful for the treat and anxious to try it again. Gracie supposed that it might remind them of their mother and that was an added bonus.

"I like Mississippi Hurricane much better," Stephen agreed. "What do you think, Dat?"

"I think you should call it whatever suits you." Typical Matthew, keeping the peace over something as simple as cake.

As if agreeing with the male members of the family, Baby pounded on her highchair tray.

"That's right," Gracie said to the baby. She leaned in and kissed the top of that sweet blond head. Then she straightened and lightly touched her stomach. In seven more months they would have another baby in the house.

They hadn't told the boys yet, hadn't wanted to get them excited too early. And Gracie wanted a little more time for Baby to be the baby. The nickname had stuck and although she still thought *Angel* might be a better one, Baby just seemed to fit.

When the time came to share their news, Gracie had a feeling Henry might not take it as well as the other boys. He was covetous of her time and attention and had taken to being something of her shadow these summer months. In a couple of weeks he would start to school, and for all his bluster and confidence she thought perhaps he was a little nervous. He had such energy and spunk that school was going to be a challenge for him. But she knew he was up for it. In time he would see it too.

"I think it's a better name too," Thomas said.

"Me too," Benjamin agreed.

"Fine by me," Gracie said. "As long as you realize that if you want this kind of cake anywhere else, you'll have to call it by its correct name."

"Deal," they chorused.

Gracie forked up a bite and held it in the air. "To cake," she said.

Only Stephen and Matthew knew what she meant. They scooped up their own pieces and held them close to hers. The other boys followed suit.

"To cake," she said again, and they all echoed the toast. Then they clinked their forks together and got down to the serious business of eating cake. And being a family.